Sarah's Gift

By Anna Jacobs

THE PENNY LAKE SERIES

Changing Lara • Finding Cassie

Marrying Simone

THE PEPPERCORN SERIES

Peppercorn Street • Cinnamon Gardens

Saffron Lane • Bay Tree Cottage

Christmas in Peppercorn Street

THE HONEYFIELD SERIES

The Honeyfield Bequest • A Stranger in Honeyfield

Peace Comes to Honeyfield

THE HOPE TRILOGY

A Place of Hope • In Search of Hope

A Time for Hope

THE GREYLADIES SERIES

Heir to Greyladies • Mistress of Greyladies

Legacy of Greyladies

THE WILTSHIRE GIRLS SERIES

Cherry Tree Lane • Elm Tree Road

Yew Tree Gardens

THE WATERFRONT SERIES

Mara's Choice • Sarah's Gift

THE LARCH TREE LANE SERIES

Larch Tree Lane

❧

Winds of Change • Moving On • In Focus

Change of Season • Tomorrow's Path • Chestnut Lane

The Best Valentine's Day Ever and Other Stories

The Cotton Lass and Other Stories

Sarah's Gift

ANNA JACOBS

Allison & Busby Limited
11 Wardour Mews
London W1F 8AN
allisonandbusby.com

First published in Great Britain by Allison & Busby in 2022
This paperback edition published by Allison & Busby in 2022.

A CIP catalogue record for this book is available from
the British Library.

10 9 8 7 6 5 4 3 2 1

ISBN 978-0-7490-2641-7

Typeset in 10.5/15.5 pt Sabon LT Pro by
Allison & Busby Ltd

FSC
www.fsc.org
MIX
Paper from
responsible sources
FSC® C171272

Printed and bound by
CPI Group (UK) Ltd, Croydon, CR0 4YY

Chapter One

Western Australia

Sarah Blakemere sat in the shade of the patio, sharing a glass of white wine with her friend Thomas, who lived across the marina from her.

'I need to write a new will,' she said abruptly.

'Really? What brought this on?'

'I had an email from my nephew's wife in England last night. Jim died suddenly two days ago, poor boy, and him only seventy, too.'

'Two years younger than me. I'm sorry to hear that.'

'I feel sorry too. I remember him as a little boy. I'd made him my heir, so now I need to find another one. At ninety-five, I can't have much longer to live myself, however hard I try, so I shall need to do the will straight away.'

She grinned suddenly. 'I'm still aiming for one hundred, though, longer if I can. I do enjoy life, even with the limitations of old age.'

He raised his glass to her. 'You're the most vibrantly alive person I've ever met in the ways that count most.'

She clinked her glass with his and took another sip of wine, then stared down into the pale liquid. 'I wrote the present will just after my Dan died. I still miss him. Well, I miss all three of my husbands, to tell you the truth. Lovely men, they were.'

He waited patiently, knowing she liked to tell stories at her own pace. He'd heard most of them before but he was happy to listen to them again, as she listened to his.

'My nephew has left his wife well fixed financially, so Josie doesn't need anything from me, but it's an annuity that stops when she dies, which isn't important when you have no children. Anyway, she's not a Blakemere born. That matters to me. I want my money to stay in the family.'

She took another sip of wine. 'Josie said Jim was worried about his two nieces. She says they both sound to be leading very dull lives with jobs that have no futures. The two women live at opposite ends of the country and have never even met one another, even though they're first cousins, because their fathers were estranged. Jim could never get his brothers to make up their differences.'

'It's sad when families do that.' He had his own sadness about the woman he'd lost, had never wanted to marry anyone else. Families and their relationships could be difficult to navigate round.

'Yes, it's very sad. The younger niece, Portia, got in touch with Jim after her father died, in case he didn't know about it, which was very thoughtful.'

Another pause, then Sarah said, 'I thought I might leave everything to the two of them jointly and try to stir them up a bit while I'm at it. They sound to be merely existing, not living life with relish.'

'Don't they have husbands or families?'

'I got someone to check them out. Fleur is forty-four, divorced a couple of years ago. She has two more or less grown-up children. The daughter is at university doing media studies, whatever that may mean, and only just coping. The lad has nearly finished an apprenticeship as a cabinet maker and is apparently very promising.'

She paused to take another sip. 'Portia is younger, only thirty-two. She was in a relationship for about a year, but they split up last year. No children. No new guy in her life. Josie says she's rather guarded in what she reveals about herself. She's working in an office but is trying to study for a childcare qualification. She doesn't sound happy.'

'How will leaving them money stir them up? They'll only thank you mentally and contact a real estate agent here to sell this house for them, then settle down quietly again.'

'Not if I can help it! I shall make it a condition that they come to live here for a year and clear out my things and the family archives before they can sell the house.'

He frowned and was silent for a few moments. 'As a former lawyer, I have to say I'm not sure you can do that legally.'

'Unfortunately, that's what my current lawyer says too. So I've written a letter to each of them.' She gave him another of her wicked grins. 'I've piled on the emotional pressure, trying to make them feel they owe it to me to do this in return for such substantial legacies.'

'Do you think it'll work?'

'Yes. They're very good letters, even in their first draft. Well, I'm fairly certain my request will make a difference.

I'll make sure Josie knows what I'm doing and will back me up in case they turn to her for advice.'

'Have you forgotten that they'll need a visa to come here? Will they be granted one, do you think?'

'That's the beauty of it. Both of them were born here so they have dual Australian and British nationality. They'll have no problem getting into the country, or staying here permanently if they want. Strange how the Blakemeres have been to-ing and fro-ing between the UK and Australia for several generations, isn't it?'

'It's surprising how many families do that. Uh-oh! You've got that look in your eyes. What do you want from me?'

'I'd like you to witness the will, if you don't mind, Thomas. I'm having it couriered here tomorrow.'

'Happy to help in any way I can.'

'Good, because I've also named you as the executor.'

'Only for you would I agree to do that! It's not a fun job and these two women are completely unknown to me.'

'You'll get to know them when they come here. I'm hoping you'll help them settle in as necessary.'

He shrugged. 'Why not? It's what friends are for. But I hope it'll be years before that happens.'

'Thank you.'

They smiled at one another for a few moments, then she said, 'I think we deserve another glass of wine today to seal the bargain, don't you?'

'Definitely.'

The following afternoon, the doorbell rang and a man poked his head inside the hall. 'Friends in Need cleaning service. Anyone at home?'

Sarah went to get a proper look at him. 'You're new. Where's Penny?'

'She's had a major plumbing emergency in her own home.'

'Do you have any ID?'

He pointed to a fancy laminated card with photo pinned to his overall, both items exactly like the ones Penny wore. 'Actually, I'm the new owner of Friends in Need. Colin Jennings at your service, but I usually shorten it to Col. I won't normally be doing the cleaning myself, but Penny was upset at the thought of letting you down, so I said I'd do the job today. Is that OK? I have police clearance if you need to check it.'

She studied him for a moment or two longer, liking what she saw. Most faces betrayed their owner's basic nature to a woman who'd interacted with so many people over nearly ten decades. His face said to her that he was honest and intelligent, but a little wary. Divorced, perhaps?

'No need for the police, Col.' She looked out through the open door. 'What made a man who can afford an expensive car like the one parked outside buy a cleaning business?'

'I had difficulty getting help with housework after my wife and I split up. Talk about an unreliable service! And some of the people who turned up were distinctly slapdash. I decided I could run a better cleaning service myself and at the same time enjoy a far less stressful working life where I could be my own boss.'

'You won't earn nearly as much as you must have done to buy that car.'

'I'm not money-hungry because my wife had a better job than me so I don't have to pay her alimony. We've simply each taken half the money from the sale of our former house, which has gone up nicely in value. And I'm about to sell that car and add the money to my investments for my old age.'

He broke off abruptly and stared at her, head on one side, looking rather surprised. 'And why am I confiding in you so easily? I don't usually mix work and private life.'

'I must have a magic touch because people often confide in me. Now, let me show you round and tell you what I need.' Which was mainly cleaning floors and bathrooms. She had trouble kneeling down these days, though she was still fine walking around on reasonably level surfaces.

He waved a piece of paper at her. 'I have the notes about what your job entails. The previous owner was old-fashioned and kept paper records, but at least she did a thorough job of it. I intend to digitise everything.'

'Elena warned me she was trying to sell her business and would be retiring soon. These youngsters have no stamina.'

'She's sixty-nine, which isn't exactly young.'

'It is to me, at ninety-five.'

He smiled at her. 'You don't look a day over ninety-four!'

As they both chuckled, she made a decision. 'I wonder if you could do me a favour before you leave? I was going to ask Penny and it needs doing today.'

'If I can. What is this favour?'

'I've been writing a new will and it needs witnessing. Would you oblige?'

He looked at her in surprise. 'Are you sure you want a complete stranger to do that?'

'I only need your signature not your soul. Besides, I like your face. You stare out of it at the world very directly. How old are you, about forty?'

'Forty-two, actually.'

'A mere youngster, in spite of the silver hair.'

He rolled his eyes and frowned at himself in the hall mirror. 'I'd prefer to keep the face I had at thirty, the one with dark hair topping it.'

'Wouldn't we all? I had auburn hair but like you I lost the colour early.' She gestured to her favourite photo of herself, which she kept on the wall in what she called her 'rogues' gallery'.

He didn't just give it a cursory glance but took the time to study it carefully, another point in his favour, she felt.

He whistled softly. 'You were a real stunner.'

'I wasn't bad-looking. And I didn't make the mistake of dyeing my hair when the silver crept in. The roots always show within a couple of days, so what's the point? My second husband disagreed about that, but I ignored him and let it turn silver. In the end he came round, said my face kept me looking young. That's Graham and me.' She pointed to another photo of her younger self hugging a man with a big, wide smile.

'How many husbands have you had?' He clapped one hand to his mouth. 'No, I shouldn't have asked that.'

'I don't mind. It's no secret. I've had three husbands. Lovely men, all of them. That's number three.'

She gave him a moment to look at it then moved things along. 'Now then, enough chatting. My other witness is coming here in a couple of hours and two people have to see me actually do the signing. In the meantime, I'll show you round then go and sit outside near the canal with my newspaper and leave you to get on with the cleaning.'

He followed her into the living room, stopping to stare through the wall of windows and let out a soft whistle. 'Wow, it must be wonderful to live on the water like this.'

'It is rather nice. This is one of the quieter canals because it's a cul-de-sac.'

She kept an eye on Col when he started working in the nearby part of the house, but quickly saw that he was doing a thorough job, so went back to her newspaper.

When he came out to tell her he'd finished, he asked, 'You wouldn't happen to have any chilled, filtered water, would you? I can't be bothered to lug a water bottle around with me everywhere but the local tap water is lukewarm in summer and tastes of chemicals.'

Another good point about him. It always amused her to see the younger folk at the shops, walking along sucking at what she thought of as baby bottles. That was what you got for being old – you lived to see a new generation displaying what you considered incomprehensible quirks of behaviour, but which they considered normal.

She got him a glass of water and watched him enjoy every last drop then put the glass into her dishwasher without needing to be told. Another good point.

'Do sit down. Thomas will be here any minute. He's always punctual.'

'I'm not in a rush to go anywhere else, Mrs Blakemere.'

'Ms. I've always kept my maiden name. It originally meant "someone who lives close to a dark pond".'

A couple of minutes later, her friend rang the doorbell and poked his head inside the hall. 'All right if I come in, Sarah?'

'Of course. This is Col, who now owns our cleaning service. Penny couldn't come today so he kindly filled in for her. Col, this is Thomas Norcott, another of your clients.'

The two men nodded, studying one another in a quick, wary analysis, as males of any species often did.

She waited for them to finish staring and relax a little before asking, 'Would you like a sundowner, Thomas?'

'Do you really need to ask, Sarah, darling?'

'No. I was just being polite. How about you, Col? Can I offer you a glass of white wine?'

He hesitated. 'It's tempting, Ms Blakemere, but I don't want to intrude.'

She flapped one hand in a dismissive gesture. 'Intrude away. You're about to do me a favour.'

'Well then, just a half glass because I'm driving.'

'We'll get the signing over and done with first, shall we?'

It took only a short time to do that, but as she signed and initialled the will, she prayed it really would change the beneficiaries' lives. She didn't like to think of members of her family living in such a tame, colourless way. She had a few things she intended to plan for them.

When they were sitting by the water afterwards, Thomas raised his glass and smiled at her. 'That will is going to throw the metaphorical cat among the family pigeons for your two great-nieces, you know.'

'Well, they sound as if they need stirring up. I trust Josie's judgement about that. My niece-in-law is a very shrewd woman.'

Thomas said, 'Not everyone has your zest for adventure and mayhem, Sarah. Maybe these two young women would rather lead a quiet life.'

'I only create moderate mayhem! Josie doesn't think those two are happy and I trust her judgement. I wish I could see what happens to them if they do agree to come here. Remember, I'm relying on you to keep an eye on them, Thomas, and nudge them a bit, if necessary.'

'I know. I won't let you down.' He raised his glass to her and took another sip.

Then they went on to more general topics of conversation that included Col, who only improved on acquaintance, she decided.

Six months later Sarah collapsed and was rushed to hospital.

Not many people die with a smile on their face, but at almost ninety-six she was a realist and had accepted for the past few weeks that her body was suddenly considering itself worn out and leaving her . . . well, permanently weary. She hadn't said anything or gone to see the doctor, because she didn't want to linger in a hospice, having to be tended to like a baby.

Thomas had noticed the difference, of course he had, but he hadn't pushed her to talk about how she was feeling and she hadn't volunteered any information, just hired a little extra help around the house. She intended to die as she'd lived, by her own rules.

Now, lying back in her hospital bed with Thomas by her side, she let out a faint, gasping chuckle.

'I've lived a nice, full life, haven't I?'

'Very full.'

'It's been fascinating. My only regret . . . is that I won't see the effects . . . of my will. One day, I hope . . . those two young women will remember me . . . with gratitude.'

Thomas raised the hand he was holding to his lips. 'I'm sure they will, my lovely friend. And I'm grateful, too. Your friendship has meant a lot to me.'

She blew a feeble kiss at him, smiled then closed her eyes. She didn't open them again, just sighed softly into oblivion.

He ignored the hovering nurse and kissed Sarah's hand one final time. 'You went off into the sunset with the same courage as you lived your life, my dearest friend. I'll keep an eye on your relatives for you. Heaven knows I haven't any other pressing duties. I'm going to miss you dreadfully.'

Only then did he leave her.

Chapter Two

Wiltshire, England

When Fleur Blakemere was asked to sign for a registered letter, she checked the address first to make sure it really was for her, wondering what on earth it could contain to need such an expensive and old-fashioned form of delivery. She looked at the address on the back and realised it was from someone in Australia: Grebe, Manyweather and Titmell. That sounded like a bunch of lawyers to her; they often seemed to have quirky names.

The only person she knew down under was her great-aunt Sarah, but she'd died last month so it couldn't be from her, because she'd have no reason to leave Fleur anything.

She suddenly caught sight of the clock and dropped the letter on the kitchen surface. She'd be late for work if she didn't leave immediately. The letter would have to wait till later.

She got as far as the carport just outside her unit, then stopped without unlocking her car and spoke aloud. 'No! I need to open it now.' If she didn't find out what the letter was about she'd worry all day. And if she took it with her to open at work, the others would want to know what it was about.

Very well, then. She'd go back and open it, just have a quick look. This was a big decision for her: it'd be the first time in two years with that company that she'd be late. Her new boss didn't deserve such immaculate behaviour from his customer relations staff anyway, unlike the old one, who'd been a delight to work with. She was thinking of looking for another job.

She went back into her unit and flung her handbag down on a chair. Picking up the large envelope, she cut it neatly open with her kitchen scissors. A sealed letter and a bundle of papers slid out.

The top paper on the bundle was a letter from a legal firm. Ha! She'd guessed that correctly! It was signed by someone called Jeremiah Grebe. Even his first name was old-fashioned.

She scanned it quickly. It said . . . no, it couldn't – but it did! She was one of two equal beneficiaries of the entire estate of the late Sarah Blakemere. The bequest included enough money 'gainfully invested' to live on comfortably, as well as half of a waterfront house and its contents, situated in a Western Australian town called Mandurah.

She gasped and looked at it again, to make sure she'd read it correctly. Yes, she had. 'Oh, my goodness!'

A copy of the will was enclosed. She might wish to show it to her own lawyer to verify that it was genuine. She didn't really have a lawyer, only a divorce lawyer and he wouldn't be an expert on wills!

Jeremiah had also enclosed a letter from their late client containing a personal request, and would be grateful if Fleur could contact them as soon as convenient after reading it in order to discuss the necessary arrangements.

Necessary arrangements for what?

She sat down abruptly at the small table, marvelling that Cousin Sarah had left her what sounded to be a small fortune, then wondering what it was her great-aunt wanted her to do. She hesitated. Should she read the will first or the letter?

The envelope caught her eye. It had her name on it in the beautiful copperplate handwriting she recognised as belonging to Cousin Sarah, who had sent Fleur's parents an old-fashioned snail mail letter with the Christmas card every year.

It was a no-brainer. She opened the beautifully inscribed envelope first.

Dear Fleur

I haven't seen you since you were a child, but I re-member clearly playing with you on the beach. You used to build such beautiful sandcastles, I was sure you'd grow up to become an architect.

Ah well, those memories will have died with me by the time you read this, but as you will have found out, I've left you and your cousin Portia half of what I own each. Had they lived, your father and Jim would have been my heirs, but now you and Portia are the only Blakemeres left who are close relatives, hence the bequest.

I hope you'll enjoy my gifts. Money doesn't always make people happy but it does give them a comfortable life, which is not to be sneezed at. I hope it will give you the chance to do whatever you most wish with your life.

I have been fortunate and had a richly satisfying life and my only regret is not being able to have children.

Now I'll get to the main point of this letter: I'd like you to do something for me. Legally, I'm told I can't insist on it, but could you please do it for me anyway?

I would be very grateful if you'd come to Australia and live in my house for a year. I need someone to sort out the family documents and photographs. I could never bring myself to do that job. I ended up in tears whenever I tried, because I'd known and loved so many of the people in the photos. All gone now. I'm the last of my generation.

Some of the photos go back four or five generations and if you and Portia don't keep them safe, who else will? We owe that to our family.

They're stored in the office on the ground floor of my home and I did get as far as writing the names of the people I knew on the backs of their photos, as others had done with the earlier ones.

If you and Portia could scan them, the digital copies could then be shared with any other family members interested in our ancestry.

It makes me very sad to think of a stranger from the lawyer's office clearing out that room and throwing away our family history.

I know it's a big ask for you to give up a year of your life, but please would you do that for me? All your fares and household expenses will be paid from the estate during this year, naturally.

Afterwards you and Portia can dispose of the house and its other contents as you see fit and get on with your lives with my blessing and gratitude.

I hope you have a happy life. Don't waste a single minute. The years go past far too quickly.

All my love
Sarah

P.S. I'd prefer you not to bring any other family members with you to Australia. My gift is only for you and Portia in the first instance.

Fleur gaped at the letter, unable to believe what it was asking her to do. She read it again, stopping now and then to think about some detail.

The biggest impact would naturally be the money. After her divorce, her share had been barely enough to buy a small town house. She had been determined not to saddle herself with a mortgage.

Her former husband had used his share to buy a luxury flat for himself, which would have needed a mortgage. No doubt he could afford it. He was still climbing the corporate ladders. Terry rarely bothered to invite his children to visit him and after the first couple of times, James had refused to go again, saying he was too busy with his studies.

Now, Marie was in her second year at university and James was about to complete his apprenticeship in cabinet making. Neither of them was based at home any longer, though they still visited her occasionally. That meant she was free to do as Sarah had asked and go to Australia – if she wanted to.

What would her children say about this bequest and how would they feel about her going away for a whole year? She wasn't going to tell them the details or Marie would pass them on to her father, who'd try to shove his nose in.

Fleur picked up the will and read it from beginning to end, even more shocked by the time she'd finished at how much she'd inherit.

The gifts from her great-aunt Sarah included not only the house but a portfolio of blue-chip stocks and shares, and a substantial sum of money, mostly on long-term deposit. The amount the shares were likely to earn for her annually literally took her breath away.

Thank goodness this had happened after her divorce. She'd have hated it if she'd had to share this largesse with that unfaithful rat when they divided their goods. Ooh, Terry was going to be furious about this.

She felt her smile fade. Could she face going to Australia on her own and living for a year in a place where she knew no one, though? She wasn't at all the adventurous type.

Oh dear, she couldn't refuse to do it, couldn't live with herself if she denied a dead woman her last wish, clearly a heartfelt one. And allowing the Blakemere family history to be destroyed would definitely be a crime.

Then she remembered the cousin who was also a beneficiary, the cousin she'd never met because their fathers had fallen out and not spoken to one another for decades. She and this Portia would presumably be sharing the house during that year in Australia. Oh goodness, living with a complete stranger might throw up all sorts of problems. What if they didn't get on?

She put the kettle on and made herself a cup of coffee, then suddenly realised that she hadn't phoned work to tell them she wasn't coming in today. She felt guilty at saying she was ill, but she couldn't deal with customers' complaints while she was in this emotional turmoil. Or with her new manager.

That call was made quickly, after which she read Cousin Sarah's letter again and then sat staring into space, worrying about it.

But she kept coming to the same conclusion. Whatever it took, she had to do as her generous aunt had requested.

Chapter Three

Newcastle upon Tyne, England

Portia Blakemere glanced at her watch as she signed for a large envelope sent from Australia by express post. She had to leave for work, didn't dare delay her departure to open this, because there was a strong likelihood of coming redundancies in her area and she didn't want to be seen as a slacker, easy to get rid of.

Flinging it on the table of her tiny flat, she drove to the office, trying to look eager and alert as she walked in.

Nothing happened during the morning and she was beginning to hope that the rumours had been wrong when she was called in to see the section manager just before lunch. Her heart sank as she walked down the corridor to his office.

Oh no! Please, no! Not me! Not again!

'Ah, Ms Blakemere. Please take a seat.' He waited till she'd sat down to say in his cold, emotionless voice, 'You may have some idea of why I've asked to see you today.'

She looked at his smug face, resenting his tone and refused to guess at what was about to happen. She wasn't going to save him from an unpleasant chore. 'No, Mr Paulson. I've been so tied up with my current project I haven't had time to listen to office gossip.'

'Ah, well. Right. There is a need for this section of the company to downsize and, ahem, I'm afraid your job has been deleted. As there isn't another job suited to your skills, sadly we'll have to let you go.'

She'd guessed correctly but it felt a lot worse to hear it put into words in such a cold tone. Let her go! Sack her, he meant. She hadn't the faintest idea how she'd cope with being out of work for the second time in a year. She'd been struggling with mild depression for a while, but this would send her even deeper into what she thought of as 'the darkness', she was sure.

He waited, then prompted, 'Do you have any questions?'

Her mind went blank. 'Not really. I presume I'll get the redundancy pay I'm entitled to.'

'Of course. But you've only been with us a few months, so it won't amount to much.'

'And then I'll have to find another job, so I'd appreciate references.'

'Um, yes. We shall, of course, give you a reference as needed. Your work has, um, been very satisfactory.'

She suddenly felt desperate to get away from him. A tailor's dummy had more life in it than he ever displayed. 'Is that all?'

'Not quite.'

He hesitated for a moment and her heart sank. What else could there be?

'The head of HR feels it's best to get this sort of thing over and done with quickly, so I'll just let them know I've told you and someone will come across to help you pack your personal possessions. You can then leave immediately.'

Her immediate thought was: make that, they'll want to check that you don't take away a single pencil you're not entitled to and then to boot you out of the door quickly to save hassles and scenes.

He picked up the phone and made a call, saying simply, 'I've informed Ms Blakemere of the situation. Thank you.'

He turned back to her. 'Someone will be here in a few moments.' He then sat drumming his fingers impatiently on the desk, not even trying to make conversation let alone say anything to soften the blow.

When the HR liaison officer came in wearing a badge saying 'Thelma', Portia stood up and left his office, only saying goodbye to him because she might need a reference. All he did was mutter something indistinguishable in response.

She walked back to her desk without a word to anyone she passed. They were mostly avoiding looking at her anyway. They clearly knew what had just happened.

There was a large cardboard box sitting on her desk now. No, not her desk any longer.

'We've provided a box for your possessions,' Thelma said unnecessarily. 'You, um, don't need to return it.'

'How kind.' Portia began throwing her things into the box any old how, and was surprised at how quickly she'd packed her stuff. It wasn't even half full.

'Do you have a car, Ms Blakemere? I can help you carry your things out.'

The double conversation continued in Portia's head. In other words, Thelma would see her off the premises.

Aloud she said, 'Yes, I do have a car. This plant is mine, too, so if you'll carry the box out for me, that'll be a big help. I can carry the plant and my handbag. I'll just put my coat on first.'

She looked round. Had she missed anything? 'Oh, I nearly forgot my mug.' She hurried across to the tea-making area in the corridor and came back to add the mug to the box. She didn't intend to leave anything of herself behind, had hated working here if truth be told.

'I'm ready.'

'Lead the way, Ms Blakemere. I presume you're in the company car parking area next door?'

'Yes.'

She set off, didn't say anything as they walked out, just nodded vaguely in farewell as she passed people she was on friendlier terms with. All she wanted to do now was get home and have a good cry.

Someone called out goodbye and good luck, but she didn't answer. Couldn't. She'd only been here for six months and it had taken four months before that to find even a lowly job after the previous business she'd worked in had gone bankrupt suddenly.

How long would it take her to find the next job? She hated being on social security, shuddered at the mere thought of counting the cost of each slice of bread again and struggling to find money to put petrol in her elderly car to get to a job interview.

'This is mine.' She opened the boot and Thelma put the box in.

'Good luck.'

She didn't bother to answer, because footsteps were already moving away. She closed the boot and got into the car, but didn't bother to look round. It took her a moment or two to pull herself together because she was determined not to cry till she got away from here. Not that anyone would see her if she did cry now. At this time of day she seemed to be the only living creature in the big, echoing space of the car park.

She was thirty-two now. It seemed harder to find these low-level jobs once you were out of your twenties. She did babysitting to earn extra money, but that didn't bring in enough to live off comfortably.

She didn't intend to study for more qualifications because she didn't want to climb any corporate ladders. She'd struggled through a basic secretarial studies course after school and had hated every minute of it. Maybe she should try to get a qualification in childcare because she didn't want to spend her life in stuffy offices and anyway she enjoyed being with small children.

The trouble was, she was dyslexic and had trouble reading quickly enough to keep up with attending a course of studies in person, let alone do exams in the time specified. She tried not to let people find out about her problem because some seemed to equate dyslexia with being stupid, which was unfair and incorrect.

She didn't think she was stupid. She'd managed to survive on her own since she left home for the second time after going back to help nurse her father through his final bout of cancer, hadn't she?

But she didn't know what to do with her working life beyond earn a meagre living and have some money for her little hobbies.

Oh, who knew anything?

* * *

When Portia got back to her tiny bedsitter on the second floor of a shabby terrace of narrow houses, she set the plant down carefully on the windowsill and stood admiring it. It was a really pretty one, had cheered her up a little in that soulless office cubicle, which didn't even have a window.

She suddenly noticed the big envelope, still sitting where she'd tossed it this morning. She walked past it, didn't want to read anything, thank you very much.

She went out to her car for the box, dumped it on the table, locked the door on the world and put the kettle on. Now that she could cry safely, she didn't feel like doing it. Instead, anger was bubbling up inside her.

Not until she was sipping a cup of her favourite coffee did she pick up the envelope and stare at it. It was from some company called Grebe, Manyweather and Titmell. Must be lawyers with weird names like that. She might as well see what this was about. They'd probably mistaken her for someone else – only, not many people were called Portia these days and Blakemere was an unusual surname.

She tore open the envelope any old how. Inside she found a smaller envelope and a pile of papers clipped together, the top one a letter.

She sighed and nearly didn't read on because she felt so weary and upset, but then told herself not to be stupid and put on the special tinted glasses that helped a bit with reading.

She picked up the single sheet of paper. When she'd finished reading it, she frowned and shook her head instinctively. This couldn't be true, surely? Was it a scam of some sort?

She read it through again slowly and carefully. Unless this was a hugely expensive practical joke, which didn't seem likely, it must be true.

The tears did come then, tears of utter relief, tears of joy – well, she thought it was joy, only she hadn't felt like this for such a long time, so had almost forgotten how it felt to have the everyday burdens lifted completely from her shoulders. Hope danced around her like warm sunshine on a summer's day.

After a short bout of fierce weeping, she realised she hadn't opened the envelope, so picked it up, not tearing this one open because it was so beautifully handwritten, a real work of art. She loved beautiful things.

She didn't recognise the handwriting but somehow she felt sure she would have liked the person who took such care to make a letter to a stranger look exquisite.

Sarah Blakemere must be one of her father's relatives but he'd died a few years ago so she couldn't ask him how they were connected. He'd probably not have told her anyway, because he hated talking about his family.

Her mother was all tied up with a new man she'd met last year and good luck to her. She deserved something good after nursing her husband through terminal cancer.

Portia read the beautiful letter slowly and carefully, gasping in shock at what the writer wanted her to do.

No way!

She'd be terrified of going to Australia on her own, utterly terrified. No, she definitely couldn't do that.

But this Sarah Blakemere had left her a lot of money, so how could she not do as the woman had asked, begged almost? How was this Sarah related to her anyway – aunt or cousin or what?

Portia sat very still as she slowly realised that somehow she had to dredge up the courage to do it, because Sarah's gift would make the whole of her life easier – and so much happier.

Only then did it fully sink in that it didn't matter that she'd been made redundant today. If she was careful with the inheritance – and boy, what a good training she'd had at making every penny count – she might never have to work in a job she hated again.

She might even be able to follow her heart and work full time at what she really wanted to do for the first time in her whole adult life.

She kept wiping tears away, tears of relief this time, and murmuring, 'Thank you, Sarah. Thank you so very much.'

Once she'd managed to calm down, Portia phoned her mother, who was bubbling with happiness about a coming weekend away with her new guy.

Eventually, her mother listened to her daughter's news, which always came second, then there was silence at the other end.

'Mum? Is something wrong?'

'This Sarah seems to have left out what remains of my generation completely from her generosity.'

Until then, that hadn't occurred to Portia. 'I'm sorry. I never thought of that. I was so excited about it because I got made redundant today.'

'Oh, darling. Not another job hunt.'

'I won't need to now. But there's something else comes with the bequest.' She explained about the year in Australia.

'Sarah can't make you do that. Speak to your aunt Josie about it. I'm sure she'll know what you should do and support you in it. If I remember correctly, I read in one of my novels that it's unlawful to put clauses like that into wills these days.'

Her mother seemed to believe nearly everything she read in the romances she'd become addicted to during her husband's long illness.

'It doesn't matter whether it's lawful or not, Mum. Sarah didn't put it in the will; she wrote me a letter asking if I'd please do it for her.'

'Moral blackmail. You're surely not going to fall for it. You've never even met the woman. You left Australia when you were only a few months old.'

'I am going to do it. It's only fair.'

'I see. Well, congratulations on your good luck. I have to go now.' She cut the connection.

Portia put her phone down. It hadn't occurred to her that her mother would be jealous, but she clearly was. Yet, her mother had been left the family house and life insurance money by her father, so was comfortably circumstanced. And she was now in another relationship, living with a guy who already owned his own house, so she wasn't exactly struggling to survive. Now she had Ross, she wasn't struggling emotionally either.

Was this inheritance going to come between her and her mother? If so, perhaps she should refuse to go to Australia. If it wasn't a legal requirement, it wouldn't affect the legacy.

Portia shook her head. No. It was a dying woman's final request and Sarah's money would make her whole life easier. She was going to Australia because it was, quite simply, the right thing to do.

But the thought of all that it would entail terrified her. And it upset her to be at odds with her mother, too.

She picked up the phone and rang her father's sister-in-law. Josie Blakemere was a nice woman, the sort you could confide in. They'd corresponded a few times since her mother had asked her to let Josie know that Portia's father had died. He had, after all, been related to Josie's husband, who'd also died.

'Josie Blakemere.'

'It's me, Portia. I just heard from some lawyers in Australia. Did you know about Sarah Blakemere's bequest?'

'Yes, dear. She told me about it a few months ago. So kind of her to do that for you.'

'Is she an aunt or a cousin?'

'Some sort of distant cousin, I think.'

'Mum's a bit miffed about it, says she's been missed out.'

'What? She's only a Blakemere by marriage, like me. Sarah wanted to keep the money and the historical stuff in the family, and I think that was the right thing to do.'

'Can you have a word with Mum about it? Calm her down?'

'Not really. She'd just tell me to mind my own business. Families can be difficult, Portia, dear. Sometimes you just have to accept that and let people get on with their thing, while you do what you think right.'

'Do you think I should go to Australia and do as Cousin Sarah asked?'

'Of course I do. It's not unreasonable when her legacy will make you secure for the rest of your life. Don't let your mother stop you showing your gratitude, dear.'

When she put the phone down, Portia sat staring into space. What a day it had been! From rags to riches – and from love to . . . what? Jealousy? Greed? She'd never been as close to her mother as her father. They were just so . . . different.

After a while she took a deep breath, checked the email address of the legal firm, who were located in Western Australia, and sent off a carefully written and spell-checked message saying she would be happy to do as Cousin Sarah wished and spend a year in Australia. She could go there as soon as they liked since she'd just been made redundant – as long as they'd be paying her fare.

She then wondered what to do with the rest of the day, but felt so tired she lay down on the bed and allowed herself a short nap.

When she woke, only half an hour had passed but she felt refreshed. She toasted the cheese sandwich she'd packed that morning for lunch and ate it slowly, half-listening to the radio news as she began to make a list of what would need doing before she left the country for a year.

For a start, it'd make sense to give up the flat and put her possessions into storage – well, anything she wanted to keep. No use paying a year's rent for this grotty flat when she wouldn't be living here after she got back. She beamed at her reflection in the speckled mirror at the thought that after she got back she'd be able to buy a nice house somewhere in the country. Her dream come true. How marvellous would that be?

But having no home to come back to would feel scary. Well, everything felt scary at the moment. Get over it! she told herself.

When someone knocked on her door just before teatime, she nearly didn't answer, then told herself not to be silly.

She was glad she had done because it turned out to be three of her former female colleagues.

One brandished a bottle of wine at her, another had a cake on a plastic plate and the third one hugged her.

'It wasn't fair to chuck you out like that without even a farewell morning tea, so we brought you some farewell drinkies instead.'

'We can all enjoy ourselves saying rude things about old po-face Paulson, which he well deserves.'

That little party lifted Portia's spirits, but she didn't tell them exactly what she'd be doing, just said she'd heard of a job in London and had a cousin there, so might look into that.

And yes, of course she'd keep in touch.

Well, she probably wouldn't, she thought as she waved goodbye and locked the door. They were nice women but she had only known them a short time. It was what you said when leaving a workplace: keep in touch. It was rarely what you did, though. She knew that only too well.

She didn't really feel certain of anything at the moment, except that she had to go to Australia.

She hoped her co-inheritor, the cousin she'd never met before, would be a nice person, otherwise it'd be a difficult year.

She'd get online tomorrow and find out more about Western Australia.

Chapter Four

When Thomas told him that Sarah had died, Col felt very sad. He'd enjoyed quite a few sundowners with her and Thomas, been invited round to her house, always her house not Thomas's, for drinks around five o'clock in the afternoon.

He'd quickly realised this was because she no longer drove and couldn't walk more than a couple of hundred yards without getting breathless.

They usually left her place around seven or sometimes later, staying to share a takeaway with her. It depended on how tired Sarah was and he'd been sad to watch as she gradually started to tire more easily.

She and Thomas didn't seem like the common stereotype (or would caricature be a more accurate term?) of old people when you got them talking. They completely changed his limited understanding of what it meant to grow older. The two of them had such a gusto for life, such interesting views of the world, that he found his own spirits picking up during a session with them.

He needed that to cope with the sadness he'd been experiencing for a while. His marriage had broken up a couple of years ago, because his wife had found someone she preferred. He still missed her, or rather, missed having a live-in companion.

The trouble was, he hadn't found another woman he wanted to live with and yet he had developed a deep longing for children before it was too late, stupid fool that he was. It was supposed to be women of his age who felt that, but he felt it very strongly.

He didn't just want children but a proper family such as you read about in books. That was something he'd never experienced. He'd had a cool and efficient mother, a university lecturer who'd never even tried to live with his father. The latter sent maintenance money but Col had only met him a few times because Jeff was American and lived near his own family.

His mother had done everything necessary to care physically for her unexpected son, Col had to give her that. Only, Jane didn't like anyone to touch her, and had rarely hugged him, let alone plonked kisses on his cheeks the way he'd seen other mothers do to their children.

Strangely, Sarah had done that a few times, scattering kisses on him and Thomas whenever something had particularly pleased her. Her obvious affection for them had felt like a wonderful gift.

After her death he felt bereft. He'd only known her for a few months but she'd quickly become the grandmother he'd never had and he found himself with tears in his eyes more than once when something reminded him of her.

Thomas had come round to his house to give him the sad news and the kind old man gave him a hug when he couldn't hold the tears back.

'I had a good old cry too when I got back from the hospital.'

Col blew his nose and mopped his eyes. 'I don't usually cry, but she was so . . . alive.'

'Everyone needs to cry when life tosses a sadness grenade at them. Will you come to the funeral with me?'

'Of course. I want to say a proper goodbye. Shall I drive you?'

'I'd appreciate that.'

There weren't many people there and that puzzled Col. 'I'd expected more people,' he whispered.

Thomas's smile was sad. 'The older you get, the more friends you lose. Most of her generation had crossed the bridge to eternity well ahead of her.'

Afterwards they went to a local hotel, where a private room had been hired for the small group of mourners. Drinks were passed round and people sipped while chatting in hushed voices.

After a while, the lawyer tapped his glass to gain their attention.

'Because this is farewell to Sarah, we'll start with a little surprise. She asked me to buy a Lotto ticket for everyone.'

There was a ripple of laughter and a couple of people called out, 'Typical!'

A smiling young woman came round with an envelope for each person, then they looked expectantly back at the lawyer.

'The will itself is very simple. She's left her estate to be equally divided between two younger women, distant cousins. They live in the UK, but she's asked them to come to Australia and sort out the family records for her, then digitise the old photos and documents.'

There were smiles and nods of approval at this.

'I'm not sure yet exactly when the two of them will arrive but quite soon, I think. Oh, and my business card is in the envelope with the Lotto ticket. Do let me know if you win anything at the weekend. Good luck.'

To Col's surprise, there was a Lotto ticket for him as well and she'd written his name on the envelope herself.

Then the lawyer raised his glass. 'I'm not going to say anything else. Sarah didn't believe in "droning on" at funerals, as she called it. I'm only going to ask you to raise your glasses and drink to her memory and the pleasure it's been knowing her.'

Glasses were raised and the name Sarah was murmured reverently.

'I hope you win a million!' Thomas whispered to Col as he tucked his envelope into his pocket and wiped away another tear.

Col blinked furiously. 'As if. I've never been lucky with these things.'

'You've never had Sarah buy you one before. She'd say you should give yourself a few days to dream of the impossible happening before you check your results.'

The following day Col was driving to an appointment when he saw Thomas walking along the foreshore in Mandurah.

The older man looked sad and was moving slowly. He would miss Sarah more than anyone.

Col decided to do something to cheer the other man up, but couldn't stop now because he was barely going to make his appointment on time.

He called on Thomas at home late that afternoon.

His friend's face brightened at the sight of him when he opened the door. 'Col, lovely to see you. Do come in.'

He did that, seeing the inside of Thomas's home for the first time. The décor was elegant and understated, yet felt welcoming. 'I've come to invite you to come out for tea. I've found a Chinese restaurant that serves excellent food, but I don't like eating out on my own, so have mostly been getting takeaways. Will you join me?'

Thomas beamed at him. 'I'd love to. Thank you.'

'If you haven't already eaten, we can go there tonight.'

'I wasn't hungry before but now I am.'

'Good. So am I. I'll drive you. Go and get ready. No need to hurry. I can answer my messages as I wait for you.'

The restaurant was peaceful and welcoming, and the food superb.

Best of all, though, Col enjoyed Thomas's company. As they left he suggested they make a habit of trying out one of the restaurants in Mandurah each week. 'Your turn to choose next.'

Thomas gave him a shrewd look. 'You're sure of this?'

'Very sure. I don't know many people here socially and I enjoy your company.'

'And I yours. I suggest we go to my favourite Indian restaurant next week if you like spicy food. Like you I've been getting takeaways, because it's not much fun sitting alone in a restaurant. And I'll drive you next time, so you can have more than one drink.'

'I'll look forward to it.'

'And Col . . . ?'

He was about to get back in his car, but turned quickly. 'Yes?'

'Thank you.'

He didn't pretend not to understand the subtext. 'We're both benefitting.'

After a quick nod, Thomas started to turn away then swung back round again and called, 'Let me know if you win anything in the Lotto draw on Saturday.'

'That'll be the day.'

Making these arrangements with Thomas somehow gave Col more hope for his own future. It also reinforced the fact that he wasn't like his mother. He did want to be with people, touch them, share lives, do things together.

And they wanted to be with him.

Chapter Five

Sarah Blakemere's lawyer told Fleur that he could start making arrangements for her to come to Australia as soon as she liked, so she spoke to the HR section, told them about her inheritance and asked when she could stop work. They said she didn't need to work her notice, given the exciting circumstances and the fact that hers wasn't a skills shortage area.

In other words, she was an easily interchangeable part. That upset her, because she'd prided herself on doing a really good job and would have liked them to acknowledge that, at least. Only they were much more interested in how much she'd be inheriting, so she said half a house and left it at that.

Even so, she could tell they were envious.

She found herself attending a farewell morning tea the very next day. A brief 'wish you well' speech, directed at 'Fiona' and after a quick nudge from a colleague, 'Sorry, I meant Fleur', further emphasised how little the HR manager knew about her.

She was still feeling somewhat miffed about that as she drove home from the office for the final time. Plus, she was beyond scared at the speed this major life upheaval was moving along, because she usually thought about important decisions carefully and took her time about making changes to her life. This one would be on a par with her divorce, or perhaps an even greater upheaval.

She was so angry she emailed the lawyer that same night to say she'd be able to come in a fortnight. Surely she could sort everything out in that time, find a tenant for her house and pack up her valuables?

There was no doubt about what she needed to do first of all, however. She phoned her children and asked them to come home as a matter of urgency this weekend, because she had something to tell them.

When her daughter said she'd made arrangements and wasn't free, Fleur told her sharply that she had some extremely important family business to discuss with them, too important to tell them over the phone and Marie could jolly well cancel her plans or miss out completely.

That won a reluctant agreement to come and one of her daughter's heavy, aggrieved sighs.

As she got ready for bed, Fleur stared round her home. Did she really want to let it and come back to an even shabbier place? If she'd had more money, she'd not even have considered living here.

Only she had money now, or would have quite soon. She'd be able to live somewhere nice.

She went downstairs again and looked through the property pages of the newspaper. She knew house prices had zoomed up lately in her area but hadn't realised exactly how much the town house would be worth now.

It didn't take her long to work out that she might as well take advantage of that and sell straight away. She didn't like living in this part of town and the house was, well, distinctly cramped after the spacious family home she'd lived in and loved during her marriage.

After she'd made that decision, she went back to bed and slept like a log.

Of course, it meant phoning the kids again and telling them that since she was selling the house, they'd need to go through their rooms while they were here and take away anything they wanted to keep, so it might be better if they stayed the night.

Marie immediately insisted she couldn't possibly do that unless she brought Cody with her because he had a car and she didn't. And anyway, the two of them were going to move into a flat together, so he was almost part of the family now.

Part of the family! Fleur had never even met him, didn't think Marie had known him long, either, so she just said OK. Marie never listened to her anyway these days.

James simply said that would be fine and he'd be able to borrow a van from his employer to take his things away in. He hoped she'd get a really high price for the house.

Two days later, her children arrived, plus Cody, who was so good-looking it made Fleur blink. More important, he seemed amiable enough and it was obvious that he was as madly in love as Marie. Whether it was the sort of love that lasted, however, only time would tell. From the way they kept pawing one another it looked more like lust.

'I wonder if you'd leave us alone for an hour or so to have a family chat, Cody?' she asked when they arrived.

'Yes, of course, Mrs Davies.'

Marie opened her mouth to protest, caught her mother's eye and shut it again.

'There's a nice café in the shopping centre. Just carry on along this road and turn right at the traffic lights at the far end. You can't miss it.'

'All right, Mrs Davies.'

'I use my maiden name now: Ms Blakemere.'

'Oh, sorry.'

When he'd driven off, Marie scowled at her. 'I don't know why you told Cody to go away, Mum. I've already said that he and I are together big time. And before you ask, yes, it's the real thing.'

'I sent him away because I want to talk to you two privately about something that's happened to me, and that is none of his business.' She took a deep breath and explained the situation.

Marie gaped at her. 'So we're rich now.'

'No, we are not rich. I've inherited some money, which is carefully invested, not lying around waiting to be spent.'

'But you can, like, give us a bit more to live off, surely? I really hate working in that supermarket at weekends. It absolutely ruins your social life.'

'I can't do that at the moment, because I shan't get the money for another year and only then after we sell the house. Though I will pay for your petrol for going back tomorrow, as a mini-celebration.'

James nodded in his usual solemn way. 'Thanks. Every bit helps, Mum. And congratulations on your inheritance.'

She smiled at him. He'd always been the sensible one. People said the oldest child was often like that. She saw that Marie was fiddling with her phone and said sharply, 'You can either listen to me or go outside and fiddle with that.'

An aggrieved sigh was her only answer, but the phone was returned to her daughter's backpack.

'As I said on the phone, you two will need to clear your stuff out of your bedrooms today. If you want me to store any of it with the things I'm keeping, I'll do that for you, but whatever it is won't be available again for at least a year.' She wasn't having Marie going rummaging among the things she was putting in storage and 'borrowing' the clothes she left behind. She'd lost two favourite tops that way only last summer.

'You're being very mean with what is really family money,' Marie said. 'We've got Blakemere blood in us too, you know.'

Fleur took a deep breath and managed not to snap at her. How had she raised such a selfish child? Where had she gone wrong?

'Why the rush, anyway?' Marie asked.

'This unit is going on the market next weekend and I'm leaving the country the week after, whether it's sold or not, so anything you leave behind here will be thrown away.'

Marie gaped at her. 'That quickly! I'll never manage it! Surely you could wait till term is over to go gallivanting off to Australia?'

'Why should I? I've given up my job and I don't want to hang around here any longer than I have to. The exact date I fly out isn't settled yet, but the lawyer seemed sure he could get me a ticket quite quickly. So, anything you leave behind tomorrow will go into the bin.'

Dead silence greeted that, then she watched her daughter's face brighten suddenly. She could guess what Marie was thinking.

'Before you ask, I'm not allowed to have family members living with me in Australia, so you're not coming out to visit me, even if you can persuade your father to give you the fare.'

It was a bit of an exaggeration to give the impression her children weren't allowed to visit, but she didn't want anyone turning up unexpectedly in Australia. It'd be hard enough to sort things out there without having other people to manage – and her daughter especially took a lot of managing.

Marie let out a scornful sniff. 'If you ask me, this old auntie of yours must have lost her marbles, making all these stupid conditions.'

'I didn't ask you and she hadn't deteriorated at all mentally. She wrote me a beautiful and very lucid letter only recently, explaining why she'd left such a will. Now, chop, chop!' She clapped her hands as she had done to get them started on doing a tidy-up when they were children and to her surprise they both turned and went up to their rooms, though James gave her a wink before he followed his sister.

When Cody came back, she sent him up to join Marie, then went back into her own bedroom and continued going through her possessions. She was glad now that she was leaving quickly, not giving herself time to worry about how she'd cope in Australia.

And to her surprise she was now looking forward to the changes coming to her life.

In the evening she took them all out for a pub meal, then when they got back, she reminded them they had to be out of the house by nine o'clock the following morning because the estate agent was coming to have a chat. So they went back to finishing work on their rooms.

It was a good thing she'd bought some extra packets of bin liners. They each went away with several bulging black bags the next morning.

At half past nine, Fleur was sitting in her kitchen enjoying a cup of tea while the dirty sheets grumbled their way through the washing cycle when her phone rang. She picked it up and frowned as she heard Terry's voice.

'Long time no see.'

'Long time no want to see. We're divorced, remember?'

'Ha! Ha! Very funny.'

She was tempted to put the phone down but curiosity made her hold on. 'Did you want something?'

'Marie just told me you've inherited a few million. Congratulations.'

'Marie should keep her big mouth shut. And for your information, I didn't actually tell her how much I'd inherited because I don't know, though it certainly isn't a few million. She's just guessing – and exaggerating.' Trust her daughter to run to her father with the news.

'Well, it sounds a generous amount to me. I know we agreed to help them, but surely you can take that over now?'

'Nope. I'm not paying more than my half of what we agreed, whether you continue to pay them or not. You're not short of money.'

'Aw, come on, Fleur.'

'I said no and I meant no. Goodbye.' She put the phone down and when it rang again, she checked who it was and didn't answer. If she never spoke to Terry again, it'd be too soon.

'Cheat me once, shame on you. Cheat me twice, shame on me,' she muttered as she'd often done when dealing with him during the divorce process.

He'd cheated on her with other women and also told lies about how much he'd been earning through the latter part of their married life, as her lawyers had found out during the pre-divorce wrangles. That had meant she got more from the settlement than she'd expected, and more than he did, which caused a few right royal rows.

She'd never give him a penny of this money, directly or indirectly, if she could help it.

As the next week passed, Fleur concentrated on sorting out what to take to Australia and what to put into storage, as well as making sure the place was immaculate, since one or two people had already been shown round it. She also had to cancel the various utilities and the house insurance.

She'd intended to give the scruffier furniture to the charity shop, but James rang up and asked if she was throwing any furniture out, because he'd had an offer to move into his employer's man cave over their garage at a very cheap rent, as long as he furnished it himself.

'You must be getting on well with him.'

'I am. Vic's getting more and more into restoring antiques and he's teaching me so much. He's already offered me a job when I finish my apprenticeship in June and I've accepted it. I'm definitely going to specialise in that area.'

'Good for you. And as it happens I am throwing quite a lot of stuff out, so if you can take it away by Thursday, you can have it. You'll need quite a big van, because it includes the beds.'

'Just a minute.' There was the sound of voices, then James came back on the phone. 'We'll be there about nine a.m., if that's all right.'

'Fine by me. Will you need all the beds or just your own?'

'I can sell anything I don't need, even if it only brings a low price. Unless you want to sell it?'

'No, I was going to give away the furniture, so I might as well give it all to you.'

That was typical of her practical son. She wished her daughter had half his common sense.

James turned up early on the Thursday with his employer. He and Vic took everything and anything that Fleur was getting rid of, even a couple of indoor plants.

As they were leaving, James plonked a quick kiss on her cheek and muttered, 'Good luck down under, Ma. Vic wants a word.'

He went out to the van while Vic lingered to say, 'I don't know if you realise how talented your son is with his hands.'

'I know he's good with practical stuff, but I'm no judge of skill levels in your area. James isn't very communicative verbally and he has never been one to blow his own trumpet.'

Vic grinned. 'I've noticed. But he is extremely talented. I've already offered him a job for after he's completed his apprenticeship – and as he'll be living over our garage, my wife and I will keep an eye on him and see he doesn't do anything too stupid. I thought that might set your mind at rest about him.'

'It will and I'll be glad to have you nearby, though James has never been rash in word or deed.'

'No. Old head on young shoulders. Well, good luck in Australia.'

She wished there were someone to keep an eye on Marie. Though she doubted her daughter would listen to anyone's advice. Well, maybe she'd occasionally listen to her father, but definitely not to Fleur.

Only failures and life experiences were going to instil a bit of sense into that girl and Fleur hoped Marie wouldn't get too badly burned in the process. She wasn't optimistic about it, though.

Fleur's house was open for viewing on the following Saturday and Sunday. There were plenty of people going round it and she sat outside in her car watching, feeling hopeful.

Sadly, there were no offers to buy. She'd feel safe leaving it in the hands of this estate agent, though, a motherly woman you couldn't help trusting, so she continued to make the final arrangements to leave.

On her last night there she camped out on a neighbour's air mattress and for tea she ate a pre-made and rather limp salad bought at a local shop. There was none of the furniture she had borrowed from her friends after James had taken hers, so she sat on a garden chair belonging to the same kind neighbour. The estate agent was bringing some professional bits and pieces to dress the house up and said they were 'getting a nice start' on selling, whatever that might mean.

Another neighbour was buying Fleur's car for his daughter, which was very convenient. She'd handed that over at teatime.

It felt weird to think she'd be leaving the following morning and never coming back to the house again. Where would she come back to?

That evening James phoned to say goodbye.

Her friends had already wished her well.

Her daughter knew when she was leaving, but Marie didn't bother to get in touch. Fleur tried not to let that upset her, but failed and couldn't help shedding a few tears.

Chapter Six

As executor, Thomas heard from Sarah's lawyer the next day. The two heirs to Sarah's estate had accepted her request to sort out the house and family records, and would be coming to Australia in a couple of weeks.

He knew Sarah would have been pleased about that. She'd looked into their backgrounds and had also hoped this trip to the Antipodes would stir them out of their ruts. Well, from what the lawyer had said, they didn't even sound to be interesting ruts, let alone comfortable ones.

He phoned Col to let him know the next day.

'What are you going to do with them, Thomas?' his friend asked. 'Did Sarah give you any hints about how to help them?'

'She had a few ideas and gave me strict orders about some things.'

'What do you mean?'

'I can't tell you all the details but she wanted me to be available if they need help, but I was not to baby them about settling in. Mostly I'm to let them find their own feet but keep an eye on them. I'll have to see what they're like. Maybe they don't have the same fire in their souls as our lovely Sarah did and will return to their ruts once their trip to Australia is over.'

'Sarah packed far more into her life than most other people,' Col said.

Thomas hesitated then added, 'She stirred up my life too, drew me out of my shell, pushed me to check a few things I shouldn't have let go.'

'You've never mentioned your family. Don't answer if you don't want to, but did you ever marry?'

'Yes, I did, but not till I was in my mid-thirties. I failed as a husband because I was too involved in being an up-and-coming barrister, and I didn't want children. My wife was a few years younger than me. Hilary felt the same about children when we married and we got on well.' He sighed and repeated softly, 'So very well.'

After a pause, he went on, 'Unfortunately, she gradually changed her mind, got broody and desperately wanted children before her body clock ran down. We had a series of rows and she left me when I refused to give her a child.'

'That's sad.'

'It's worse than sad, it's tragic. I was an idiot. I realised later that I did wish I'd had children, but only with her.'

Col ventured another question, this one out of sheer curiosity. 'Is your ex still living in Australia? Did she find someone else to give her the children? You might enjoy getting in touch again.'

'I don't know where she is. She made me promise not to try to track her down after she left. And I was foolish enough to agree to that. Later on I met Sarah and she taught me how wrong I'd been, how it made it look as if I didn't want to see Hilary again. I did want her back if I could find her. No other woman ever made me feel as alive as she did. But by the time I admitted it to myself, the trail had gone cold and I felt if she'd taken the trouble to hide, she truly didn't want to see me again, so I backed off.'

He sighed and stared into space.

Col gave him time to recover, sipping his drink and gazing out at the canal. Thomas had as good views of the waterway as Sarah, but from the opposite side of this cul-de-sac canal.

Col was thinking of buying a house for himself because his business was ticking along nicely and he was enjoying living in Mandurah. But he wouldn't be able to afford a canal-side house like this one. Pity.

In spite of his promise to check, Col completely forgot about the Lotto ticket till he and Thomas went out for their Indian meal a few days later.

'How did you go on in the Lotto draw?' Thomas asked once they'd ordered.

'Oh, hell. I completely forgot to check it, I'm afraid.'

'Well, after we've eaten, you can check the numbers on your phone. I won three hundred dollars with my ticket. First time I've ever won anything.' He raised his glass of wine. 'Thank you, Sarah.'

After they'd finished eating, Col checked. He froze as he circled numbers on his coupon one by one, holding his breath after the fifth one, then letting it out in a gasp as he circled a sixth. Then he went back and checked that he was looking at the right date of draw, before going over the numbers again.

Thomas watched him. 'You've won something too, haven't you? Trust old Sarah. She had a magic touch with everything. Which division have you won?'

Col's voice came out hoarse. 'First division.'

There was dead silence then Thomas said, 'That's . . . the big one.'

'I know.' Col held out the coupon. 'Will you check this for me, please? I daren't believe it.'

A few moments later, Thomas looked up. 'You were right. It is Division One. Congratulations! I wonder how much the prize will be for this draw and how many will share it.'

'I have no idea. I don't normally buy Lotto tickets. When can I find out about the winners?'

'Tomorrow, I think.' He picked up his wine glass and raised it. 'Here's to Sarah.'

They clinked glasses.

'And here's to you winning a very large amount of money.'

Col clinked glasses again but was still finding it hard to take this in. He had never won anything in his life, hadn't come from a wealthy or even comfortable background. Everything he'd achieved had been gained by sheer hard work.

The following day Col went to his local newsagent and asked them to check his ticket.

The assistant put it into the machine and a siren suddenly started wailing, then lights began flashing above the counter.

'Congratulations, sir. You've won the big one and there's only one other Division One winner.' She whipped out a camera. 'Could I please take a photo? The other customers will love to see that someone won from here.'

He was incapable of speaking for a moment because Thomas said that'd mean it was a lot of money, but he managed to shake his head. 'Sorry, no photos.'

She looked disappointed but put the camera down. 'Shall I find out how much you've won?'

'Yes, please.'

She did that and whistled softly as she told him. 'A couple of million dollars, give or take. Congratulations!'

He didn't know what he was going to do, seemed to have lost the ability to think or speak coherently.

'You should go to their head office and lodge your claim, sir. This is the address.' She offered him a card and he took it without even looking at it.

'Drive carefully. You're in shock,' she said softly. 'It can take people a while to settle down again.'

He nodded, took the coupon back from her and put it with the card folded inside it into the inner pocket of his jacket.

He hadn't driven here because his office was nearby. He walked slowly back to the SUV he now drove. He didn't tell his secretary his news, just asked her to cover for him because he had to go up to Perth on urgent private business.

Then he set the satnav and left. He hardly even reached the speed limit anywhere on his journey because he was driving so slowly and carefully.

*　*　*

Once again, the people who checked his Lotto ticket wanted to use his win for PR purposes, and once again, he refused. All he wanted was to get the money into his bank account and then leave it there while he came to terms with his changed circumstances.

The following morning, he felt more able to face the world and of course wanted to chat to Thomas about what to do with the money. However, he suddenly remembered that his friend would have gone to the airport that morning to pick up the two Blakemere women.

He wondered how they'd felt when they found out they'd inherited so much money, far more than he'd won by the sounds of it. Like him, they had Sarah Blakemere to thank for it.

He'd be interested to compare notes about their reactions. Well, he would if they were anything like Sarah. Did kindness run in families?

In the meantime he was doing nothing and saying nothing to anyone except Thomas till he'd got used to it. Perhaps he would use the money to buy a waterfront house.

Chapter Seven

Portia had to give a month's notice on the bedsit or pay rent in lieu, which left her very short of money. She'd also had to pay six months in advance for storage of the few possessions she wanted to keep and was beginning to wonder how she'd pay the cost of getting to the airport to fly out to Australia.

She'd have to renew the storage towards the end of that period but hopefully by then she'd have some more money. The lawyer had mentioned an allowance while they were in Australia and she'd be very careful with it.

That meant she'd be going to Australia with little money to fall back on if something went wrong, which also worried her. In fact, this whole inheritance thing was getting scarier and scarier.

To her amazement, the Australian lawyer booked her a business class flight – not only that, but had got her on the non-stop flight to Perth, for which you had to pay extra again. When she checked the actual cost online, it made her gulp and feel almost nauseous at the waste of money.

She emailed him to say it wasn't necessary to spend so much on just one flight, but he told her that her aunt Sarah had specified it. He emailed again, almost as an afterthought, to tell her that he'd arranged for a car to pick her up at home and take her to Heathrow airport early on the day of departure. The limousine company would be in touch.

A limousine too! All the way from Newcastle. She could easily have gone by coach. Still, at least that solved one problem.

What next? she wondered.

Well, at least she would be able to take more luggage in business class without paying extra for it and would have no trouble carrying it around if she went there in a limousine. That meant she had to buy another suitcase from the charity shop. And when she saw a scuffed leather carrier for rolled documents standing forlornly in one corner of the shop, she bought that too.

Some of her art things fitted into her luggage now and that cheered her up. It was like taking old friends with her. She'd need a hobby while she was there, would have more time to devote to it, in fact. That'd be blissful.

On the last night she camped out on the floor of the flat, borrowing a blow-up mattress and an old sleeping bag from a neighbour she chatted to occasionally. She'd given Louise her two houseplants and her leftover bits and pieces of food as a thank you. Louise was on social benefits and struggled to cope, and yet she still tried to help anyone in trouble. It was good to be able to help her in return.

The limousine looked incongruous when it drew up next

to the shabby two-storey group of flats. Portia waved to the driver from the door and started carrying the first suitcase down the concrete stairs. He came running up and insisted on carrying them for her.

'We'll be there in plenty of time,' he said cheerfully as he set off.

'Good.'

She was glad he picked up on her mood and didn't try to chat because now that the time had come, she felt numb with fear about flying.

She had no job now and nowhere to go if she chickened out. She could only carry on grimly, using an old motto that had helped her in a few challenging situations before: One step at a time. And she was finding travelling to Australia very challenging indeed.

At the airport the driver put her cases and the leather document holder on a luggage trolley and wished her a good flight.

She blurted out, 'I'm sorry, but I can't afford to tip you.'

He looked in puzzlement at her luggage labels.

She could feel herself blushing. 'Someone else is paying for my trip. Um, thank you for driving so carefully.'

His expression softened. 'It's all right, love. Good luck in Australia.'

She nodded and set off. The airport signs were excellent and she easily found her way to the check-in counter for business class clients. There were no queues there, as there were at all the nearby check-ins, and she felt like an imposter to be travelling in luxury.

Well, she assumed it'd be luxurious on the plane. What did she know about such things? Only what she'd seen in films and on TV, that's what. She'd never expected to travel to faraway places. It was hard enough managing to steer your life through a place where you knew how things were done.

She went through customs with barely a pause then found the business class lounge for her airline. She felt pared down to basics in everything with only her cabin luggage left now, one rather shabby backpack.

The huge lounge amazed her, as did the arrays of refreshments. A smiling attendant saw her hesitating and asked if she could help.

It came out as a whisper. 'There are no prices on the food.'

The smile didn't falter. 'It's included in the price of the ticket. So are the drinks.'

'Oh. Thank you. It's my first time business class, you see.'

'I hope you enjoy the extra comforts.'

Portia wandered round. There were alcoholic drinks of every description and food of all sorts. She'd thought she didn't feel hungry, but now her appetite picked up a little. She got herself a cup of tea, a bowl of fruit and a luscious-looking pastry because she hadn't had breakfast beyond a final cuppa with her last teabag. She didn't want to faint on the poor flight attendants, after all.

She had to force even this small amount of food down because the next step was approaching, and it felt enormous: getting on the plane and letting it swoosh her away from all she knew.

She'd brought along a book, one with large dark print that was easier to make out, but she couldn't settle to reading it as she waited to board the plane. She found herself going over the same page several times and in the end put the book back into her pack and settled for watching people.

It was happening, it really was. And the word that came into her mind to describe how it felt was 'inexorable'.

Heathrow airport was crowded and Fleur was relieved to find the business class check-in for her airline quite easily. She'd never have booked to travel like this – well, she'd never had the money and even her ex hadn't wasted his on 'posh flying', which he'd said scornfully only lasted a few hours so didn't give you a worthwhile return on your spending. He flew business class for work, though, because his company paid.

This time her fare had been paid by the law firm handling her aunt's estate before she realised what they were doing. When she'd protested that it was a waste of money, they'd said her aunt had specified business class. So she decided, with a feeling of both guilt and delight, that she might as well enjoy the extra comfort and luxury.

She was feeling nervous, not because of flying but the fact that she was flying into an unknown situation.

The lawyer had also mentioned that her unknown cousin Portia would be travelling on the same flight but she had no idea what the woman looked like and hadn't thought to ask if he had a photo. She actually knew very little about her cousin and had been too busy getting ready to leave to try to find out more.

It had always seemed sad to her that, even though they were brothers, their fathers had fallen out big time and the younger brother had moved his family to the northern end of the country. The two men had died without ever speaking to one another again. That was wrong. Families should stick together through thick and thin, in her opinion. And it had only been some minor difference of opinion, though she suspected, from things her father had occasionally let fall, that the brothers had never got on particularly well.

She wandered along the displays of food, which looked beautiful, getting herself a glass of apple juice and adding some fruit and cheese. She found a seat and enjoyed her refreshments while watching what was going on around her.

As she studied the other passengers, she kept coming back to one who looked a bit like the women in her family. She had dark wavy hair similar to Fleur's own, and yes, there seemed to her to be a resemblance. Like her own and her daughter's, it was a face that you'd never call girlishly pretty but you might call it striking. Well, it would have been if it had showed more animation. At the moment all this one showed was fear.

Was it possible that this woman could be her cousin Portia? It'd be easy enough to go across and ask. Did she dare do that?

Oh for heaven's sake, Fleur Blakemere, stop being such a coward! she told herself. That woman isn't going to shoot you if you've guessed wrongly. She got up and walked across before she could chicken out.

'Excuse me, but you wouldn't be Portia Blakemere, would you?'

The woman looked at her in surprise. 'Yes, I am. Are you Fleur?'

'Yes. Strange way to meet, isn't it?' Fleur paused. 'Are you all right? You look rather pale.'

'I've never flown before.' She looked more than a bit nervous.

'May I join you?'

'Please do. I'm afraid I won't be very good company, though.'

'I'll just get my refreshments.'

Fleur brought her drink across and sat down, speaking in a deliberately gentle tone of voice, 'I've never been on a long-haul flight before, but I've done a few short flights to France and Italy. It's not all that frightening. Since this one will take about seventeen hours, it'll probably be boring rather than anything else once we're up in the air. I'm hoping to sleep for at least part of the journey.'

As they sat looking at one another, Fleur tried to think what to say next. 'Did you, um, know Cousin Sarah?'

Portia shook her head. 'No. Apparently she held me a couple of times when I was a baby but that was it. My parents came back to England when I was a few months old because my mother was homesick in Australia. Then they fell out with your father, so we moved to the other end of the country: Newcastle upon Tyne.'

'I knew they'd fallen out, but not why. Do you know?'

'No. I've often wondered.'

'So have I. My father always refused to say. He worked for a multi-national and was offered a promotion in Australia. We lived there till I was about ten, so I do remember Cousin Sarah. She was very kind and played games with me, which were great fun.'

She smiled at the memories that brought. 'Dad could fit in anywhere and chat to anyone as if they were old friends. I always envied him that.'

'I'm not good with small talk.'

Fleur had noticed. There was another uncomfortable silence as if to confirm it, then they both started speaking at once.

'Can you—?'

'Is there—?'

They broke off at the same time and Fleur said quietly, 'It's awkward when you've never met someone before, isn't it? We'll know one another quite well by the end of the twelve months, I should think.' She smiled and added, 'I'm not argumentative, by the way.'

'I'm not either. At least I don't think I am. But twelve months seems rather a long time to clear out the family documents. Do you think it'll take that long?'

'I don't know. Don't you think you'll want to stay for the full year?'

'I don't know what to think about how I'll cope with a strange country.'

'Have you left someone important behind?'

'No, there's no one important these days and I'm not looking for another relationship. The last one became – rather difficult. But I thought we might finish clearing the house early, or get homesick or something.'

There was an announcement just then that business class passengers should board the plane and they found themselves joining the first group.

Fleur didn't know whether to be relieved or sorry when she found that though they were sitting together in the middle two seats, they weren't crammed as closely together as they would have been in what her father had always jokingly called 'cattle class'.

She studied her seat, pleased that she would actually be able to adjust it and lie down properly with her lower legs extending into a little tunnel under the seat in front. That would be so much more comfortable when she wanted to sleep.

After taking off her outdoor clothes and heaving her backpack up into the overhead locker, she settled in, keeping her smaller bag beside her. She accepted a glass of champagne from the flight attendant and sat sipping it, even though it was still early morning UK time.

She enjoyed watching the bustle around her as other people settled down. Some did it efficiently and others seemed to scatter belongings around before they'd even taken off.

Poor Portia was still looking extremely nervous but the attendant dealing with the passengers along the other aisle seemed to have realised that. He showed her how things worked and explained when refreshments would be served.

At last the plane took off and Fleur glanced sideways again, seeing Portia stiffen and clutch the arm rests so tightly her knuckles proved how accurate the phrase 'bone white' was.

Fleur leaned back, not worried about the take-off, wondering now what their life would be like in Australia. Would there be a car so they could get to the shops and to wherever else was needed? They couldn't sit inside the house all year, after all, and they'd want to do some sight-seeing. Oh, there was bound to be one, surely? If Cousin Sarah had insisted they travel business class she'd also have made some provision for a vehicle.

More important to Fleur would be finding ways to meet people and perhaps make new friends down under. She was going to miss the people she'd left behind.

Once they were up in the air, she checked the films available to passengers and found there was one she'd been wanting to see. Oh, good.

They were bringing refreshments round now, and she hoped they'd remembered to provide a gluten-free meal. They had. The food was rather bland, but seemed safe and when she'd finished she sipped her glass of wine, which was a good quality Chardonnay. Thank goodness her food problems didn't include wine.

It was rather nice to be fussed over.

Afterwards she settled down to enjoy the film. By the time it was over, she was feeling tired, but to her annoyance and for all the comfort of being able to lie down properly, she had difficulty falling properly asleep.

All she managed to do was to doze a little, wake with a start, then doze again. In the end she gave up trying and sat up to watch another film.

She kept an eye on Portia, amused and envious to see her cousin sleeping soundly for several hours in spite of her nervousness.

It seemed a long time until they reached Western Australia. It might only be just under seventeen hours but when you were the only one awake in a darkened plane, it felt more like seventy.

And even that wouldn't be the end of their journey. They were being met at the airport but still had to travel to Mandurah, which was apparently about an hour south of Perth.

Chapter Eight

As Thomas walked into the waiting area at Perth airport to meet the two heirs, a yawn took him by surprise. Well, he wasn't used to getting up at three o'clock in the morning, was he? It had taken a hot shower and some strong coffee to make him feel alert enough to drive safely.

He looked at his watch. Nearly half past five. Then he studied the flashing sign on the arrivals list. Good timing. The plane was just landing. He'd be able to grab a quick coffee before its passengers got through customs and out of the restricted zone.

He found a seat near where they would exit from the luggage retrieval area and sat sipping the surprisingly good coffee. He'd been right to set off in plenty of time. You never quite knew how heavy the traffic would be when you were travelling up to the capital from Mandurah – could be just over an hour, an hour and a half, and he'd known it take even longer at the end of the working day when there was a three-car pile-up blocking traffic.

He didn't have photos of the two women but he'd made a sign on a piece of card and as people started to trickle through into the waiting area in ones and twos, he held it up whenever a woman who looked roughly the right age came out through the automatic doors. The two heirs might or might not be together.

After a rush of people had come out into the public area and with only an occasional person now appearing, he began to worry, especially when several minutes passed without anyone at all coming through. What had happened to the heirs? If they'd missed the plane, surely someone would have contacted him before now?

He was just wondering whether to ask an official when two dark-haired women come slowly out, looking round uncertainly. They weren't pushing a trolley, which puzzled him, but he held up his sign, just in case.

The one who looked slightly older nudged the other and raised a hand to signal to him.

Thank goodness! He waved back and moved forward. 'Blakemeres?'

'Yes, that's us. I'm Fleur and this is Portia.'

'I'm Thomas Norcott. Don't you have any luggage?'

'We started off with some but it didn't come off the plane. And we weren't the only ones missing bags.'

As if to prove that, a family came out into the waiting area just then, looking annoyed and exchanging sympathetic glances with the two women.

Fleur answered. 'The official told us it must have gone astray and they'd send it on to us once they'd located it and brought it to Western Australia. They think it might have inadvertently been put on a plane going to Sydney, but they won't be sure till they locate it.'

'What rotten luck!'

'We may have to buy some underwear and a few items of toiletry to get us through. We're both feeling in need of showers now.'

Portia nodded agreement.

'There are unused toiletries in the guest bathrooms at the house, so no need to buy those.' He stepped back a little and studied them. 'What's more, you both look to be about the same size as Sarah to me. Nothing of hers has been cleared out so there will be plenty of clothes to choose from if your luggage is delayed for too long.'

The younger one gaped at him. 'Use someone else's underwear?'

'It's all clean and if I know Sarah, there will be some new stuff that hasn't been used. She had a weakness for pretty things and used to buy them online. It was one of her rules to buy nice clothes when you see them, not when you need them.'

Portia was still looking dismayed. 'We can't use her things!'

'Why not? She wouldn't mind.'

Fleur took over. 'We may have to, Portia. And if a piece of underwear hasn't been used, I don't see any problem.'

Someone said, 'Excuse me!' in an annoyed tone and three flight attendants edged past them, wheeling small suitcases and looking as smart as ever.

'Let's get out of the way, shall we?' Thomas led them to a space behind the rows of seats, which were filling with new groups of people presumably waiting for arrivals from other planes.

'Did you know our aunt well?' Fleur asked.

'I was a very close friend of hers, which is why she made me the executor for her will. You look exhausted. Didn't you get any sleep on the plane?'

'Portia did, but I didn't manage more than a doze or two, Mr Norcott.'

He chuckled. 'We don't use surnames very often in Australia. Just call me Thomas.'

They nodded, looking at him oh-so-patiently and politely, and waiting for him to give them a lead conversation-wise. Sarah would never have been this hesitant.

'I'm afraid we have just over an hour's drive before us, maybe a little longer if we encounter heavy traffic. It's the morning rush hour now but more people will be coming into the city than heading south, so we won't encounter the worst of it. Let's get you out to my car.'

He led the way, wondering if sheepdogs felt like this about their charges, watching every move, ready to nudge them in the right direction. Resisting the temptation to fill the silence with empty babble, he set a brisk pace.

The footpaths through the car parks were narrow and they had trouble overtaking a woman tottering along at a snail's pace. Once they were past and out of earshot, he whispered, 'Those high heels are utterly ridiculous. Your aunt and I used to joke that they make women walk like pregnant camels.'

Portia let out a snort of laughter and seemed to relax a little. 'I couldn't even begin to walk in them.'

'I wouldn't do it if I could,' Fleur said. 'I value my spine and feet too much to harm them.'

Thomas glanced at his companions' footwear with approval. They were wearing sensible light sneakers and walking along easily, but he didn't think much of the dark, nondescript clothes that both were wearing.

Sarah would have been wearing sensible shoes too, but also something vivid to add style and colour to her appearance. A surge of sadness went through him at the thought of her. His loss still caught him sharply at times.

As they left the covered areas, the brightness of the early morning sun hit Fleur like a blow and she wished she had her sunglasses with her. She reached up to shade her eyes.

'It's not far now,' Thomas said. 'That's my car, the silver one at the far end of this row. Who wants to ride in the front?'

'I don't mind sitting in the back,' Portia replied quickly.

Fleur guessed this was to avoid struggling to make small talk. She didn't mind and as she settled into the front seat, she wriggled about in pleasure. The car was some sort of Mercedes from its badge and the seats were extremely comfortable.

'I'll just go across to the ticket machine to pay for my stay, then we'll be off.' Thomas walked across to a payment point.

'What a lovely car!' Fleur said.

'Must have cost a fortune. He can't be short of money.'

'Neither are we now.'

'I still can't get my head round that.'

Thomas came back and settled in quickly beside her, giving Fleur a smile. 'If you fiddle around in the glove compartment you'll probably find an old pair of sunglasses. You're welcome to borrow them. Sorry I haven't got two pairs, Portia.'

Fleur put them on. 'Ah. That's a lot better. Thanks.'

'Good. I should have said it before: welcome to Australia, both of you. I hope your stay here will be very happy, in spite of the sad reason that brought you here and the inauspicious start with the luggage.'

'Thank you.'

He set off, weaving in and out of the traffic with an ease that spoke of many hours at the wheel of a car. 'The weather forecast for today is 30 degrees Celsius, which is about 86 Fahrenheit.'

'Oh, goodness. That'll be dreadfully hot!' Portia exclaimed.

He chuckled. 'Out in the open, perhaps. We don't sit out in it, baking ourselves brown like a lot of Poms do, especially in the middle of the day. Most of us have air conditioning in our houses and cars, and the shops and cafés all have it, so we hardly feel the heat.'

'That's a relief. I'm no good at sunbathing anyway. I get bored.'

'So would I. Yesterday afternoon I checked everything out at the house and the air conditioning was working just fine. I set it to come on about now at 25 degrees Celsius, which is my favourite temperature. It'll be pleasantly cool inside by the time we get there, not icy cold.'

'Thank you.'

'I also took the liberty of buying some basic fresh food for you. I should think the last thing you want to do today is go grocery shopping. There are also unopened tins and packets of food in the pantry, and quite a few things left in the freezer, not to mention plenty of bottles of wine.'

His voice wobbled on the word 'wine' and he fell silent abruptly. Fleur glanced sideways and could see that he was looking deeply sad. 'You must miss her greatly.'

'Yes. She was my best friend. We used to have regular sundowners together at her house.'

'Sundowners?'

'Drinks at the end of the afternoon, at the going down of the sun, more or less anyway. We didn't always wait for it to go down at this time of year. It doesn't go dark till early evening in high summer.'

'It's strange to be coming from mid-winter to high summer.'

Fleur saw him pull himself together visibly and he began making occasional comments on what they were passing.

'The road to Mandurah isn't one of the prettiest,' he said as they slowed down for another group of vehicles. 'You have to head further south than Mandurah to find beautiful scenery, such as the wine country in the Margaret River region. You must go and visit it at some point. Book in on a wine-tasting tour and buy a few of their excellent wines. Unless you're not drinkers.'

'I enjoy an occasional glass of wine,' Fleur said. 'How about you, Portia?'

'I couldn't afford to drink very often. I like the taste of white wine, though not so much the reds.'

'We're compatible, then.'

'Whites were Sarah's favourites, too.' Thomas smiled slightly. 'I'll introduce you to some of her favourite wines and you can see how you like them. You can work your way through what's left of her collection. She'd hate it to go to waste. She was generous to a fault, though careful not to waste anything. Said it came from living through the shortages of World War Two.'

He seemed to be a kind man, Fleur thought. The ultra-comfortable car was making her feel a bit sleepy now, but she tried to stay awake and respond to his comments.

He chuckled and she jerked upright, wondering what had amused him.

'You were nodding off there for a minute or two, Fleur. If you'll take my advice, it's best to try to stay awake and fit in with the local time straight away when you face such a big time change – though you might not last past teatime today.'

'I think I may have trouble staying awake even that long. I didn't get much sleep on the plane. I've been so busy for the past few days, putting my house on the market among other things, that I haven't had time to wind down.'

He shot her a quick, surprised glance. 'You've already decided to sell your UK house?'

'I didn't much like it or the location, but it was the best I could afford after my divorce a few years ago. I was utterly determined not to get into a mortgage, you see, because I've never been a high earner. I shall be glad not to go back to it.'

'Very sensible to sell it, then.' He raised his voice a little. 'What about you, Portia? Did you have a house or flat to sell?'

'No. I'm just a lowly clerk. I've never been able to aspire to owning my own home.'

'Well, you can aspire to it now. Sarah was clever with money and you two are going to be very comfortable financially. Once her estate is settled there will be a nice annual income just from her portfolio of shares. In the meantime, the lawyer and I will be giving you a comfortable living wage while you're sorting out the house, as Sarah suggested.'

The figure he named made Fleur gasp in surprise. 'We shan't need that much, surely?'

'Well, if you prefer to save some of it, no one will stop you, but it's what Sarah wanted you to have, so that you could enjoy yourselves. She doesn't expect you to work non-stop on the family records. All work and no play makes for a dull life. For a start, there are some excellent restaurants in Mandurah, which is a tourist town.'

He waited a moment then added, 'I thought I'd take you to choose cars tomorrow morning if you're up to it. You'll need vehicles to get around here because there aren't a lot of bus services, compared to the populous parts of the UK, from what I remember of my visits there, anyway.'

'That'll be great,' Fleur said. 'Just something small and economical will be fine.'

'Ah. Well, that's another of Sarah's conditions. She was a bit bossy, in a caring sort of way. She wanted to make sure you two had comfortable vehicles and small ones aren't as safe, so as per her instructions, you get a choice of which car we buy for you, but not an unlimited one.'

Fleur couldn't think what to say to that. You could hardly complain about being made comfortable and safe, could you? But if it was a new car, she'd be terrified of damaging it. Not that she was prone to accidents, but she'd never even driven a new car before.

Terry had reserved that privilege for himself and his had been a company vehicle so not available to her anyway.

She let herself close her eyes, just for a minute or two. This car was so comfortable.

Chapter Nine

Fleur was amazed when Thomas shook her gently and said, 'Wake up, sleepyhead. We're here.'

'Already!'

'You've been asleep for a good forty minutes.'

'Oh, my goodness! How rude of me. I'm so sorry.' She blinked and wriggled her shoulders and feet.

'If you haven't slept for a day and a half, it's perfectly understandable that you'd doze a little.'

She turned to smile at Portia. 'Did you fall asleep too?'

'No. But Thomas said to let you have your nap.'

Fleur glanced out of the window. 'Is this the rear of the house?'

'Sort of. It's the street side of it. I always think the real fronts of these canal houses are at the other side, looking out onto the water. I live just across the canal from Sarah's house. She used to wave to me from her patio and hold up a glass to invite me over for a drink.'

'That sounds fun.'

'Yes, it was. Come on, let's go inside.'

He got out and waited for them to join him, then locked the car. 'It makes an easy target for thieves to leave a car unlocked when you can't keep an eye on it.'

'I won't be likely to forget,' Portia said at once. 'I had a problem with that sort of thing where I lived in England, even though my car was an old one.'

He led the way to the door and unlocked it, then opened it and gestured to the two women to go in first.

Fleur looked at him in puzzlement. 'Wouldn't it be better if you led the way?'

He gave them a rueful glance. 'My instructions are to let you inside the hall, point out a few things from there then leave you to explore the house at your leisure.' He wasn't as certain as Sarah had been about this being the best way to start, but he wasn't going to go against her wishes.

Again it was Fleur who spoke. 'You mean, you're not even going to show us round or explain how the appliances work?'

'I promised Sarah to bring you here, give you a few basic details and leave you to it. She thought you'd like to explore the place on your own.'

He stepped into the hall and gestured to them to walk past him. 'That door to the right leads into the garage but there's not been a car there for a few years, not since Sarah stopped driving at the age of ninety-three. She was almost ninety-six when she died.'

'Well done her. I hope her final years were happy!' Portia said.

He smiled. 'Oh, yes. She was a very positive person, used to say that you could choose to look for the good or bad in life, and she preferred to focus on the good side of it all.'

Portia stared at him, mouth slightly open. He'd guess that this reply had resonated with her, but she didn't say anything. She seemed very guarded in what she said.

He was glad when Fleur continued the conversation.

'I remember Cousin Sarah from my childhood as great fun to spend time with. She and I kept in touch for a few years, then a couple of years after my marriage she stopped writing. I wondered if she'd died or had a stroke, so my husband looked into it and told me she'd passed away a few months before.'

He looked at her in surprise. 'She's only just died.'

There was a pregnant silence and he continued slowly, 'She didn't stop writing till you'd stopped responding for a year or two. She was always sad to have lost touch.'

'I responded to every letter I received.' Fleur frowned then whispered, 'My ex must have done this on purpose. I shall never forgive him for separating us.' She closed her eyes for a moment or two, looking like someone holding back extreme anger.

None of the family had approved of her husband, from what Sarah had told him, and the more he learned about this Terry, the more he found to dislike. He didn't say that, of course, but then he didn't need to from the expression on her face. 'You're right that Sarah was fun to be with, Fleur. Even as she was taking her last few breaths she was chuckling about something.'

'You were with her when she died?' Portia sounded surprised.

'Of course. I couldn't let her go through it alone.'

'You must have been exceptionally good friends.'

'We were. Though she was more like an aunt to me in some ways. There were, after all, over two decades of living between her and me.'

He fell silent for a moment, then took a deep breath and continued his explanations. 'You need to know a few things about the house. This is the control box for the reverse cycle air conditioning, which heats or cools the house as needed. You can switch it off in the zones of the house you're not using to save wasting energy. The zones are listed on the keypad. Basically, with a house this big you need to remember to think ahead, because it takes time to cool or heat such large spaces.'

They nodded but to his surprise, it was Fleur who looked less confident this time.

She caught his glance and grimaced. 'I'm not good with guessing about technology.'

'You'll get used to it. Also, there's a box of instruction manuals for all the household equipment in that cupboard under the stairs.' He pointed along the hall and got more nods.

'Another thing to remember is that there are flyscreens on all the windows and doors that open – I think you call them "insect screens" in the UK, don't you? It's better not to leave any of the flyscreens open; you should close them even if you're only going to be outside for a minute or two, because Mandurah is home to a few zillion mosquitoes. It varies how numerous they are according to the time of year but they seem particularly fond of tender pink flesh that's just arrived from the UK. And they go for some people more than others.'

He opened a door further along the hall. 'Sarah found this lift helpful for the last few years, especially when she was carrying up heavy objects or shopping. You might want to take up your luggage in it when that arrives, and any furniture or boxes you want to move around the house. Remember, you two own this house now and you have every right to change things. Sarah would want you to make yourselves feel comfortably at home here.'

He pointed to another door. 'The living area is in there. You go through it to get out to the patio. I think you'll like sitting out by the canal. Part of the patio is flyscreened so you won't get bitten, either. During the warmer months, Sarah spent a lot of her time out there watching the boats go past and the dolphins sometimes, or just reading the newspapers and magazines. She never quite adjusted to reading them online. She was an avid reader so you'll find plenty of books scattered round the house to choose from.'

Fleur beamed at that. 'Oh, good! I love reading.'

Portia grimaced as if she didn't like reading. Now, why was that? he wondered.

'Do dolphins really go right past the house?' she asked. 'I love watching them! They have such kind faces.'

'You'll see plenty of them here. And finally . . .' He went across to the stairs and picked up two small, padded envelopes that were on the lowest step. 'These are your house keys. They're all labelled. There's a spare set in the freezer.'

They stared incredulously. 'In the freezer?'

He laughed. 'Sarah thought it was a safer place than hanging them on a hook where anyone could see them. She had a few quirky ideas like that.'

He waited and when neither said anything, he took a step towards the front door. 'I'll leave you to explore and choose your bedrooms.'

Then he stopped and looked back at them. 'Oops! Nearly forgot. I'll come round about nine o'clock tomorrow morning, if that's all right with you. Your luggage should have been delivered by then, but if it hasn't, we'll phone the airport to ask about it before we go out. I'll take you to look at cars first. She made provision for you to have one each.'

They both gaped at that news.

'After that I'll show you the big shopping centre, which is a good place to buy groceries and most other things you might need. The shops on the foreshore, which is a lawned area that runs along the estuary, are mainly for tourists and there are plenty of cafés there too. Ciao!'

He walked out, hoping that Sarah had been right and that simply tossing the two women into the house would help them to start bonding. It was sad to think of cousins never having even met. He hoped these two would get on well.

Chapter Ten

Fleur looked at Portia as the front door clicked shut behind Thomas. 'Just like that, he's gone. I bet we'd have had a lot of things to ask him if he'd bothered to walk us round the house.'

'I suppose he feels he has to do as Cousin Sarah asked. She had some strange ideas about welcoming us, didn't she? And fancy putting the spare keys in the freezer. Shall we make a start on exploring?' Without waiting for an answer, Portia opened the second door on the right and stepped into the room beyond it. 'Oh my! Look at this! It's a huge room, just like the property shows on TV.'

The living area was a square space with a large kitchen to one side of the rear. An eight-place dining table stood next to it and comfortable seating, plus a TV and stereo were placed in two groups near the wall of windows that overlooked the water. They walked towards it and stared out at the beauty of the water sparkling in the sunlight, with the neighbouring houses reflected in it.

'It's absolutely gorgeous,' Portia said softly. 'I can't believe we own it.'

'Neither can I. We'd better not go outside yet or I'll not want to come back in again.'

'Shall we explore the rest of the ground floor first or go upstairs and check out the bedrooms?'

'Let's have a quick whizz round the rest of the downstairs next. I should think that door leads to them.' Fleur led the way across the room and they found that the door opened into the other end of the hall through which they'd entered the house.

The three rooms along the side of the house were less imposing, rather dusty and with an unused feel to them all. The end one overlooking the canal was full of boxes, books and piles of papers; the other two were completely unfurnished.

'It's warmer in these rooms, feels quite stuffy. I bet this air conditioning zone is switched off. She mustn't have used these rooms much.'

'Let's go upstairs and sort out bedrooms for ourselves.' Fleur hesitated and added, 'We can look for some clean underwear, too. I'm desperate for a shower after that long plane flight.'

'Me too.'

'Let's try out the lift.'

Portia hesitated. 'I've never used a house lift before. What if we get stuck?'

'Why would it suddenly not work?' Fleur looked at her in amazement, wishing her cousin wouldn't be so negative. That'd be hard to live with. But if she'd been made redundant twice in a year, perhaps she was depressed. Who wouldn't be?

She opened the lift door and peered inside at the control panel. 'There's an emergency button and a phone plus directions to call for help if you get stuck. See for yourself.'

'Oh, good. That makes me feel a lot safer.' Portia followed her inside it and closed the door.

Fleur pressed the button with '1' on it and as the lift took them upstairs she stole a glance at her companion, who was standing clutching the handrail tightly.

Portia saw her watching and said, 'I don't like to be shut in small spaces.'

The lift bumped gently to a stop upstairs and they got out, standing looking round the landing.

'I feel like an intruder,' Fleur confessed suddenly.

'So do I.'

'Look at all those doors. However many bedrooms do you think there are?'

'Five or six. And to think I was living in a grotty little bedsitter in England only two days ago.'

'After my divorce all I could afford was a squinchy little town house with small rooms and one claustrophobic bathroom. It was in a row of eight and had a little yard behind it, not even a proper garden.'

'Squinchy? What does that mean?'

'It was a word my daughter used to describe it. She thought she'd made it up but the dictionary calls it "a small arch used to support a spire". She hated living there after our big family home.'

'What about their father? Couldn't she have lived with him or didn't he have the money for a big house either?'

Fleur scowled at the thought of Terry. 'The rat seems to have plenty of money now the divorce is over. I bet he had some stashed away. He bought himself a big luxury flat, but didn't give his children the choice of living with him. He doesn't often invite them to visit him, either, and our son wouldn't go anyway. The two of them don't get on very well, especially lately.'

'Why lately?'

'Because Terry seemed to change after we split up, grow more arrogant and unreasonable somehow.'

She decided she might as well finish the tale. 'There was a big bust-up because Terry didn't want James to do an apprenticeship, but to study business. That's the last thing my lad would ever be interested in, so I supported him.'

'Not everyone's good at academic subjects. I'm not, for one.' Portia sighed.

'What are you good at?'

'Nothing, really. I'm very ordinary.'

'There are other things in the world besides universities. My dad said that when I didn't want to go to one. Well, I couldn't have. I got married very young. Terry was older than me and I was dazzled. My father always said so-called ordinary people are the backbone of the world and without them everyday life would grind to a halt. Dad told James people needed furniture more than university degrees when the boy developed a passion for working with wood.'

Portia was staring at her as if she'd said something astounding, so Fleur's father's simple wisdom must have struck home again. She gave her cousin a moment for it to sink in, then went on quietly, 'Living here is going to be rather different for both of us, eh?'

'Very different indeed.' She glanced out of the landing window. 'I love the brightness of the light here.'

'So do I. And I'm looking forward to missing the rest of the English winter, too.'

'Let's use bedrooms on the canal side of the house. I'd love to lie in bed looking out at the water.'

'Me too.'

There were three bedrooms along the canal side, all with walk-in wardrobes and en suites with showers.

'Three en suites,' Portia said in a whisper.

Fleur chuckled. 'What are you whispering for?'

'I don't know.'

They both fell silent when they went into the end room, which had clearly been Sarah's. Her clothes were still hanging up in the wardrobe and filling the drawers.

'We'll have to clear it out,' Fleur said. 'Let's use the other two bedrooms.'

Portia went to her bedroom window and called, 'Oh, look! They've all got little balconies. Wow, I've never had a room half as grand as this.'

Fleur dumped her backpack on the bed and turned round in a circle. The room felt light, airy and was beautifully furnished.

Then she peered into the en suite, which had a large walk-in wet area. 'I feel desperate for a shower. Let's go and look at Cousin Sarah's clothes, see if Thomas is right about her having some new, unused underwear. Even if I wash my own things for tomorrow, I'm not walking around with no knickers or bra till then.'

'We could always tumble them dry.'

'And hang around half naked waiting for them? No thanks. Let's at least have a look.'

She led the way back to Sarah's bedroom and began opening and shutting the drawers. When she got to the bottom drawer, she exclaimed, 'Bingo! Thomas was right. This one is full of new clothes, still in packets.'

They pulled out more than a dozen unopened packages.

'This underwear isn't at all what you'd expect an old woman to wear,' Portia said.

'How do you know what old women wear? I certainly don't.'

'I just – didn't expect to find such pretty things.'

'You're stereotyping oldies there,' Fleur protested. She sympathised with people who were treated unfairly because she'd been told many times that no one was really gluten sensitive and she was stupid to fall for that idea.

'I suppose I am. Silly of me. It's sad, isn't it, that she never got the chance to wear these? They're in my size.'

'Mine too.'

'She had excellent taste.'

'It's sad in one way to see them, but think of the optimism of someone buying new things she didn't really need at the age of ninety-five. She must have remained as lively as I remember. Thomas clearly adored her.'

Portia sighed. 'I wish I'd met her. Let's share the new underwear between us – and keep them. It'd be immoral to throw such beautiful things away.'

'You're right. We could take it in turns to choose.'

Once that was done, they turned to look at the clothes hanging in neat groups. 'We might as well see if we can find some clean clothes as well. Oh, look at this skirt! Isn't the material beautiful?'

'Those colours would suit you, Portia. Why don't you take that one?'

'Should I?'

'We'll need to clear out her clothing as well, remember. I don't think I could throw away something as pretty as that.'

'I don't actually have many clothes.'

'I've seen a few that I love the looks of.'

They looked at one another, then Portia said, 'I shall feel a bit guilty taking them, but I'd feel a lot more guilty if I threw away good clothes.'

'That's settled, then.'

They walked out of Sarah's bedroom with an armful each of underwear and clothing. Portia looked down, her face glowing with pleasure. 'These will be the prettiest things I've ever owned.'

'Ever?'

'Yes. My mother went for practical things when I was a child and she's colour blind, so hardly anything she bought me ever matched or looked good. She used to say they were practical and cheap, and you had to buy bargains when you saw them. We never had a lot of money.'

'Is she still alive?'

'Yes. I haven't seen her for a while, though. She's got a new guy and she's busy with him.' She smiled suddenly. 'He teases her about her lack of colour sense and goes clothes shopping with her. He's quite nice, actually.'

'Do you get on well with her?'

Portia shrugged. 'We've drifted apart since Dad died. She wants me to get married and give her grandchildren. After my disastrous relationship, I'm not jumping into anything.'

'I agree. Being married to the wrong person is . . . horrible. I got married far too young and let him boss me around.'

Portia patted her arm in sympathy and they smiled at one another.

'Right then. See you downstairs in about half an hour. I'm hungry but I'd rather have a shower before I eat.'

'I would, too.'

When she got into her bedroom, Portia went to smile at herself in the mirror as she held up one of the new tops, then a skirt.

This was the last thing she'd expected to be doing here. She'd never be pretty but she could look nice.

Fleur closed her bedroom door and leaned against it for a moment, letting out a long sigh of pleasure at the prospect of a little time to herself. It was good that they were sharing details about their lives, a hopeful sign for the future.

She strolled round the beautiful room, touching things here and there. The walls were off-white, with turquoise and white curtains and a plain turquoise bedspread on a small double bed. In one corner a large vase of flowers stood on a plant stand, so realistic she had to walk across and touch them to prove they were artificial. She'd rearrange them a little later, something she was good at. There were too many bunched together.

She walked over to the walk-in wardrobe and put her new clothes away, except for the ones she was going to wear after her shower.

Thomas had been right. There were toiletries and a pile of lovely fluffy towels in colours that would go well with turquoise. She shook one out, put a bathmat in place and slipped out of her clothes, having to leave them on the floor in one corner because there was no container for dirty linen. She'd have to start a list of things to buy.

Turning the shower on, she adjusted the temperature and walked under it. Such bliss to stand there and let the warm water wash away the travel staleness. The soap smelled heavenly and there was both shampoo and conditioner to go with it.

When she went downstairs she found Portia already in the kitchen, also with damp hair, exploring the contents of the fridge.

'That skirt and top look good on you,' she said.

Portia stroked the material. 'I love them. She had good colour taste, didn't she?'

'Yes. What have we got to eat?'

'Salad stuff, a cooked chicken, fruit and a loaf. Thank goodness it's wholemeal. I hate eating white bread even if it is often the cheapest.'

'I shan't be able to eat the bread but the rest is OK.'

Portia looked at her. 'Oh yes. You said something about that food problems before, I think. Are you coeliac?'

'No, but similar. There's another category: non-coeliac gluten sensitive. I'll have to buy some special wheat-free bread for myself. It's more expensive than ordinary bread so I tried to make it myself once, but I'm not the world's greatest cook, especially when it comes to baking.' She chuckled at the memory. 'It came out all crumbly and turned into a heavy brick overnight.'

'We could find some recipes online and I could have a go, if you like. I love cooking – when I've got anything to cook with, that is.'

'Wonderful. Thanks. You can't be worse than me. Let's look in the freezer as well. We'll need at least one more meal today after this one.'

The freezer contained a lot of food, and plenty of neatly labelled ready meals. Fleur flipped them over. 'These must have been made specially for her. They're not commercial ones. The contents are listed but they're handwritten.'

She began going through the list carefully, saw Portia staring at her impatiently and explained, 'I have to check the list of ingredients carefully every time I buy something I use a lot at the shops, because the makers rarely signal changes in the recipe. I've been caught out by that more than once when I've forgotten to check and it made me ill.'

Portia picked up some of the packets of pre-prepared food, screwing up her eyes as if finding it difficult to see what was written.

'Did you leave your reading glasses upstairs?'

There was dead silence, then, 'You're bound to find out that I'm dyslexic.'

'I have a friend with that problem. The tinted glasses don't help her so she makes a joke of it.'

'You don't – well, think less of me because of it? My mother hates it. She used to get furious with me when I was a kid for taking longer than she thought necessary to read something.'

'Why should I think less of you? You didn't choose to be dyslexic and I know what it's like coping with a problem, just like me and gluten. It's a nuisance at times, but no one is perfect.'

'Thank you.'

'What for?'

'Saying that.'

Fleur saw that her cousin had tears running down her cheeks and put an arm round her instinctively, as she would have done with one of her children.

Portia sniffed and fumbled for a tissue. 'I've been dreading telling you.'

'Do you mind that I'm gluten intolerant?'

'No, of course not. You can't help it.'

'Well, there you are, then. I don't mind that you're dyslexic. You can't help that, either. It's just how you are. Now, stop sniffling and let's get something to eat. I'm famished.'

Something had eased between them with that exchange and Portia had relaxed markedly.

After they'd eaten, the day seemed to drift past slowly. Neither of them could settle to anything because their bodies were craving sleep. They sat outside for a while, enjoying the warmth and watching the occasional boat go past. When that palled, they wandered round the house, on their own or together.

Each lingered in the room where documents and boxes were piled but admitted afterwards that they weren't looking forward to sorting it out. There were so many piles of folders and papers and who knew what else. No wonder Cousin Sarah had not wanted to deal with it.

As the afternoon passed, they switched on the TV and when the controls baffled Fleur, Portia took over, channel surfing till she found some news. Some of the things it talked about were new to both of them and it was fascinating to see another view of the world. Some of the Australian stories were incomprehensible.

Fleur studied the bookcase in the living room, found a novel she'd been wanting to read and settled down to read it for a while.

Portia found a book about Mandurah, one with a lot of photos, but she spent more time staring out of the window at the water and the sea birds coming and going nearby than she did looking at the book.

They made a simple meal in the late afternoon, or rather Portia did. She decided on a quick risotto to cater for her cousin's intolerances. It was delicious, too.

'You're a good cook,' Fleur said.

Portia beamed at that compliment. She clearly wasn't used to them.

Just before six o'clock they both yawned at the same time, laughed and Fleur said, 'That's it. Let's go to bed.'

'Definitely.'

Chapter Eleven

In England, Terry Davies was fretting. He couldn't believe his mouse of a wife had inherited so much money. He should have stuck with her, then he'd be in clover, never have to work again.

He'd have to see if he could find some way of nudging them back together, nothing too obvious, but it was worth a try.

In the meantime, he'd have to rely on Marie to let him know what was going on. She wasn't best pleased about her mother being rich, and considered Fleur selfish for not sharing it. Well, Marie took after him, wasn't a fool who put others first, which was why he was quite fond of her. Chip off the old block, she'd be, when life had toughened her up a bit.

The bequest puzzled him. From early on in his marriage he'd had all their mail forwarded to his 'business address', a private PO box, and that had come in useful several times. It had been easy to spot and destroy the letters from the aunt. What idiot still used pen and ink in this day and age? A senile one, that's what. He'd destroyed the old fool's letters though she'd kept writing for a while at Christmas.

He hadn't realised the old witch was swimming in lard, though! Where had she got all that money from? He should have checked her finances more carefully.

In those days he'd needed Fleur to run his house and take care of the practical details of life. Why else would he have stayed married to such a colourless female for so long? She wasn't the best cook in the world, but she knew what to buy ready-made that would please his guests. And she'd made his guests feel welcome.

About time he checked up on her again. He picked up the phone and rang his daughter. 'Hi, love. Just keeping in touch. You all right?'

'Why shouldn't I be, Dad?'

'I thought you might still be upset about your mother being so selfish.'

Her voice grew sharper. 'Tell me about it! Who wouldn't be upset?'

'Look, I can spare another pound or two a week, say twenty quid a month, just to give you a bit more.'

'Thanks, Dad. You're a star. All contributions gratefully received.'

'Heard from your mother yet?'

'Just a quick text message to say she'd arrived in Australia. No details.'

'Has James heard from her?'

'I asked him and he got the same message, so she didn't even take the time to give more information to her little pet. Did you know she gave him all her furniture, except for those creaky old things that had belonged to her father's family? She kept those, so I suppose they're valuable.'

'But ugly.'

'Definitely ugly.'

He let her chat on for as long as he could stand it, then said he had an appointment. 'Let me know if you find out anything else about what your mother's doing down under. And I won't forget to put the extra money in every month for you.'

'Thank you so much. It's great to catch up with you, Dad.'

'Yes. Absolutely. I'm sorry I get these busy patches and don't always manage to keep in touch.'

He switched his phone off. It was good to have a pretty daughter, and photos of her to show people, but she was a bit of a yawn to chat to. And he had a very special package to pick up tonight.

Chapter Twelve

Fleur was woken at ten o'clock that evening by her mobile phone ringing. A woman said brightly, 'I'm calling about your luggage. Good news, Ms Blakemere. We've found it and can deliver it to the address you've given in Mandurah at about six o'clock tomorrow morning.'

'Oh, thank goodness!'

'Is the other Ms Blakemere at the same address?'

'Yes. I can give her the message if you like.'

'I'm afraid I have to speak to her myself.'

'I'll go and wake her.'

But Portia was already awake and standing in the doorway of her bedroom. 'Is there a problem?'

'On the contrary. They've found our luggage and someone needs to tell you that personally.' She held out the phone.

When the message had been duly delivered, Portia said, 'I'm thirsty and we have to be careful not to get dehydrated after the flight. I'm going down for a glass of water. I should have brought one up.'

'I'm thirsty too. I'll come with you.'

In the kitchen, Portia beamed at the huge fridge. 'I love that there's this tap on the fridge to provide chilled, filtered water. The water in my bathroom came out lukewarm and tasted horrible.'

After they went back to bed, nothing woke them till their alarms went off to wake them early so that they could receive their luggage.

By the time Thomas was due to arrive, they'd unpacked and done a load of washing, which was now hanging out on some lines they'd found by the side of the house. It seemed silly to use a dryer when it was so beautifully sunny and hot already but both pegs and washing lines were dusty, as if Cousin Sarah had stopped using them.

'I wonder what sort of car she wanted us to get?' Portia said as they waited.

'Who knows?' Fleur looked at her watch for the umpteenth time. She hadn't told Portia but she was rather nervous about driving in a foreign country. She'd not done a lot of driving till after her marriage broke up, because Terry hated her driving him. He'd told her many times that she wasn't a good driver.

She guessed now he'd been lying, just to upset her. She wasn't a bad driver, and had never been involved in an accident. She hadn't realised, till they separated, how much Terry had put her down. It seemed ages till they heard the sound of a car stopping outside.

Thomas looked fresh and alert. 'Good morning, ladies. I hope you slept well.'

'Very well. And our luggage arrived this morning at six.'

'Great to hear. Do you have some form of identity with you, like your passports? There will be all the paperwork for the car.'

'We can get them,' Fleur said.

They were back almost immediately and he drove them to a car dealership full of expensive-looking vehicles. He'd let the salesman know they were coming and the man showed them the cars Sarah had specified.

When the price of these was mentioned, Portia looked aghast and tugged Thomas's sleeve to get his attention while the salesman was responding to a colleague's question. 'These are too expensive,' she whispered. 'What if I have an accident?'

'The insurance will cover that. Why should you, though? Are you a nervous driver?'

'Not normally. I'm . . . not a bad driver, actually.'

That probably meant she was a good driver, he thought. 'Just try them out,' he coaxed.

When the salesman took them to a quiet part of town to have a go at driving the cars, it was Fleur who looked nervous. She stepped back, flapping one hand at Portia. 'You have first go.'

As Portia got into the driving seat, checked the various controls and set off, Thomas watched carefully from the back seat. She was actually an excellent driver, careful and yet not timid. When he told her so, she flushed.

'I mean it,' he insisted.

'Oh well, thank you. It's a lovely car to drive.' She'd blushed bright red, clearly wasn't used to compliments.

He turned to Fleur. 'Your turn next.'

She drove over-carefully, not in the same league as her cousin skill-wise, though safe enough. 'That went well.' He saw her relax a little and added, 'How did it feel?'

'Too big. I've only ever driven smallish cars.'

He got out Sarah's list of cars and showed it to the salesman. 'Is one of these smaller?'

'A couple of them are. Come and see.' He took them outside and found one that suited Fleur better.

However, when Portia tried it, she said she admitted she preferred the first car.

'It's your choice.' Thomas turned back to the salesman. 'What sort of a discount do I get if I buy them both – cash?'

His three companions all gaped at this.

'You're buying both cars, sir?'

'I am if you'll give me a tempting price; otherwise I'll go elsewhere. They're presents from the ladies' great-aunt, but she said to make sure I got a good bargain.'

After a bit of haggling, they settled on a price.

'Can they be ready to be picked up tomorrow?' Thomas asked.

'Yes, of course. What about insurance?'

'I can sort that out with them when you come to pick up the cars.'

Both women seemed dumbfounded by all this and were rather quiet as he drove them back to their house. 'I think we should start off from here again so that you'll know your way to the supermarket and back.'

'Oh yes, that's a good idea,' Fleur said at once.

As they set off, he told them another of Sarah's conditions. 'It's another of Sarah's wishes that I only take you to the shopping centre the first time, then leave you to find your own way to and from it afterwards. I'm afraid she had very definite views about this and everything else. Which didn't mean she wouldn't listen to other people and change her mind if they had a more convincing argument. Only, she wanted you two to lead an independent life here.'

The two women exchanged worried glances.

'I'm rubbish at finding my way somewhere new till I've been there a few times,' Fleur confessed.

Thomas could only shrug.

Portia turned to Fleur. 'We can go together the first few times. I'm usually able to remember the way, even if I've only driven somewhere once.'

Well, Thomas admitted to himself afterwards, Sarah's rules seemed to be doing what she'd wanted, nudging the two women to co-operate with and help one another. They might both need a little push here and there but perhaps she'd been right about tossing them in the deep end together.

But he'd keep an eye on the situation. If her plans needed tweaking a little, he'd do it, and was sure she'd want him to.

Thomas drove slowly round the shopping centre car park. 'I'm trying to find a place under a tree so that we can park the car in the shade and keep it cool.'

'I've seen people do that in films!' Portia exclaimed.

He succeeded in his quest and led the way across the huge car park to the nearest entrance to the shopping centre.

'The air inside is nice and cool,' Fleur commented. 'I'm beginning to see what you meant about not having to endure too much heat.'

'Yes. Why don't we stroll round the whole place first to get a feel for it?' No mistaking their relief at that even before they spoke.

'Oh, yes. Good idea.' Fleur relaxed visibly.

'Are there any foods you need in particular?'

'Yes. I'm gluten intolerant, so I need special bread and baking ingredients. Is there a health store at this centre?'

'Yes, though I don't know what it's like because I've never been inside. This place is so big I should think there will be every type of shop you need.'

'Good.'

He noticed that Fleur studied the lists of ingredients on all the packets of food she picked up, discarding some with a regretful sigh.

'It must be hard to cope with an intolerance towards a common food like wheat,' he said.

He saw her frowning over some ingredients that were particularly hard to read and pulled his reading glasses out of his top pocket. 'Why don't you use these as a magnifying glass?'

She held them over the list. 'That's a big help, thank you. I didn't remember to bring my little magnifying glass with me today. I don't know why they use such tiny lettering, anyway. If I can't read the ingredients properly, I don't buy the food. It's too risky. And if people are badly affected by an item because they couldn't read the ingredients, they won't buy it again. So either way, it means the manufacturers could be losing custom.'

To their relief the health store sold all sorts of strange (to him) flours but Fleur knew what they were and also bought a strange-looking loaf.

'We should get a gluten-free cookery book,' Portia said.

When they spoke to an assistant who seemed to be very knowledgeable, she recommended a cookery book with a bread recipe that she assured them was easy to make.

Fleur took a quick look at it, nodded at the list of ingredients in one or two recipes and passed it to Portia, who followed her example and went through a few of the recipes.

By the time they'd got everything they could think of from the shops, the boot of Thomas's car was crammed full of bags and packages, and the two women were both looking weary.

'I don't think I've ever spent so much money on food in one fell swoop,' Portia said as she got into the car.

'Can you summon up just a little more energy to go to the bank? It's on the way home from here. Your debit cards should be waiting for you there and money will be paid into your accounts each month.'

He named the sum and they both gasped.

'There's also a set-up sum in case you want to buy any furniture or laptops or whatever.' He told them how much and watched Portia's mouth drop open literally and her eyes glaze with shock. He wondered if Sarah had known how short of money the younger woman was. Had she always been?

His friend must have known something about these two Blakemeres, or she'd not have made them her heirs. Kindness had been Sarah's middle name, he'd always teased her.

After they'd finished at the bank, he drove them home and helped them unload the shopping. 'I'll leave you to get on with the rest of the day. We'll need to pick up the cars tomorrow morning at eleven, so I'll call for you at quarter to. Then you can drive them round on your own for a while and get properly used to your new chariots.'

He saw the panic on Fleur's face and steeled himself not to give in to it and make things easier for her.

'How about coming round to my house for a sundowner at about four o'clock tomorrow afternoon? I'm at number twenty-three. You won't need your cars. Just turn left when you leave the house and keep walking till you get to my place. The street is a U shape, built along the sides of a watery cul-de-sac, so you can't lose your way.'

'That'd be lovely,' Fleur said.

Chapter Thirteen

At the house they put the food away and Portia volunteered to do most of the cooking.

'I can't ask you to do that,' Fleur said.

'You said you don't enjoy cooking, but I love it, only I haven't been able to afford to do anything fancy for years. It'll be fun to experiment with gluten-free cooking, too.'

'Fun? It drives me mad trying to stay safe.'

'There you are, then. I'm happy to take over. But I'll let you clear up.'

'Fair enough.' The doorbell rang. 'I'll get that, shall I?'

Fleur answered the door to find a man wearing bright red overalls with Friends in Need Cleaning Services printed on the front and back. 'Can I help you?'

'It's the other way round. You must be one of Sarah's heirs. My company does the house cleaning here. The normal cleaner has an emergency dental appointment, so I said I'd take over for her today.' He waited, head on one side.

'I don't think we'll need a cleaning service. There are only the two of us.'

'Your aunt wanted me to continue working here, so that you'd be free to enjoy yourselves, so she arranged for payments to be made automatically.'

Portia had come to join them and her face brightened at that comment. 'I'm not fond of cleaning. Let's just accept it as a welcome gift, Fleur.'

'But—'

Portia gestured to him. 'Do come in, Mr—'

'My name's Col. And I know my way round, because I've been here many times before, not only to clean but to enjoy Sarah's sundowners.' His voice grew gentler. 'I really miss your aunt. I'm so sorry for your loss.'

There was silence for a minute. Fleur wondered whether, if she dropped dead, her friends would miss her as much as he and Thomas were obviously missing Sarah. Perhaps her son would. She was less sure of her daughter and there were no other relatives she was close to on a personal level. Well, there might be one if she and Portia got on well.

It made you think, being alone in the world did.

'How long does it take you to go over the house?' Portia asked.

'About three hours because some rooms are not in use. This is the day we usually do the bigger clean-up but we can change the day if it isn't suitable. We do another shorter clean as well in between, just an hour and a half. In warmer weather Sarah used to go out and sit on the patio while the cleaner worked. We have a key to the front door but you might prefer us to return it to you.' He waited patiently for an answer.

Fleur found herself beginning to relax. He clearly knew the household and had an honest face, not good-looking but attractive. Well, that was better as far as she was concerned. She was suspicious of men who were good-looking after living with one for so many years.

Terry had been vain about his looks and he'd used them shamelessly to charm people, especially women. As the years passed, he'd stopped bothering to charm his wife, though, just taken her for granted.

She'd had to listen to people saying what a lovely man he was – only he wasn't. He wasn't nice in any way that counted, as far as she was concerned. She'd put up with him for the children's sake when they were younger and she couldn't understand why it'd taken her so long to realise that they'd all be better away from him.

She suddenly realised that Col was still waiting for her to say something. 'Sorry. My thoughts wandered for a moment. I'm a bit jetlagged, I'm afraid.'

Portia stepped in. 'How about we follow Cousin Sarah's example for the hours you need to come and then we can change it later if necessary? And if she could trust you with the keys, so can we. Is there anything else or shall we leave you to it for today?'

'Nothing else.'

He went into the garage and came back with various pieces of cleaning equipment that must have been in one of the cupboards at the far end. They were still learning what was in this house.

The two women got themselves some chilled water in an insulated jug they'd found earlier and went out onto the patio. It was warm but not too hot for comfort and a light breeze was stirring the air.

'I might do some sketching,' Portia said suddenly. 'I'll nip upstairs and get my pad.'

She was back within a couple of minutes with a large pad and a pencil case. But before she started she stared out at the water and the boats passing in the main canal at the end of theirs and sighed in pleasure. 'Talk about living in luxury: new cars, house cleaners, plenty of money. I haven't got my head around it yet. Am I dreaming? If so, don't bother to wake me up.'

'If you're dreaming, so am I.'

They settled down to a restful time but both fell asleep after a while and Col had to wake them up to say he was leaving.

'He does a good job,' Fleur said as they walked round the house afterwards.

'He seems a nice guy, too. I'll just put a simple tea together, shall I? Salad and some of that roast pork all right for you, with rice biscuits?'

'Whatever is convenient. Thank you.'

Portia went to the kitchen, leaving her pad on the outdoor table. A breeze lifted the edges of the pages a few times then a stronger gust blew the top one completely open. Fleur couldn't resist looking at what her cousin had been doing.

The sketch was charming, featuring a cormorant perched on the next door's jetty. The wind lifted the next page, showing two seagulls squabbling over some titbit. They were all so lifelike. Goodness! Portia had hidden talents.

Fleur felt guilty for even this amount of peeping, so moved away. She wasn't surprised when her cousin came out and said, 'I'll clear away my mess,' and took away the pad.

She didn't say she'd seen the top couple of sketches. It was up to Portia whether she shared her work with others, but she was clearly a gifted artist and should be proud of her talent.

They managed to stay awake until nearly eight o'clock, then yawned at the same time, laughed and agreed it was time for bed.

'We should be into local time in a couple of days,' Fleur said.

The following morning, they woke early and got ready mostly in silence, both admitting to feeling rather nervous about driving, especially a brand-new car.

Portia signed. 'I wish we knew the highway code here.'

They looked at one another and Fleur said, 'I wonder if Cousin Sarah's computer is still online. Let's go and find out.'

'How stupid of us not to try it yesterday!' Portia said.

The computer came on straight away.

'What a relief to have the internet working here already. Why didn't Thomas tell us we'd also inherited a desktop computer?'

'I think we're supposed to use our initiative,' Fleur said.

'I've never been known to have much of that.'

'You will have by the time we've finished here,' Fleur said darkly. 'I'm beginning to think Cousin Sarah is manipulating us even though she's dead. I wonder what else she's planned. We're going to have to fumble our way through the first few weeks. I hope we don't make a mess of anything.'

'I'm sure her efforts were kindly meant.'

'Yes. My childhood memories are of a kind woman. But it still isn't easy, is it? I'm glad you're here. I'd not like to have faced this alone.'

'I'm glad you're here, too.'

They gave one another uncertain smiles, then Portia did a search online and found the driving rules for Western Australia. They pulled up chairs and read them carefully, not finding much difference from the UK ones.

After that, Fleur sent quick emails to her children, but Portia said there was no one who really needed to know about her.

'Not even your mother?'

'She's away on holiday with Ross. She doesn't usually bother to pick up her emails when she goes away. She's not addicted to going online.'

'Are you?'

'Not unless there's a good reason. And there usually isn't.'

How sad was that? She watched Portia stare blankly into space so didn't hesitate to interrupt.

'I think we should try out the garage door and see if there are remotes. We'll need to put the cars inside it when we get back today.'

The garage was a big, shadowy space that they'd not bothered to explore yet. It had room for three cars and then a whole series of big cupboards covered the far side wall. The remotes were sitting openly on a workbench at the rear.

Portia fingered a couple of the tools on the shelves behind them and nodded approval. 'These may come in useful.'

'I haven't a clue how to use a drill.'

'I have, though only to do simple things. It's not hard. Let's try out the ponglers.'

'The what?'

'Oh, sorry. "Ponglers" is what I called remotes as a child and I still think of them by that name.'

'It's cute. I like it better than "remote".'

Portia picked up one 'pongler', aimed it towards the big double door and pressed the button. The door slowly rose and then obeyed her electronic command to close again. The third pongler opened the single garage door at the end, but they wouldn't need that so they left it behind.

Fleur looked round in satisfaction. 'That's another daily detail dealt with.'

Chapter Fourteen

Thomas arrived exactly on time and drove them to the car dealer, where they were each given a lesson on the features of their vehicle. After providing a few details for insurance purposes they were turned loose to drive them away.

Fleur could feel herself shaking with nervousness and for a moment her cousin's hand lay on her shoulder, then Portia whispered, 'You can do it.' She wasn't so sure she could, she got lost so easily, but that hand had felt comforting.

Thomas stood to one side as they were given their lessons, but now re-joined them. 'Ready? Good. Do you remember the way back?'

'I think so,' Portia said.

'No. I definitely don't.' Fleur was so nervous about driving back in sole charge of an expensive vehicle that she could hardly remember which way was up.

He stared from one to the other, then said, 'Hang it! I'll break Sarah's rule this time and lead the way back.'

They both spoke at once. 'Thank you!'

When he drove slowly away, Portia gestured to Fleur to go next.

The traffic wasn't heavy and at first things went smoothly, but they got into trouble at the second set of traffic lights. As Fleur followed Thomas's vehicle through, the lights changed and Portia had to stop. Since there were 'No parking' signs along the street and traffic was quite heavy, the others couldn't stop and wait for her. Fleur could only hope that her cousin would catch up.

But though she kept a watch in her rear-view mirror, so many other vehicles turned in to the streets after them that they lost sight of the other car. Once they got home, Thomas parked to one side of the drive and waved to Fleur to go inside.

She sat frozen for a moment, then muttered, 'Pongler,' found the remote underneath her handbrake and used it to get into the garage.

As she stopped the engine inside, she shuddered and buried her face in her hands briefly. She'd done it but she'd been afraid all the way back. Absolutely terrified.

That thought made her suddenly raise her head and frown. When had she become so timid? Years ago. Partly thanks to Terry, partly thanks to her own cowardice in not standing up to him. She had to do better than this from now on, couldn't go through the rest of her life panicking at every slight change of routine.

'You all right?'

She looked sideways and saw that Thomas was standing beside her car, watching her in concern. She opened the door. 'I was just recovering from my challenging experience.

I shan't be as frightened of driving next time.' She wouldn't let herself be.

As she got out of the car, he nodded approvingly but she had the feeling he'd guessed how panicked she'd been feeling.

'Good girl.'

There was the sound of a car turning in to the drive and Portia edged into the space next to Fleur's car, beaming at them.

She positively bounced out of the car. 'I did it! Only made one mistake and managed to head in the right direction and find my way back here once I realised what I'd done. I didn't even need to stop and ask for directions.' She patted the steering wheel. 'It's a beautiful car to drive.'

'Well done, Portia!' Thomas smiled at them like everyone's favourite uncle. 'I'll leave the two of you till later. You haven't forgotten that you're coming round to my place for a sundowner, have you?'

'I'm looking forward to it,' Fleur said. And actually, she was.

They grabbed a quick snack and went to sit outside.

'We did it!' Portia smiled at her cousin. 'Don't look so worried. I'll help you till you know your way round the centre of Mandurah.'

'Thanks. I'd be grateful.'

After a restful few hours and another involuntary nap for Fleur, the two women got ready for their first ever sundowner.

Portia had chosen a plain navy-blue skirt from Cousin Sarah's wardrobe worn with her best top, a red T-shirt. She hoped they looked reasonable together but if not, too bad.

When she joined Flour, she felt underdressed because her cousin looked so elegant. She wasn't wearing any of Cousin Sarah's clothes, either, just a neat matching summer top and skirt with a string of pretty beads. How could such simple clothes look so right?

Fleur stared at Portia, eyes narrowed. 'You need a scarf with that to finish it off; a patterned red would be best.'

'Well, I don't have one. And I'm not borrowing one. I've already borrowed the skirt but it's very plain, not too recognisable to Thomas as Cousin Sarah's, I hope. This is as smart as I can manage.'

'I have a scarf I think will work well with it. You're welcome to borrow it. Wait a minute.' She didn't wait for an answer but ran lightly up the stairs and came back with a long scarf in a pretty red and navy pattern.

She twisted it round Portia's neck. 'There. Looks good.'

Portia went to stare at herself in a mirror. It did add a rather smart touch. 'That looks much better. How did you know to use it?'

'I just know that sort of thing. Don't you have ideas about clothes that suit you?'

'Sort of, but I'm rarely sure, and until now, the colours have mainly depended on what they had for sale in the charity shop.'

'Well, I think we should definitely use Sarah's things. It'd be so wasteful to throw good clothes away. They're hardly worn and she had excellent taste. Luckily we both seem to be the same size as her. I always wished I had a sister to share clothes and accessories with and now you and I will be able to do that.'

She paused because Portia had suddenly pulled out a handkerchief and was blowing her nose. Her cousin had tears in her eyes. What sort of life had she led in the past few years to get emotional over a simple remark like that? Charity-shop clothes and struggling to get by.

She waited till Portia had put away the handkerchief to say, 'We decided to give ourselves five minutes to walk to Thomas's house, so let's make a start. Ready now?'

'Yes. Um – ought we to take a bottle of wine?'

'Oh, heavens! I'm not sure.' After a moment's thought, she shrugged. 'Not this first time. We'll invite him here for drinks another day and see if he brings one then.'

'And maybe we can invite Col to join us as well.'

'Good idea. He seemed really pleasant when he came here to clean.' More than pleasant: attractive. Oh heavens, where had that come from? She'd given up men since her divorce and had refused all invitations to go out on dates. She definitely wasn't getting involved with a man again, so shouldn't even be eyeing him in that way.

Outside they found that the sun was warm still, but the day had cooled down a little so it was pleasant to walk the short distance to number 39.

The door opened before they reached it and Thomas stood there smiling at them. 'Welcome!' He led the way inside another lovely home, not quite as big as their aunt's, but still large, with spacious rooms. It was situated on the other side of the same stretch of water and they could see their house from here.

A man stood up as they followed Thomas out to the patio. This time he was wearing a smart, short-sleeved shirt and jeans, not overalls.

'I think you've already met Col, haven't you?'

Fleur nodded. 'Yes. Nice to see you again.'

'Nice to see you, too. I was always the one in charge of the drinks at Sarah's, so Thomas and I thought we'd carry on the tradition.' He flourished a mock bow. 'What can I get you, ladies?'

'A glass of white wine would be nice.'

Portia hesitated, then said, 'I'll have the same. Just a small one, though. I'm not used to drinking.'

'How about a white wine spritzer, made into a long drink with soda water? And I'll use less wine than usual.'

'That sounds just right.'

He smiled at her. 'You don't have to drink alcohol at all if you don't want.'

'No, what you said sounds fine, with maybe about half the usual wine in it.'

'Your wish is my command.'

Thomas had gone back into the house and now returned with a platter of finger food.

This was a similar sort of set-up to the 'drinkies' that Terry had sometimes organised for useful acquaintances. Fleur froze for a moment at the memories that brought flooding back: his scorn when he didn't like the nibblies she'd provided, or the clothes she was wearing, or the way she'd done her hair. There had always been something wrong, but none of it ever his fault.

She had to ask Thomas to repeat himself. 'I'm sorry. I was just remembering something.'

'Not pleasant by your expression.'

She shrugged, not trying to explain. Nothing as boring as listening to tales of an ex's faults.

As the conversation got going, she soon realised this was nothing like Terry's social affairs. No one was telling risqué jokes or bad-mouthing a business rival or acquaintance. And her companions weren't drinking quickly, either, just taking the odd sip, as if in no hurry to pour alcohol down.

Sometimes she'd wondered if their guests had slipped away to indulge in a drug because she was sure she'd seen traces of white powder round their nostrils, but Terry had said she was imagining things and even if they were, it was no business of hers. The main thing she needed to know was that he wasn't stupid enough to waste his money on an expensive habit like that.

She hadn't simply taken his word for that but kept a sharp eye out for any tell-tales, but he had never shown the slightest sign.

Portia didn't say much but she listened and her occasional smiles were increasingly relaxed. It was, Fleur realised, like watching a flower unfold seeing her cousin enjoy herself. Thomas was particularly skilful at engaging the younger woman in conversation. No wonder he'd been a close friend of her aunt. He too was a kind person.

When Col said it was time to leave Thomas in peace, Fleur glanced at her watch, amazed to find that two hours had passed. She stood up as well. 'Goodness! I hadn't realised what time it was. We'll leave as well because we're still getting sleepy in the early evening. It's been lovely, Thomas.'

'Thank you so much for inviting us,' Portia said. 'You must come round for a sundowner at our place next time. You too, Col.'

Both men nodded and said, 'Love to.'

'I'll walk you ladies back,' Col offered as they went outside.

'There's no need. It isn't dark yet and there are two of us.'

'I'll enjoy stretching my legs.'

He strolled beside them, not forcing conversation but able to name a couple of pretty flowering plants that Fleur had wondered about on the way there. When they got home, he stood and watched them go inside via the garage. He waved and started walking away as the door rolled down.

'Tonight was so different from my ex's idea of casual gatherings.' Fleur explained how.

'That's what you were thinking of when you fell silent soon after we arrived.'

'Yes. I used to hate them and the sort of people he invited. This one was really enjoyable, though.'

'I wasn't sure how I'd cope, because I'm not good socially, but there was nothing to cope with, was there? The silences flowed as easily as the conversation so I didn't have to worry about what to say next.'

'They're nice men, aren't they?'

'Very nice.'

After all the nibblies, the two cousins didn't need a meal, just a small snack.

As she switched on the TV news, Fleur said, 'Should we start on the records room tomorrow? What do you think?'

'I suppose we'd better. It's what Cousin Sarah brought us here for, after all.' She wasn't looking forward to showing how hard it could be to read some documents. She'd have to use her special glasses.

'I think I'll take a little drive out on my own tomorrow as well. I'll find a map online first and plan my route.'

Fleur sighed. 'Even if I find a map, I don't seem to translate it very well into where I end up. They will change the roads and make streets one-way at the drop of a hat. Terry always said I was a rubbish driver and this is one time when he was right.'

'He sounds to have put you down a lot.' After a pause, Portia added, 'And you're not a rubbish driver, just not a brilliant driver.'

At her bedroom door she had another thought and stopped again. 'I think we should dress in our oldest clothes tomorrow. That room is very dusty.'

'Will do.'

After his guests had gone, Thomas cleared up, which didn't take long, then went to see if he had any emails.

There was one and he nearly deleted it because he didn't recognise the sender, but luckily part of the first sentence showed before he opened it.

> If you're the Thomas Norcott who knew Hilary Patterson, could you please . . .

He was eager to open it then, because he'd tried to find Hilary a year or two after they broke up and had never discovered even the slightest sign of her. He'd always wondered what had become of his ex, had wanted to see her again and at least apologise for being such a poor husband.

The email came from a lawyer in Melbourne. Lawrence Jenkins was very brief. As he read it, Thomas exclaimed, 'Oh, no!' and tears came into his eyes.

Hilary was dead. He'd never be able to apologise to her now. For some weird reason, he'd always thought that one day he'd meet her again.

When he read on, he found that her lawyer was asking whether he wished to make contact with her family. She'd suggested that he might find that of great interest. If he did, she'd left him a letter. If not, she wished him well.

He glanced at his watch. He could reply to the email but he'd not hear back till the following day because Melbourne was two hours ahead of Western Australia timewise and they'd have finished work for the day over there ages ago. In any case, there was no rush because he needed to think carefully before opening up old wounds. Did he really want to do that now that she was dead?

Of course he slept badly, wondering why she had contacted him and suggested meeting her family. Why on earth should it be 'of great interest' to him?

Maybe he'd do it, just to get as close to saying goodbye as he could now.

Only . . . what family was she referring to? She must have married and had the children she longed for. Hilary had always been very practical.

This request must have been made for a good reason or she'd never have sent the letter.

What most directed his decision in the end was the realisation that if he could do anything for her, he would, even after all these years, because he had never met a woman to match her.

It took him half an hour to write and rewrite a very brief response to Mr Jenkins, saying he'd be happy to read her letter and to make contact with her family. He nodded as he sent off the message. It felt like the right thing to do.

Terry found the following day that he had an appointment near the city where his daughter was at university, so decided to contact her and offer to take her out to lunch. It always pleased him that Marie preferred him to her mother.

He texted an invitation and received a response only minutes later expressing great delight.

When he turned up at the restaurant she was waiting outside and beamed when she saw him. He studied her, pleased that she was so well-dressed and pretty.

She looked at him hesitantly and when he held out his arms, she gave him a hug. He'd hated the small child years, but it was rather nice to have a grown-up daughter who did you credit.

'I shall be dining with the prettiest woman in the restaurant,' he said.

And it turned out to be true.

'New outfit?' he asked idly after they'd ordered.

'Goodness, no. I can't afford new clothes. I bought this from a charity shop and altered it myself. It's a really well-known clothing brand.' She stroked the sleeve.

'You're into dressmaking now?'

'I've always liked sewing, because I like nice clothes and Mum was mean about what she bought me.'

'Well, whatever you're doing looks good.' She did him credit and she was a very good listener too, asking intelligent questions.

All in all it was a very pleasant meal and he slipped her another twenty-pound note as they said goodbye.

He watched her walk away, nodding. She definitely took after his side of the family, even though she resembled that stupid mother of hers with that long, dark hair.

Chapter Fifteen

The next morning after breakfast, Fleur and Portia went to the documents room, stopping just inside the doorway to stare at the clutter.

'Where on earth do we start?' Fleur wondered aloud.

'I can't imagine.'

'Well, we'll not get anywhere by standing here doing nothing. Let's work in two stages. First we'll make piles of things that look similar and then we'll go through each pile piece by piece and sort them out properly. What do you think?'

'Sounds like a plan.'

That turned out to be easier said than done, however. Even sorting it into piles sometimes meant looking inside folders and envelopes, some of which inevitably caught their attention.

By lunchtime they were both feeling sneezy after inhaling so much dust, and the piles for initial sorting didn't look much smaller.

Portia went to wash her hands and splash water on her face. 'Half a day of that is enough. We should buy some masks.'

'Oh, I agree.' Fleur sneezed again and followed her cousin's example by washing her face as well as her hands.

As they sat eating their midday meal, Portia began fiddling with a piece of bread, not meeting her cousin's eyes. 'I've been thinking – would you mind if I took over one of the spare rooms on the ground floor?'

'Not at all. We both need somewhere of our own. I'll take over the other empty room. I don't mind which that is. What are you going to do with yours?' Fleur felt she could guess and that was confirmed a minute later.

'I want to use it as an art studio. I always wanted a separate room for my drawing and painting, so I don't need to keep clearing my things away each time I stop for the day. I'll need to buy some art supplies first, as well as a table and an easel. I thought I'd try to find a second-hand shop. You can buy lovely, solid old furniture really cheaply.'

'You've got the lump sum from Cousin Sarah. You can afford to do things properly.'

Portia looked horrified at that. 'I don't want to spend it all at once. We don't know what we're going to need during the year.'

'We'll be getting an allowance every month.'

'Even so.'

'Well, I peeped into the bedrooms at the street side of the house this morning. There are two empty chests of drawers in one of them, on either side of the bed. We're not going to be using them so we could bring them down and take one each. You'll need somewhere to store your art supplies. But you'll definitely need a big table and a proper, professional easel.'

Portia hesitated. 'You don't think that'd be extravagant?'

'Not at all. You obviously enjoy sketching. You looked truly happy yesterday when you were doing it.'

'Did I? Well, it does make me happy, happier than anything else I do, I must admit. It's been my main hobby all my life. Do you have any hobbies?'

'I've never had much time to indulge myself. Terry was a rather demanding husband for business events and such, yet he didn't help with the housework, refused point-blank. Why did I let him get away with it for so long?'

'You don't always see what you're doing wrong till something forces you to re-evaluate.'

Fleur's tone was bitter. 'Like finding out that your husband has been unfaithful more than once and boasted about it to his colleagues? One of their wives told me in the end because he was nudging her husband to follow his example. She also hinted at something else going on, something I'd wondered about before: drugs. Only he'd said he didn't waste his money on such things.'

'Is that what happened to break you up? You found out about him being unfaithful? How terrible.'

'It was the main thing, yes. Terry and I had a huge row, absolutely huge, yelling and screaming. In the end I threw things at him and told him to get out and stay out.'

'Served him right.'

'I thought so. After we split up, we sold the joint house and I bought a small one. I was busy working full time and being a single parent to teenagers in their final years of high school so I was often stressed. I feel guilty for thinking it, but in one way it was a relief when they went away to college, especially my daughter, who was a lovely child but a bitch of a teenager. My main relaxation during those years was reading, but that's not exactly creative, is it?'

'Not everyone can be creative, Fleur.'

But she had an idea, had been thinking about it on and off for a while. 'No, but I started making up stories in my head, even mentally changing the endings to novels I'd read when I felt let down.'

She hesitated, then admitted her secret dream. 'I might buy myself a new laptop with some of my lump sum, Portia. I've always fancied writing, so maybe I could try to write a short story or two. After all, if I turn out to be hopeless, no one will need to see them except me, will they?'

'I doubt you'll produce rubbish. You seem to me to have a clear way of thinking about the world these days. Though actually, that's what I feel about my sketching, so I rarely show it to anyone but I get huge pleasure from just doing it.'

Fleur decided to tell her what had happened. 'Well, when you left your sketchbook outside yesterday, the wind blew the top pages open and I couldn't help seeing a couple of the drawings.'

'Oh. Right. Well, I know from my mother that I'm not all that good, so you've no need to tell me that. I still get the urge to draw things. It not only gives me a lot of pleasure, it doesn't cost much.'

Fleur stared at her in surprise. 'I don't agree with your mother at all. I thought your sketches were excellent, not just how they were drawn but the compositions.'

The words came out as a near whisper. 'You did? Really? You're not just saying that?'

'I meant it. Why would I lie to you?'

Portia clapped one hand to her mouth, then blinked at her cousin and said in a wobbly voice, 'You've made my day.'

Fleur patted her arm. 'Good. You should see if there are any art classes or groups and join one.'

'I can't afford to pay the fees and I— Oh! But I can afford it now, can't I? I'm still not used to that.'

'Yes. And what's more, from what Thomas has said, I think Cousin Sarah would be pleased if you used her money that way. Why don't you go out this afternoon and buy some art supplies from that place at the shopping centre? And an easel, a really good one. Go on your own and take your time. We'll find a second-hand shop for the furniture another day, because I'll need some pieces too.'

'You won't mind me leaving you alone?'

'Of course not. We're not glued together at the hip. Go forth and buy!'

'I will. I'll do it.'

Portia had a little happy cry in the privacy of her bedroom as she was getting ready to go out. She might not be a good enough artist to sell paintings, but she was good enough to make herself proud and win praise from a woman who definitely wasn't stupid.

She knew somehow that Fleur wouldn't lie to her. What she didn't know was whether her cousin was a good judge of art or not.

Did she dare believe that she could one day produce reasonable work, work that people might want to buy and hang on their walls? She'd try, oh, she would.

She felt to be stumbling along in a strange new world, still half-expected to wake up and find she'd been dreaming. Life had been so bleak since her father died. And though breaking up with her partner had been the right thing to do, it had left her very lonely because she'd spent some of her precious savings keeping up with him. She'd shared half of all expenses when he had been responsible for at least three quarters of the food eaten, the greedy pig. After she left him, she hadn't been able to afford to go out in order to put something by for a rainy day. Only it had seemed to rain, metaphorically speaking, most of the time, and she'd been in despair after being made redundant a second time.

When she went down to the garage she murmured, 'Thank you, Cousin Sarah,' as she patted the steering wheel before starting her lovely new car.

It was ages since she'd been in an art shop. Her old car had needed repairs only a few weeks ago so she'd not been able to afford anything except minimum food supplies for a while.

She shook off the memories and enjoyed driving to the shopping centre, having no trouble finding her way there. It was wonderful having the freedom to go where she pleased and not have to count the cost of the petrol. Today she would indulge herself. Just a little. No need to go mad.

She parked the car under a tree and got out. Perhaps she'd splurge on a professional easel. And a whole new set of paints and pencils. Did she dare spend that much money?

She stopped dead as she was walking towards the shopping centre. Of course she dared. She was an idiot even to hesitate. Cousin Sarah was paying them each enough money for her to buy whatever art materials she fancied, not just the bare minimum.

Smiling at her own reflection in a shop window, she walked on briskly. When she went inside the art shop, she was surprised to find that it went back a long way, so there was more to see than she'd expected. She walked slowly round, studying the goods, writing down any items of interest for future reference, together with prices. It was how she always did things if she got the choice: found her bearings and learned as much as she could to make sure she wasn't going to be cheated or couldn't get an item more cheaply elsewhere.

She didn't buy anything but spent a blissful hour in the shop. Fleur was a lovely person, but sometimes it was good to have time on your own, especially when you needed to think clearly about something that mattered so much.

By that time Portia was thirsty, so went off to buy a coffee, another delightful extravagance, and plan exactly what to buy.

On the way out of the shopping centre, she was tempted and bought a smartphone that came with a special bargain package for the first six months.

She was full of mixed emotions as she hurried out to her car, feeling both guilty and delighted, not to mention terrified of spending too much and needing the money later.

She knew rationally that it didn't matter now, but the fear was irrational, ingrained in her after years of counting every penny.

* * *

When the sound of Portia's car had faded, Fleur made herself a cup of hot chocolate then went to sit by the canal, enjoying the feeling of being alone and at peace. She hadn't decided yet what to do with the rest of the morning, needn't do anything if she chose not to.

She really ought to practise driving her car, only she was frightened of getting lost. She thought she might be able to find the shopping centre, but wasn't sure enough to try. She'd ask Portia to go with her once more, to be sure.

What she really needed was an old-fashioned book of street maps.

However, she'd better do something more active physically. She could go out for a walk, perhaps. Walking was healthy. It didn't seem as hot today so if she used sunblock and put on a shady hat, she ought to be all right. She'd seen a bottle of sunblock in the laundry room off the kitchen and she'd seen several hats in Sarah's wardrobe.

But first she'd look at a map of this area online and try to work out a route. She set off ten minutes later, enjoying the fresh air, even if it was a little warmer than she'd wish.

An SUV with a logo she recognised on the side drove past, stopped and waited for her to catch up with it. As she got closer she saw that Col was driving it and smiled at the coincidence. She only knew three people in Western Australia and here was one of them.

He got out. 'Are you lost?'

'No. Just taking a walk and starting to get my bearings in the neighbourhood. I didn't feel like driving because I'm still jetlagged and don't feel alert enough to remember my way to the shopping centre by car, or even the way back.'

'If you like, I could drive you round the waterfront area a few times. I've just been checking out a new customer and I'm free for an hour or two.'

'Are you sure?'

'I wouldn't have offered if I wasn't.'

'Then I accept. It'd be so helpful. I was just wishing I had a book of street maps. Do they do those any more?'

'I don't know. I used my satnav to find places when I first came here, but I know my way round the main parts of the town now.' He reached across to open the passenger door and then pressed a button and the window closed. He gave her a mock bow. 'Your carriage awaits, my lady.'

'Thank you, kind sir.' She bobbed a curtsey and got in.

They went round a couple of the longer nearby streets, then did it all over again.

'I think I've got that area straight in my mind now, Col. I see the connections in my head as patterns when I'm driving. Does that sound stupid?'

'No, of course not. We all view the world differently. Let's go a few streets further and you can fit that into your schema as well.'

As they started on a new patch, he stopped suddenly. 'Oh, look! There's a house open for viewing and it's on the water. Would you mind if I went in and had a quick look round? It's about time I bought myself a proper house but having seen Thomas and Sarah's residences, I'm a bit spoiled.'

'I wouldn't mind at all. In fact, I'll join you if I may. I love looking round houses.'

The estate agent greeted them with a professional smile but wanted Col's name and phone number before he'd let them further inside. Once he had that information, he told them the price, gave them a plan of the house and sent them off to wander round.

It was a lovely house, smaller than Cousin Sarah's but far larger than the town house Fleur had been living in back in England. Best of all, it had a cosy feel to it. When you had the choice, you bought houses mainly by emotional feel, she always thought. Some people called that sense of rightness 'good feng shui'. Whatever its name, it was the most important aspect of selecting a house, in her opinion.

But only if you had enough money for the sort of house you longed for, like this one.

'I like it,' Col said as they finished a second walk-round. 'I'll make arrangements to come back and bring Thomas to look at it. He's a very shrewd chap.'

'He is, isn't he? And so kind. I'll wait for you outside.' She felt it more tactful to leave him to chat to the estate agent on his own, because the man was treating them as a couple and that was a bit embarrassing.

Col re-joined her shortly afterwards. 'I'll take you home now then go and check things out at the office.'

'Before you do that, do you know of any second-hand furniture shops where Portia can buy furnishings for making an art studio?'

'She can afford new stuff, surely?'

'New would be a bit of a waste if it's going to be covered in splashes of paint, wouldn't it? Besides, we'll be leaving within the year. I want to buy some office furniture too.' She held up one hand to stop him. 'Neither she nor I have the spending-freely gene.'

'Do you need an art studio too?'

She could feel herself flushing but made herself speak out. She really must stop being so timid. 'I want to try writing stories now that I don't have to earn a living, but I'm not buying new stuff till I'm sure writing every day gives me the pleasure I think it will. I shall need a new computer as well.'

'There's a shop selling computers near my office. The woman running it is very savvy, and it's good to give your business to small traders, don't you think?'

'Yes. Could you give me the address, please?'

'I'll do better than that. I'll take both you and Portia out tomorrow and show you where to shop for your computer and afterwards I'll take you to a big second-hand furniture warehouse where you're bound to find what you need.'

'Oh, that'd be wonderful. Only I feel guilty for taking up so much of your time.'

'Please don't. I haven't made many friends in Mandurah yet because I've been too busy getting my business up and running. All work and no play can make for a pretty dull life, believe me.'

'Then I'd love to take you up your offer and I'm sure Portia will too.'

To Fleur's surprise, there was no sign of her cousin at home, nor was there any sign of parcels in the room designated as her studio. Portia had been out a good while. Her cousin couldn't have got lost, surely?

She wandered round, not sure what to do with herself. She didn't like to sort out family records on her own, somehow. They hadn't discussed what they were having for tea, either, and though the afternoon was half over, she didn't like to start on any preparations because Portia was a far better cook.

She was finding that you tended to tread carefully when living with someone you didn't know very well.

Half an hour later she heard the garage door rolling up and went to check that it was indeed Portia.

'Thank goodness you're back. I was getting a bit worried about you.'

'I always do a lot of what I call "eye shopping" before I buy anything. Look what I found on special because it had been used as a display!' She lifted the hatchback and gestured to the big easel that had only just fitted into the car. 'Voilà!'

Her hands were as gentle as a lover's as she carefully eased it out.

Fleur moved forward to help her and duly admired it when it was fully unwrapped from the bubble plastic protection.

As it stood in solitary pride in the middle of the embryonic studio, she remembered Col's offer to take them shopping and when Portia agreed instantly, Fleur phoned him to set a time that suited him the next day.

She put the phone down and turned to Portia triumphantly. 'Tomorrow morning. He understands how eager we are to set up our personal spaces.'

'That's great. Now, let's find something to eat. I'm famished.'

Chapter Sixteen

The following morning Thomas received a phone call from Lawrence Jenkins, Hilary's lawyer.

'I'm just letting you know that I've got your email and will forward Hilary's letter immediately by express post.'

'Just a minute. Presumably you know what's in it?'

'Well, yes. More or less anyway. I helped her draft the basics.'

'Then please open it and scan it, then email it. I'd like to have it today, within the hour if possible.'

'Are you sure you don't mind me seeing it?'

'Very sure.' What could there be that was so private anyway? They hadn't seen one another for – what? More than three decades.

'I'll do that straight away, then, Mr Norcott. And you can be sure that I'll treat the information as confidential.'

'Thank you.'

That meant Thomas couldn't settle to anything until a few minutes later he received an email with the scanned document as an attachment. He printed it out instantly but resisted the temptation to read it until the whole two pages were in his hand.

He took them outside, sitting in his favourite armchair looking out across the water. Finally, taking a deep breath, he began reading the letter from the woman he still thought of as his lost love.

He was shocked rigid as the information it contained sank in, then as he read on, alternated between feeling furiously angry at her and at himself too.

Dear Thomas

I'm so sorry to do this to you, but my son needs help and I'm dying of cancer so I shan't be here to give it to him. If you've come as far as agreeing to read this letter, I feel fairly sure you'll help him.

When I left you, I didn't intend it to be such a complete break, but then I didn't know that I was expecting your child.

Thomas gasped and re-read that bit. Expecting his child! How dare she have kept something that important from him? All these years, wasted!

Once I did realise it, I thought long and hard before deciding to keep it from you.

'No!' He thumped one clenched fist on the arm of his chair, then did it again, muttering, 'Damn you, Hilary! That was so wrong!'

You were so sure you never wanted children and I'd deliberately stopped taking the pill, so it was my fault – and therefore ultimately I decided it was my responsibility to deal with it.

I never regretted having the baby but lately, as the cancer eats away at my future, I've felt guilty for keeping Ethan's existence from you and your existence from him.

My death will mean I'll be leaving him without any close family to help him because my parents are both dead.

To make matters worse, fate struck again: like mother, like son. Ethan got a woman pregnant by mistake when he was barely twenty and when she didn't really want children, we agreed to take the child. She wasn't totally sure until it turned out to be twins. That sent her running for the woods within a week of giving birth.

She has never once attempted to contact my son or her daughters, let alone offered him any payments towards their maintenance. I've made enquiries and found out that she's now living in America and is married to her job. So I'm not going to give you her name, let alone try to ask her help.

Our son is a delightful human being, not without faults, but then who is perfect? He looks very like you. You will have no need of DNA tests to believe he's yours.

The twins are delightful as well. I've helped him raise them – both financially and literally – until recently.

Ethan has found it hard to cope with the finality of my illness and is depressed. He needs help and so do his daughters, Nicole and Liane. You'll see why when you meet them. There is no one left to appeal to except you – and anyway I should have given you the choice before. Perhaps this will make up for that a little.

If you are at all interested in becoming a grandfather, please come and scoop them up. Then take them all back to Western Australia to make a fresh start and banish the sad memories.

I made enquiries about you too and I gather that you've had a very successful life serving the law. That's no more than I expected.

If you want to help, my lawyer will give Ethan a letter from me to 'introduce' you as soon as you let him know.

All the best and thank you in advance – that's how sure I am that you'll agree to help. Not 100 per cent sure, but maybe 95 per cent.

Always your Hilary

P.S. I took the surname Smith soon after I arrived in the eastern states. Imaginative, eh?

Thomas read and re-read the letter, getting tears in his eyes more than once. An hour later he contacted Jenkins and asked how best he could help his son and grandchildren.

'As Hilary has suggested, you should perhaps take them to Perth and help them start a new life there. I've got to know Ethan quite well as we settled his mother's affairs. He works in IT and can do that mainly from home, so he could live anywhere in Australia.'

'Should I send him some money?'

'He doesn't need financial help as he's Hilary's sole heir, but he does need another sort of help plus emotional support. He and his mother were very close.'

'It might be best to take him by surprise. What do you think? I could fly over to meet him. I didn't treat his mother well and I don't want to give my son a chance to refuse to know me.'

After a short silence, the lawyer said, 'Sounds a good plan. In the meantime, I'll give him his mother's letter.'

'It's rather cloak-and-dagger stuff, isn't it? Did she think he might refuse to see me?'

'She didn't confide her reasons to me, but I think . . . Yes, from what I understand about the family, you should come as soon as you can get a flight. Let me know when you'll be arriving and I'll have a hire car waiting for you and—'

'Make it a limousine and chauffeur. I'm not fond of driving in Melbourne traffic and I'm not short of money.'

'Very well, Mr Norcott.'

'Call me Thomas. I'll fly across as soon as I can, tomorrow if I can get a seat.' And if that wasn't going to be possible for several days, he might even charter a plane. What was money for if not to help those you cared about? He had plenty of money but no one left to care for now Sarah had passed on.

Hilary shouldn't have kept his son from him! Thomas dashed away more tears, then sat down and made a quick list of what needed doing, thought for a moment about priorities and started by trying to book a seat on the early morning flight. He was lucky. There had just been a cancellation and when he claimed urgent family business in connection with a bereavement, the booking officer allowed him to jump the queue of stand-by passengers and take that seat.

He emailed the lawyer to let him know the details, then phoned Col to explain the situation and ask him if he'd mind taking over the informal task of keeping an eye on the two cousins.

'I'm happy to help in any way you need. You get on with your packing. I'll tell them what's happened tomorrow.'

So Thomas went on making arrangements to fly to Victoria, eager to meet his son and yet afraid – no, make that terrified – of how Ethan Smith would receive him.

He wouldn't accept being turned away, though. He was going to be part of their lives from now on, whatever it took to persuade them to get to know him and give him a chance. He'd camp on their doorstep if he had to.

Hilary hadn't mentioned a husband. Had there ever been one? He should have asked the lawyer about that.

There were going to be a lot of questions to be answered. He'd have to jot them down in his pocket notebook as they cropped up.

He couldn't help wondering what Hilary's son was like – his son as well. She'd said Ethan resembled him. How closely? He had to keep reminding himself that he had a son; it was such an unexpected and marvellous shock.

But how would Ethan take the news that his father was alive? Would his son want to move over three thousand kilometres away from Victoria? Hilary had seemed to consider it necessary. Why? What did she know that caused her to say this?

She'd made a big move across the country in the opposite direction when she left Thomas in Western Australia and moved across to Victoria, changing her name as she began her new life. She'd been a feisty, independent woman and he'd bet that had never changed.

He blamed himself more than her. He realised now that he'd been a very selfish person in his first four decades of life. Her leaving him had changed him gradually as the loneliness set in, made him more mindful of other people's needs and feelings and he met Sarah, who had taught him to care for others.

Oh, what was the use worrying about all that now? You couldn't go back, only move forward and try to do better afterwards each time you made a mistake, even a huge one like this.

He finished packing, set an alarm to wake him and tried to get some sleep before his early trip from Mandurah to Perth airport.

He found it hard to stay asleep, and got up even before the alarm sounded.

This would be the most important trip he'd ever made in his whole life.

Ben Peyton had a rostered day off and decided it was time to go to the supermarket to stock up on all the basics. Since his mother-in-law wasn't able to look after his little daughter that day, due to a medical appointment, he took Mandy with him. He loved spending time with his child. At four, she was delightful (well, most of the time), coming up with the most amazing comments on the world.

He shook his head in bafflement as he got her ready to go out, as he had many times before. His ex-wife was out of the action most of the time as a parent, claiming to be 'too busy this week' or that 'something important just cropped up at work, I'm afraid'. She was missing so much, but then, Kylie was the most un-maternal woman he'd ever encountered, even her own mother admitted that.

He'd married late and rushed into it, feeling a sudden, urgent need to settle down. It was a good thing she'd accidentally got pregnant, or he'd never have had a child to enjoy because he wasn't getting married again. He'd never really been married in one sense because Kylie had been married to her career and had just used him and their home as a convenience for when she was in Perth. He'd even had to bribe her financially to keep the baby.

But he wished the child had some proper mothering. She had an excellent grandma so she wasn't completely lacking the feminine touch, but his mother-in-law was older so not able to play with her much physically.

A mother-daughter relationship should be special and fun too, but his little Mandy was never going to experience that.

He smiled at the mere sight of the child getting her handbag ready to go out. 'Come on, munchkin! Let's get going.'

She picked up the tiny, pink, glittery bag and closed it carefully. 'Ready now, Daddy.'

At the supermarket, he insisted she held on to the trolley and didn't move away on her own. He also refused to let her put things that caught her eye into the trolley and wouldn't buy her a packet of some sickly-looking sweets, something he suspected his mother-in-law did at times to keep the peace.

Afterwards they took the shopping home and Mandy 'helped' him put it away, which meant it took twice as long, but hey, he didn't mind that.

They went to the local park later on, once the heat of the day had abated. He let her play in the sandpit, which was in a shaded area.

All in all, he had a thoroughly enjoyable day off and managed to tire Mandy out so that she'd sleep well.

When he'd got her to bed, he put a wash in the machine and sat in front of the TV to watch the news while waiting for the cycle to finish. In the evenings the loneliness bit harder than at other times. He missed social encounters with people his own age, men and women both. He'd emigrated to Australia when he married Kylie because she wasn't prepared to live in the UK and face the winters there. His IT skills put him in a high priority category as a migrant and it had felt like a great adventure – till the gloss started to wear off their relationship.

That meant that he didn't have any long-time close friends in Australia and no relatives at all. And since he didn't often go out for a drink because of not wanting to impose on his mother-in-law for additional babysitting, he had no easy way of meeting people.

He shrugged and picked up his library book. Thank goodness for murder mysteries. He'd become addicted to them.

He smiled. And of course he was addicted to his little daughter.

But still . . .

Chapter Seventeen

Ethan Smith got up early, as he usually did. He liked some time to himself before the day rushed at him.

The girls were still asleep. At twelve they were almost teenagers and very mature for their age. Lovely young women with their mother's dark hair and his mother's hazel eyes. They'd had to mature quickly during the past two years and they'd risen to the challenge.

He was hoping there wouldn't be as much angst during those coming years. His mother had guided them through childhood brilliantly, nudging them into better behaviour when necessary. She'd been brilliant at defusing situations. To his surprise, there was a knock on the door before they even got up and when he opened it he found Lawrence Jenkins standing outside.

'May I come in?'

'Well, yes, of course. My goodness, you're early. The house is in a bit of a mess, I'm afraid.'

'That doesn't matter. You're not far out of my way into work.'

'Come into the kitchen and I'll make you a cup of tea. I remember that you don't like coffee.'

'Thank you.'

Ethan gestured to one of the bar stools and put the kettle on. 'I hope nothing is wrong to bring you here at this hour?'

'No. But something has cropped up and I wanted to tell you in person, answer any questions you may have and give you as much time as possible to think about it before – well, something important happens later today.'

He pulled an envelope out of his inner pocket and held it out. 'Your mother left another note for you. I was to give it to you if what she hoped for actually happened. And it has done. She would be so glad about that.'

Ethan stared at him in surprise. 'I know she tried to make plans for me, for after she'd gone, but she was a bit vague about what they were.' He paused for a moment to fight back the tears that often welled when he thought of her.

'She did her best for you, always. This was her final plan – well, the final one that I know of. Let me finish making the tea while you read the letter, then you can ask questions. I know a little about the, um, general situation.'

He busied himself in the kitchen and left the younger man to sit near the table and read in peace. He'd come early because Ethan had once mentioned getting up early to enjoy an 'hour of peace' before his daughters woke up.

Ethan opened the letter from his mother. Unusually for her, it was handwritten. He touched it with his fingertips before he started reading, feeling as if that brought him closer to her.

He went through it slowly and carefully, letting out an involuntary exclamation at suddenly finding out what she had refused to tell him all his life: the name of his father and something about him.

Thomas Norcott. Former barrister.

He sat staring into space when he'd finished, trusting that Mr Jenkins would leave him to think about it. Then he read the letter all over again, this time even more carefully and slowly, weighing every word and phrase to try to understand the subtleties that lay behind them.

When Mr Jenkins brought across a mug of tea and joined him at the table, he looked up. 'What if I don't want to meet this man?'

'It's a bit late for that. He's flying here from Western Australia today and will be arriving in the early afternoon. Your mother told me to give him your address if he asked for it, and he did.'

'She should have told me about him herself, and done it a long time ago when I first started asking. It was the one big thing we disagreed about.'

'I think she was afraid of losing you. Norcott was a lawyer so when I was helping her with her will, I made it my business to find out about the man he'd become. He's well-respected by those who know him and has great personal charm. Not ambitious for status or money, didn't want to become a judge, seemed to enjoy helping people legally.'

'He'll still have to earn my respect,' Ethan said sharply. 'I always thought he'd abandoned my mother, but now I find it was the other way round.'

'I'm sure he'll not try to rush things. I don't know whether I should tell you this . . . no, I'd better. It may help you to avoid hurting him about one thing. His dearest friend died recently, apparently, a neighbour of ninety-five, who had been almost a mother to him. He's now completely alone in the world as far as close relatives are concerned.'

'Except for me and the girls. I see. Similar to our own situation, in fact, except that we have one another.' Ethan began stirring the tea round and round, not drinking it, staring into space, then stirring some more. 'I don't think you get much closer as a relative than a son or daughter. If you're lucky.'

He fell silent again, seeming to need time to process all this information, so Lawrence sipped his own tea and waited.

A few minutes passed, then Ethan looked up. 'Sorry. I'm absolutely knocked for six by all this. I don't know what to think, except that I wish he weren't coming today.'

The lawyer could only shrug. 'I think your mother would have wanted you both to get a difficult meeting over quickly and not think things into it that don't yet exist, probably.'

Ethan managed a faint smile. 'Mum did tend to dive into things, didn't she?'

'Yes. Very decisive woman. Um, what shall you do?'

'Open the door and invite him in, I suppose. I can hardly raise the drawbridge. Besides, I've wanted to know what my father was like all my life.' After another pause, he added quietly, 'And what the girls will say and do, I can't guess. In fact, I'm finding it hard to think clearly about my own meeting with him. This has been – well, a difficult year.'

'For him as well as for you. He not only lost his best friend but suddenly found out about your existence.'

'Surely he had some idea?'

'No. None whatsoever. I'm quite sure of that.'

Another silence followed. In the end, Lawrence stood up and put his mug on the draining board. 'If you have no more questions, I'll leave you in peace to think about it.'

'Yes. Thanks.' Ethan looked down at the wheelchair. 'And I've still got another few months before I'll be rid of this damn contraption.'

'How's it going?'

'Slowly, so very slowly. But I am improving. I'll still need another minor operation, a minor adjustment, they call it. That drunken idiot made a good job of messing up my life and my body, didn't he?'

'He paid for it with his own life.'

'I tell myself that, but it's not much consolation because I'd never wish such a drastic comeuppance on anyone.'

He sighed and closed his eyes, shutting out the world for a moment or two, as he had sometimes needed to do since the accident. Even his lively daughters knew to give him a few moments' space when he did that. They were an amazing mixture of tactful understanding and leaping in feet first, had been wonderful since the accident.

When he looked up, Mr Jenkins had left. A few seconds later there was the sound of a car starting up outside the house.

After a while there were sounds upstairs. Should he tell the girls or wait till he'd met the man who'd sired him?

He smiled wryly. That was a no-brainer. They'd make a right royal fuss if he didn't keep them in the loop from the start. They'd cope, whatever happened, though. They seemed to have inherited his mother's determination and courage.

There wasn't much to tell them yet, though. The crunch was still to come and that was something he would be facing alone first.

Ethan's daughters came downstairs together as usual, yawning. They grunted a greeting and headed straight for the fridge.

He stayed out of the way. They had worked out a morning routine now that he was in a wheelchair and they weren't at all civil till they'd put some food in their bellies.

'Got a busy day?' he asked once they'd sat down with platters of fruit, cheese and toast in front of them, put together rapidly in a well-choreographed and rehearsed mock ballet round the kitchen.

'So-so. Why?'

'We have an unexpected visitor coming later today, so you may want to come straight home and if necessary you can use one of the taxi vouchers I gave you. He's flying over from Western Australia specially to see us.'

They both paused, frowning slightly, waiting for more information.

'I only found out this morning that my father is still alive.'

They gaped at him like two little birds with beaks open ready to be fed, but with information, not food, this time.

Nicole, the older by a matter of minutes, spoke first as usual. 'Gran kept her secrets well, didn't she?'

'It sucks to have kept you from him!' Liane said.

Nicole kicked her sister under the table. 'So how did you find out, Dad?'

'Your gran left me a letter. Mr Jenkins brought it round this morning. She'd apparently told my father about our existence in another letter and asked if he wanted to meet me. If he hadn't wanted to, Mr Jenkins would never have told us about him.'

They'd recovered enough to take a big mouthful of fruit each as they waited to be fed further titbits of information.

'I only know a few things about him,' Ethan warned. 'He's called Thomas Norcott and he lives in Western Australia. Not only did he want to meet us, he booked a flight over here for the very next day and he's arriving this afternoon.'

'Well, that sounds a fairly positive reaction to our existence, anyway,' Nicole allowed. 'A good start.'

He shrugged. 'We won't really know how he feels about us till we meet him. There must have been some reason Mum never told him about me and—'

'You always were the cautious one, Dad.'

Nicole jabbed her sister in the ribs this time to shut her up. 'Let him finish.'

'I'd have liked to check him out before I told you, but he's coming today so there won't be time. I shall have to dive in the deep end with him and he'll most probably be here when you get back from school.'

'We could stay at home today?' Liane suggested hopefully.

'No. I want to meet him on my own the first time. I need to.'

They considered this for a moment, then each nodded.

'OK. Fair enough. But we're coming straight home by taxi, not waiting for the school bus,' Nicole said.

Ethan would be hoping with all his might that the man would be acceptable and would not upset them. They were still raw about losing their grandmother. As was he.

He looked at the clock. 'Get cracking. You don't want to be late for school. And don't leave your rooms in a mess. It's Mrs Murab's morning to clean.'

When they'd gone, the house seemed to echo with emptiness and he wished he had let them stay at home.

No, he didn't.

Oh, hell! He didn't know what he wished.

Chapter Eighteen

When Col picked up the two women the following morning to take them shopping, he told them about Thomas's sudden discovery.

'There's a lot goes on beneath the surface in this world,' Portia said. 'I hope everything goes well for him. He's such a kind man.'

'He must still be in a state of shock,' Fleur said quietly. 'Would you rather postpone our shopping trip, Col? He might need your help with something.'

'I doubt it. I'm not really involved in this. No one is but him and his newly discovered son, with some help from his ex's lawyer. Thomas is very good with people and it's my guess that he'd prefer to sort this out alone. Though I'm fond of him, I've only known him for a few months. Sarah would have been much more use to him, I'm sure.'

He waited a minute or two as they took this in, then added, 'For the time being, if you need to find out anything you'd have asked him, about how we do things in Western

Australia or anything else more specific to dealing with your inheritance, don't hesitate to turn to me instead.'

They nodded, looking as solemn as two rather pretty owls. He found himself wanting to give them a hug sometimes; they both sounded like they had been alone for the past few years. He'd like to do rather more than just hug Fleur, actually. She was a very attractive woman in a quiet way, just the sort of person he preferred to spend time with.

He corrected himself mentally. Look where those thoughts were leading him! Down a path he'd vowed never to tread again, that's where. He was not getting into a permanent relationship ever again.

'Shall we get going?' he asked and led the way to the door without waiting for their answer.

He took them to the computer shop first and both women seemed unsure of what they were looking for. He knew what would suit his own skill levels and needs, but not what would be best for them.

The owner of the shop clearly and quickly worked out their difficulty and began to question them about what they'd mainly be using their computers for. She suggested one or two that she considered reliable and straightforward. 'They're set up to go, but do you need me to help you sort out your files?'

Both shook their heads. They had already decided they could manage that, because Portia had more experience than Fleur and had done it before. She was confident enough to volunteer to make sure her cousin's computer was set up properly, but not confident when buying a brand-new computer, as most of hers had been passed on by friends or bought second-hand.

'James did it for me last time,' Fleur told her cousin with a sigh. She was already missing her son, missing the thought that either of them could visit the other. Even though he'd not been living at home for a while, he had always been ready to come back and help her with major stuff.

She'd not miss her daughter nearly as much, which was sad. You could do your best as a mother but you couldn't dictate how your child would grow up and interact with the world. Or whether they'd prefer the parent who did the least for them as they grew older, which Marie did.

Damn Terry and his facile charm!

Fleur shook off those thoughts and forced herself to pay better attention to what was going on around her. They'd now parked outside a big warehouse away from the town centre. She followed the others inside and stopped for a moment in the doorway. It was full of second-hand furniture and looked very promising.

To Col's amusement, both women were absolutely at home with this sort of shopping. They had lively discussions about desks, office chairs, filing cabinets and he listened with interest. They were certainly good at spotting bargains. He'd never have looked twice at some of the pieces they agreed were 'good value'.

They bought carefully and seemed happy about their purchases.

Afterwards he dropped them at home and left them to wait for their new furniture to be delivered. He had a business to run and a house to go round for a second time.

Would it make a good home? Did he like it enough to risk spending his Lotto money on it? If he did, it would be like having a marvellous gift from Sarah.

Important too was whether that particular house would be a good investment if he needed to sell it. He wished Thomas, who'd lived in the area for years, were still available to advise him.

Fleur had made approving comments about the house and seemed to know what to look for. Maybe he'd take her with him again the second time.

And maybe he'd better not.

The bottom line was that he liked it and could afford it, thanks to Sarah's parting gift. His business was now profitable, so he could indulge himself in a home he'd fallen in love with.

On the plane, Thomas yawned and tried to stretch but there wasn't much room in economy class for such luxuries. Good thing the flight to Melbourne was only about three hours. He was lucky to have chanced upon a seat at such short notice and must console himself with that, though he'd normally have travelled business class, not just because it was more peaceful but because his legs were too long to be comfortable in a seat like this.

Older bodies became uncomfortable more quickly than young ones, he decided with a sigh, trying once again to find a more comfortable position. The young chap next to him tapped his arm. 'Do you want to swap seats, granddad, and sit on the outside edge? I'm only going to snooze.'

'How kind of you. Yes, please.'

The young fellow amazed Thomas by falling asleep within a couple of minutes in a crumpled tangle of arms and legs.

In spite of the improved comfort of an aisle seat, he was deeply thankful when the flight ended. He was not travelling back in economy class. No way!

After he'd retrieved his luggage, he went out into the public area of the airport, where he saw a sign saying Norcott held up by a man in a very smart chauffeur's uniform. Thank goodness! He was far too weary after his poor night's sleep to feel he could drive safely in the busy city traffic of Melbourne.

He gave the driver the name of his hotel and when they got there he went in to register and freshen up. He told the driver he'd be out in half an hour and slipped him some money to buy himself a coffee.

He phoned the lawyer before he did anything else and luckily caught him in the office. 'I'm here in Melbourne and ready to go and meet my son. Do you want me to pick you up? I have the driver standing by.'

'Thank you, but no. I'll meet you at the end of their street in say, forty minutes.' He gave the registration number of his car.

'I forgot to note the reggo of the limo,' Thomas admitted, 'but I doubt you'll mistake us because there aren't usually many luxury cars hanging round on suburban street corners.'

He liked the looks of the lawyer, who had a warm smile. You could tell a lot about people from their smiles.

Lawrence said, 'Before we go to the house, Thomas, there's just one other thing I haven't mentioned that you ought to know. Ethan was involved in a car accident caused by a drunken driver a few months ago and he still has to use a wheelchair much of the time. He's had a couple of major operations and will still need a minor adjustment plus more physio, but he's getting better all the time and isn't likely to be in the wheelchair permanently.'

'That was rotten luck.'

'Yes.'

Thomas shook his head sadly, wondering if that was why Hilary had thought Ethan needed help. Well, if he did, Thomas would definitely step up to the mark. There was a visceral feel to someone being your child.

Lawrence waited a moment, then asked, 'Shall we go now?'

'Yes.'

When the two men reached the front door, however, Thomas's nerves seemed to kick in big time and he felt it hard even to breathe smoothly.

His companion shot a quick glance at him. 'You all right?'

'Not exactly. What if Ethan refuses to acknowledge me?'

'I don't think he will from what he said this morning. I've always found him and his mother very reasonable to deal with, though she was more impetuous than him.'

He couldn't help smiling. 'Yes. I remember that about her.'

Lawrence pressed the doorbell but there weren't footsteps inside, only a faint whining sound.

When the door started to open, the lawyer tactfully stepped to one side and left Thomas and his son to take centre stage.

The two men stared at one another.

When his companions continued to stare, making no attempt to move, Lawrence asked, 'May we come in?'

'Oh, sorry!' Ethan edged the wheelchair skilfully backwards and led the way into a comfortable sitting room. He gestured to a sofa and his visitors sat down.

He and his father began staring at one another again, looking as if neither knew what to say, so once more Lawrence broke the silence.

'There's a strong resemblance between the two of you.'

'Yes. You look like photos of me when I was younger,' Thomas said. 'Good to meet you, Ethan. I wish I'd been able to do that sooner.'

'Mmm.'

Lawrence could have shaken the pair of them, so said firmly, 'I'm not going to stay long but Hilary asked me to be here to introduce you. Do you have any questions before I leave you to get acquainted?'

'It's a wonder Mum didn't leave us a list of conversation starters,' Ethan said. 'She was good at organising people.'

'I could do with some question prompts now,' Thomas said. 'You think you're ready for something as important as this, but I'm not sure where to start.'

Ethan nodded agreement.

Lawrence stood up. 'Well then, in that case I'll leave you to progress at your own pace. I can see myself out, Ethan. Don't hesitate to get in touch if you need anything.'

When they were alone, Thomas took the plunge. 'I want to say up front that I'm very happy indeed to find I have a son. I may not have wanted children when I was younger and very selfish but I found later that I did wish I'd had them.'

'You didn't marry again?'

'No. Hilary was . . . special. No other woman ever measured up to her.'

Ethan stared at him in obvious surprise. 'That's the last thing I expected to hear. I thought you'd be angry at her.'

'She had more reason to be angry at me. I'm surprised she didn't marry again.'

'She had occasional male friends but her main focus was on me. I was fortunate to have a wonderful mother, who made a good life for me.'

'And you have twins, I gather. No wife?'

'There never was. I was careless and got someone pregnant. I had to persuade her to carry the baby to term, or rather, Mum did. And when it turned out to be twins, my friend left once they were a week old and signed a legal document giving me complete custody. She wasn't the maternal type. I never realised someone could be so disgusted by the whole childbearing process and wouldn't change nappies if they were dirty. She's missed a lot. The twins are amazing.'

There was the sound of the front door opening.

Ethan smiled. 'Talk of the devil. Here they come, home from school early. They're brutally frank, I'm afraid. Don't let them upset you.'

* * *

The front door banged shut and a voice called from the hall, 'Is he here?' Two girls in school uniform stopped in the doorway of the sitting room, gazing avidly across at the stranger.

Thomas knew they were twelve from what the lawyer had told him, but they were taller than he'd expected and looked older than that.

They came across the room to plonk kisses on their father's cheek, then went back to studying the stranger openly.

'You look like Dad will look one day when he's old. Nice to meet you. I'm Nicole.'

She held out one hand but Thomas took hold of it between both of his rather than shaking it. 'I'm more delighted than I can say to meet you both. Two days ago I didn't even know any of you three existed, thought I was without any close family.'

'Were you lonely?' she asked.

'Yes.' His voice shook a little as he spoke. He couldn't help it. He turned to the other girl, realising they must be identical twins. 'And you're Liane.'

'Yes. What do we call you?'

'Whatever you like – as long as it's reasonably polite.'

'Pops, then,' Nicole said. 'We already agreed that's what we'd like. Is it OK with you?'

'Absolutely wonderful.' He had never before fully understood what women meant when they said 'happy crying'. He did now because he wanted to do it.

'We need something to eat. Shall we make you two a cup of tea or coffee or something?'

'I'd prefer tea if that's all right. Milk but no sugar.' He watched them go into the kitchen and turned to his son. 'They're a good-looking pair. Hair the same colour as Hilary's used to be, almost blue-black.' Once again he couldn't prevent his voice from shaking.

Ethan said quietly, 'That was a good start. They must have liked the looks of you.'

'Really?'

'They offered to make you a cup of tea, didn't they?'

'Yes. And I certainly liked the looks of them.' His voice was still wobbly with emotion.

Ethan reached out to pat his hand. 'Relax. We can take this slowly.'

'I didn't expect to be so overwhelmed. But then, I didn't expect the wonderful gift Hilary has left me. There's a French word for how I feel: bouleversé. It sounds better than "knocked for six", don't you think?'

'A lot better. Nicer than "gobsmacked", too.'

They were making rather meaningless conversation, Thomas thought, but there was more going on underneath the words and in the visual communication: curiosity and mini-assessments taking place at each step.

Conversation flowed more easily when the girls came back in with mugs of tea and a plate of chocolate biscuits.

Liane looked at her father challengingly. 'It's a special occasion so I opened the special biscuits.'

'Excellent. My daughters are turning into good hostesses since this happened.' Ethan gestured towards his wheelchair.

'You coming here is going to solve one problem anyway, Pops,' Nicole said.

Thomas waited, hoping it really would. Anything he could do to help them would make him feel happy. Anything at all!

'Dad's put off his next operation because of not knowing what to do with us while he's in hospital. He can book in now and you can look after us for him. Not that we couldn't look after ourselves, but there has to be an adult hanging around or the teachers at school might report us to social services.'

'I'll have to find another surgeon first,' Ethan said. 'The one who did the first operations retired last month.'

That made a difference to what was possible, Thomas thought, looking round. This was a fairly small house by his standards. 'How many bedrooms are there here?'

'Three,' Nicole said. 'Ah. I can guess why you're asking and I don't think Nicole and I would fit into one bedroom. They're quite small.'

'Have you three put down deep roots in this part of the world?'

'We only moved to this suburb a couple of years ago, Pops,' Liane said. 'To be near the hospital for Gran as well as Dad after the accident. And the hospice later.' She sighed and reached out for her twin's hand at the same time as Nicole reached for hers, both blinking their eyes rapidly.

'Then it might be better for you all to move across to Western Australia. I have a large house on the water and you can live with me either temporarily or permanently. It's got five bedrooms, each with an en suite, and there's an internal lift, which will be helpful.' He and Sarah had both been in agreement about lifts making things easier in old age, if you could afford one and they could.

His three companions gaped at him, then Nicole spoke, taking the lead once again, 'That sounds brilliant, Pops. Our present school isn't very good so we won't miss it. We're quite bright, you see, and they don't have any special courses for gifted students like our other one did, so it gets rather boring.'

'You didn't tell me that!' Ethan exclaimed.

Liane patted his hand. 'You had enough on your plate with Gran being ill and then you getting injured.'

The two girls must have needed to grow up quickly, Thomas thought. He looked at Ethan. 'I'd really love to have you stay with me.'

'How can you tell so quickly?'

'I have to do things quickly at my age, dive in and take chances. There aren't as many years left for me as for you.'

'How old are you?' Nicole asked.

'Seventy-two.'

She whistled softly. 'What's it like being that old?'

'Good to have a wide experience of life when making decisions, sad to keep losing old friends and difficult to gradually lose your own physical ability to do some things that were easy in your youth.'

'You must have a lot of money if you've got a house that big.'

'Yes. I really wanted to live near the water. But money is no consolation for being alone.' His voice wobbled again, dammit.

Nicole exchanged nods with her sister. 'That's settled, then. We'll come and live with you.'

Ethan's voice also sounded a bit shaky. 'Don't I get a choice?'

'We can slow down the decision-making if you prefer it,' Thomas offered.

The girls went to stand one on either side of their father's wheelchair. 'No. Don't slow down, Pops. Do it straight away. Dad really needs the next operation ASAP so he can finish recovering. Anyway, Gran chose you as a husband and always spoke well of you, so you can't be too bad. She was an excellent judge of character.'

'She left me in the end, though – and I deserved it in those days. I've regretted my selfishness many times since.' Thomas looked at his son. 'I can arrange things quite quickly, if that's all right with you. I have contacts who'll find a skilled surgeon and rehabilitation specialists for you in the west, and we'll find a really good school for the girls.'

Ethan gave him a long, assessing stare, then spread his hands in a helpless gesture and shrugged. 'Thank you, then.'

Thomas stayed there till after tea, for which they had a pizza and salads delivered. Later on he called the chauffeur, whom he'd sent off to find a café, and asked to be taken back to the hotel.

He didn't want to leave the warmth of the small family he was tiptoeing into.

He barely managed to hold back the happy tears till he was alone in his room.

When the room phone rang a couple of hours later, he heard his son's voice.

'It's me. I didn't wake you, did I?'

'No. I was sitting thinking.'

'You're still sure about this?'

'Totally sure, son.'

'Then please start making arrangements immediately . . . Dad. The girls are very eager to move and none of us cares two hoots about our present house. I can arrange to have it sold.'

'Do that. And Ethan, I couldn't be happier.'

When the call ended, Thomas felt to be almost bursting with joy. He shed some more happy tears, but not for long. He already had a list started and planned to make a lot of arrangements the next day. If he'd ever been a whizz at organising things, now was the time to apply his skills.

He even did a clumsy little dance round the bedroom before he got into bed.

'You're a fool,' he told himself, catching sight of the capering old man in the mirror.

A very happy fool, though.

Chapter Nineteen

In the end Col told himself to stop dithering and phoned Fleur to ask her to go with him to see the house again. 'I'm seriously thinking of buying it and would appreciate a second opinion. You seem to know what you're doing when looking at houses.'

'I'm not surprised you're thinking about it. That's a lovely house. I'd enjoy going round it again with you.'

'Are you free today?'

'Yes. I can go right now if you like, or any time that's suitable. I've nothing planned.'

'Now would be perfect. I'm suddenly impatient for my own home and the realtor said he'd be free for the next couple of hours. Bring Portia too if she wants.'

She let out a lovely gurgle of laughter that made him smile with her.

'I don't think she will. She's trying out her new easel and only speaking in monosyllables. Shall I meet you there? I can remember the way.'

'I'll be going near your house so I can easily pick you up. Ten minutes?'

'Fine by me.' It felt good to have somewhere to go, someone to speak to. She wasn't a person who relished solitude, especially at this stage of her life. Being on your own left you too much time to think.

The real estate agent was waiting for them. He let them into the house and said he'd wait for them in his car. 'Take as long as you like to go round it. I can get on with some other little jobs.' He waved his phone at them.

They walked slowly round the house, which seemed to be unoccupied even though it was fully furnished, because the fridge was switched off and completely empty. Once again they quickly agreed that the house had a very welcoming feel to it.

'I feel more at home in a smaller house like this,' she confessed. 'Not that it's small by normal standards like the town house I had in the UK. That one was very cramped, especially with two teenagers scattering debris wherever they went. Only it was all I could afford.'

They seemed to have quite a few of the smaller things in life in common.

'Anyway, to me Cousin Sarah's house is too big. The silence seems to echo around you sometimes.'

'I know what you mean. That house feels very different now she's not there.'

As they walked into the next room, she had a sudden thought. 'Do you have enough furniture to move right in?'

He shook his head. 'No. Hardly any, in fact. I got rid of a lot of older stuff when I moved over here from the eastern states and I'm renting a furnished flat at the moment. I shall have to get a couple of things and camp out for a while.'

'Then you might want to check whether this furniture is for sale as well as the house. You can replace it gradually but if you want to move in quickly, it'll give you an easy start. It's fairly neutral, so shouldn't irritate you too much, either.'

She went back into the kitchen, opening and shutting cupboard doors. 'They've even left the crockery and cutlery. Maybe the owner died and if so, he or she has left good vibes behind.'

'I agree. I shall offer a little less than the asking price. What do you think?'

'I don't know enough about house prices here to figure out what's likely to hit the target. I don't even know yet what Cousin Sarah's house will be worth when we sell it.'

'Getting on for a couple of million, I was told.'

She let out a long, slow whistle of breath. 'Phew. I'm still not used to the idea of having so much money. I had no idea she was going to leave half her estate to me.'

'Were you thrilled?'

She smiled. 'Yes, of course – "thrilled skinny", as a plump friend of mine used to say.'

He chuckled. 'I like that phrase.' He looked at his watch. 'I'll put in an offer, then we could go and have lunch somewhere to celebrate. Unless you're busy, of course.'

'On the contrary. I'm not used to having so little that urgently needs doing and time can hang rather heavily. Lunch would be lovely, as long as they can cater for someone who's wheat intolerant.'

'I had a colleague with that problem. Bit of a nuisance, isn't it?'

'Lot of a nuisance. Some idiots seem to think we do it on purpose to be different, and could perfectly well eat wheat. I wish!'

'I don't think that.' He took a deep breath. 'Well, here goes my first offer, then.'

He and the agent came back inside together, so she moved back and listened to them bargaining.

Col said quietly, 'I expect a reduced price because it'd be a cash sale.'

The estate agent beamed at that. 'Ah. That does make a difference, though not as much difference as the price you've offered. If you can wait for a few minutes, I can write out the offer and let you sign it straight away, then we'll leave it up to the owners to come back with a counter-offer.' He cast a shrewd, questioning glance at Col as he said that.

'As long as it's near my offer and below the asking price. You go ahead and sort that out.'

'I hope you don't get gazumped,' she whispered as they waited.

'It's not like the UK house sales system,' he told her in a low voice. 'Once the offer has been accepted, the sale is legally fixed and can't be gazumped.'

'Wow. I wish it had been like that when I bought my current house. I was on tenterhooks for several weeks till the sale went through. And mine was a cash offer, too: it took nearly all my divorce money, but I managed not to need a mortgage. Terry used his share to put a deposit on a luxury flat. I thought he must have taken out a big mortgage to buy that, but now I wonder if he had some money or valuables stashed away.' She sighed and added, 'Water under the bridge now.'

After a moment's thought, she added, 'My UK house is for sale at the moment. If I can afford to buy a bigger place after I go back because of this legacy, I'll be a lot happier.'

She couldn't resist walking across to the canal-side window and staring out at the water sparkling in the summer sunshine. A tour boat full of holidaymakers passed by because this house wasn't on a cul-de-sac canal like Cousin Sarah's. The tourists looked so happy it made her smile too. Every day she'd been here had been sunny so far. She wasn't missing the English winter at all.

'I'm going to ask for an accelerated settlement,' Col said. 'They can do them in a couple of weeks if you press for it.'

'That quickly? How wonderful!'

The estate agent cleared his throat to get their attention. 'Would you like to read the offer and sign it if you're satisfied, Mr Jennings?'

After Col had done that, the agent added, 'I'll get back to you by eight o'clock tonight at the latest with a response. And I'll ask them what they want for the furniture. I know they don't intend to keep any of it. In fact, they were going to have to pay someone to clear the house. They live in Queensland so they'll be glad to be rid of it so easily. All this was an inheritance from an old uncle, you see.'

When they walked outside, Col grabbed Fleur's hand and waltzed her across to the car, twirling her round and giving a flourishing bow, which made her laugh. He was a good dancer, too.

'I can't thank you enough, Fleur. You were so helpful. If I get the furniture as well, I'm moving straight in. I'm so eager to have somewhere to call home.'

Then he realised he was still holding her too closely and stared at her for a moment before letting go. 'Oops! Sorry.'

His closeness had set her heart racing and it took her a few moments before she could speak calmly. 'You're allowed to get excited about something this important.'

In the car he asked, 'My coeliac friend says Indian or Chinese food is easiest for him. Would one of those suit you and if so, which?'

'Whichever you prefer. You're right. I like them both and can usually find something safe in either of those cuisines.'

'How about Chinese this time?'

He didn't get her home till after three o'clock in the afternoon because they found the restaurant really did understand her needs so they ordered a banquet for two. They sat chatting at a table by the window as they worked their way slowly through a series of small courses.

Afterwards they went for a walk along the foreshore because they both admitted to feeling guilty at eating so much.

When Fleur arrived home, Portia was still in her studio and didn't even seem aware of what the time was. She looked blissfully happy, which was good to see.

Only, if her cousin was going to get lost in her art, Fleur decided she'd better put making friends closer to the top of her list and mark it 'urgent'.

Around teatime, an email from Marie arrived, wanting to know how she was getting on. It contained several very specific questions about the inheritance, which puzzled her. It was unlike her daughter to show any interest in what she was doing, let alone ask such detailed questions about financial matters.

Fleur frowned and re-read the message. It sounded as though Marie was trying to find out exactly what her mother's inheritance amounted to. Why?

Well, her daughter wasn't going to get her hands on it. She was lazy enough now. More money would only encourage that trait.

Or was someone else pushing her daughter to ask such questions? Yes, of course. Why had she taken so long to realise that?

Surely even Terry wasn't arrogant enough to think he could charm his way back into Fleur's life? Hell would freeze over before she would ever take him back. The man she'd married had been bearable but the man he'd turned into had become – well, a little strange.

She looked at the message again. Marie was also suggesting an app that might make chatting easier for them. It wasn't one Fleur had ever heard of before and the mere thought of diving into that made her frown.

She didn't reply to Marie immediately, but decided to send a joint email to her children the next day, giving them both some vague details about the house and its location, and leave it at that. It was all they needed to know about her new life because she wasn't going to pay for them to come and join her in Australia for a holiday. At this time in their lives, they needed to get their tertiary education done and dusted.

Portia came out of the studio just then and asked what she wanted for tea.

'What? Sorry, I was deep in thought. I'll get myself a snack later, thank you. I ate far too well at lunchtime. Just sort out something for yourself.'

'I'll try one of those pre-cooked meals, then.'

Fleur was relieved to find a good film on TV that evening, one she'd been wanting to see for a while. She was even more relieved when it turned out her cousin also liked musicals, so she wouldn't have to watch violent films like the ones Terry had loved.

After the film ended, Fleur went to bed early with the songs humming happily through her.

She dreamed about Col that night and woke feeling embarrassed at the sort of dreams they had been. She'd been too long without a man, was still young and healthy enough to want . . . well, a normal love life.

She felt sure Col had only danced her round and kept hold of her hand by accident, because he was excited about his house. It had meant nothing. But he was interesting to chat to and that was important in a friend.

She might try a dating site once she'd settled in, as she knew female friends who had used them. She considered what that would involve and shuddered. No, she had never been able to face putting herself out online, still couldn't.

Unless fate intervened and she met someone special, she'd have to be satisfied with friendships.

As if fate was thinking about her need for friendships, Fleur met some of the nearby neighbours a few days later when a man and woman passing by in a smallish boat saw her sitting on the patio, waved to her and stopped at her jetty. She went out of the flyscreened area to find out what they wanted and was delighted when they introduced themselves as Emma and Aaron Buchanan, nearby neighbours.

After finding out that Fleur and her cousin were newcomers to Australia and knew practically no one, Emma immediately invited them round for a sundowner that evening.

She and Portia went by, climbing over the low dividing wall. They spent a lovely chatty hour and got on so well they stayed for an impromptu supper.

Another night, Fleur invited Col round for a sundowner and would have invited the Buchanans as well, but they'd said they were going away for a few days, driving round the vineyards further south. That sounded a lovely way to spend time, so Fleur noted it mentally as something to do before she returned to England.

She could already tell that she and her cousin's social life would be mainly left for her to organise. Portia was rather shy and didn't seem skilled socially, though she was pleasant enough company when Fleur organised something.

Another night Col rang to see if they were in, and came round with a bottle of Prosecco to celebrate his settlement date being arranged for the new house. He didn't stop beaming the whole time.

'Only another few days to go. Here's to moving in ASAP!' He raised his glass to clink it with each of theirs. 'I can't wait.'

He looked at Fleur. 'And it's thanks to you that it's going to be relatively easy to move, because there's plenty of furniture there already. In fact, too much.'

'I was happy to help.'

Their eyes met and for a few moments it felt as if they were somehow connected, then Portia said something and the spell was broken.

Had she imagined it? Fleur wondered afterwards. She hoped not. The more she saw of Col, the more she enjoyed his company.

She didn't dare hope for more than friendship, though. Life had a way of hitting you on the head if you hoped for too much. Well, she'd found that anyway.

Most mornings, Portia and Fleur continued to put in a couple of hours going through the various family records. To say they found chaos was putting it mildly.

'I'm not enjoying this, are you?' Portia asked.

'No. Not really. And it looks as if it'll take much longer than I'd expected.'

They contemplated the contents of today's box-to-be-emptied, as they'd started calling them. 'Still, we owe it to Sarah to do as she wished.'

'I know. She's given us so much. Most importantly to me, my freedom.'

'That's pretty important to me too.' Portia looked up towards the sky. 'Thank you, Cousin Sarah.'

Her cousin echoed her words, but followed them by a sigh. So they continued doggedly.

Thomas was still away and Fleur had received a couple of emails from him explaining what was going on with his newly acquired son and granddaughters. She shared these with Portia.

She was surprised how much she missed him. He had somehow been a unifying force for the two cousins and had started connecting them to people in the town, even in the short time they'd known him, not to mention bringing Col to interact with them all, making a group of friends as well.

Since they knew Col was busy packing up his possessions and arranging the other things like taking over the utilities in his new house, they tried not to disturb him.

When he got permission to go through the contents of the house in the few days before moving in, on condition that he didn't dispose of those he didn't want until after settlement, he dropped in to tell them.

'You haven't got much time to do that. I'll come and help if you like,' Fleur offered.

He gave her a long, serious look. 'That's a generous offer but I'm taking too much of your time.'

'I seem to have too much time on my hands, to be honest. I'm used to keeping busy. Truly, I'll be happy to help you.'

'I'll help as well. Let's go and put in a couple of hours now and see how long it might take,' Portia added.

She drove them round and stopped outside to look at the house for the first time before going inside. 'This is a more normal-sized home. Who lived here before?'

'An old man whose only relatives were over east. That's why they were happy to sell the contents to me for such a reasonable amount. They thought they'd have to pay someone to clear the house out.' Col grimaced. 'I'm not enjoying the thought of going through his personal possessions, though, especially his clothes, but there you are. This sort of job has to be done.'

'I'll do that if it creeps you out,' Fleur volunteered. 'I can wear plastic gloves and chuck all his clothes in a bin liner bag.'

As they set to work, she gradually became aware that Portia was stealing glances at the two of them every now and then and was embarrassed at what her cousin was obviously thinking.

'He's just a friend,' she said firmly after they got back home.

'Tell that to the fairies!'

She didn't argue. You couldn't stop people speculating about relationships if you were a single woman and so much as spoke to an eligible man. She'd found out when she and Terry split up that the best way to deal with them was to deny there being any new relationship, do it only once and thereafter ignore any insinuations.

Not easy this time, though. For once she found the man in question very attractive and the more time she spent with him, the more she wished he had shown signs of wanting to get to know her in that way.

Chapter Twenty

In England, Marie picked up the phone. 'Dad! How lovely to hear from you again.'

'Just making sure you're OK now you haven't got your mother to keep an eye on you. How are things going?'

'Oh, you know. Studying sucks. They want you to read such long, boring books, and working in the supermarket sucks even more.'

'Your mother isn't sharing her inheritance at all, is she? She wasn't selfish before but money can change people.'

'Tell me about it. She's been a bit of a pain ever since you moved out, actually, wanting everything done just so. And why she chose that horrid little house, I'll never know.'

'Did you, um, find out more details about what she inherited? I can't advise you properly unless I have all the facts.'

'I did ask, but she's ignored my questions. I do wish you two were still together, Dad. Life was so much nicer when I was living at home and you were around.'

He winced at the memories of the rows between Marie and her mother but that didn't stop him letting out a carefully calculated sigh. 'I sometimes wish we were still together, too.'

'You do?'

'Yes. Nothing is perfect, but our relationship had a lot of good points. Fleur was very easy to live with. I know it's old-fashioned to say she was a good housewife, but she was. I didn't realise I'd miss having her to run things, miss the comfortable home she created.'

'Maybe you should try to get together again.'

'I doubt she'd even consider it . . . unfortunately.'

'I suppose not. But if you ever think of some way to try and I can help you, you have only to ask.'

'I know, darling. You're a good daughter to me. Well, must go now.'

When she put the phone down, Marie was thoughtful. Her life had definitely been better when her parents were still together. And studying wasn't her cup of tea at all, was even worse than she'd expected. She'd thought she could put up with it and just do enough to get through a degree, but getting pass-level marks was harder than she'd expected.

The annoying thing about Cody was that he was into studying big time. He didn't even want to go out most nights, so she had started going out with her own friends.

She was seriously considering leaving him and dropping out of university. Only, then she'd have to find somewhere to live, pay the full rent on it if she wanted her own space, and for that she'd have to find a full-time job. She had no idea what sort of job she could do if she did drop out. She'd only be able to get a miserable, lowly job without qualifications.

Why was life so hard?

Her mother had made it clear when Marie left school that she wasn't going to support her daughter in idleness, even though she'd begged for a gap year, because she needed some quiet time to find herself.

You'd think inheriting a lot of money would have made a difference to that, but it hadn't. Her mother was just plain mean, hadn't even raised her allowance, unlike her father, who had sent her an extra twenty pounds this month, just in the nick of time to buy her share of the food.

The least her mother could have done was invite her children out to Australia to visit her in the holidays, give them a break in the sun, away from the hassles of studying and the chancy UK weather.

Marie had said that to James but her brother had told her not to act like a stupid child. He couldn't have left his studies at the moment and neither should she. She should buckle down to work at it. It was only for three years, after all, and her course was one of the easy ones.

'Well, I don't find it easy; I never have been good at studying.'

'Well, life is always full of hassles, whatever you're doing, sis. You just have to get on with it and do your best. And don't tell me you are doing that, because we both know you're not.' He interrupted what she was going to say to add, 'And what's more, people who claim to be adults shouldn't still want their parents to support them.'

As their row progressed, she cut the phone call off. She could do without being hassled and lectured. He took after their mother, James did. He was boring. She might as well not have a brother. It was a good thing she had her father to turn to.

She went back to her sewing. She'd found a really nice skirt in the charity shop. It just needed altering to fit her, one of the few jobs she did enjoy.

For the next few days, Thomas spent the first part of every morning in the hotel's business suite where he was able to rent a computer by the hour, a small cubicle of office space and secretarial assistance.

With the help of a very capable woman who was more of a general factotum than a secretary, he began making arrangements to move his family across the country with him. She also helped him find out about a relevant medical specialist in Western Australia.

He passed the name to Ethan, leaving it to him and his GP to look into the woman's background. If she seemed suitable, Ethan would get a referral and make an appointment to see about having his next operation done in Western Australia as a matter of urgency.

'Do you have private health insurance?' Thomas asked.

'Yes. I've managed to keep up the payments but my accident meant I haven't been earning nearly as much and I'm getting a bit short of money now to pay for the gap in cover for any further operations. Unfortunately I still need to take those painkillers sometimes, but they dull the brain as well as the pain so I can't get as much work done, let alone concentrate on sorting out my life.'

The look of embarrassment and shame on his son's face hurt Thomas and he went across to sit beside the wheelchair and clasp Ethan's nearest hand. 'I've got plenty of money and no one to spend it on, so I'm happy to help you financially and in any other way you might need.'

'I know and I'm grateful, but I still can't help wishing I didn't need it. If I had my mobility back again and my brain working properly, I'd not be taking this much from you.'

'But you will accept my help?'

'Yes, of course. I'm not stupid enough to reject a way out of the impasse.' His voice grew harsher. 'It's totally embarrassing to lose your independence so completely at my age, though.'

'It's not through any fault of your own.'

'I know. But still . . .' His voice tailed away and he shrugged his shoulders.

'We all need help at various times in our lives, Ethan. Besides, you really are helping me in return.'

'How am I doing that? All the girls and I seem to be doing is costing you money.'

Thomas didn't usually speak of his innermost feelings, but somehow he could talk about them to his son, as he had been able to do with Sarah. 'You're driving away the loneliness that's iced over my life since my friend Sarah died, not to mention banishing how upset I've been at the lack of a future for my genes. I'm arrogant enough to think they're worth passing on, you see.'

Ethan looked startled. 'I've never heard an older person talk like that before. Does it matter so much to pass yourself on, as it were?'

'As you get older, yes it does. You desperately want something of what makes you to carry on. Well, that's what I've found anyway and other people I respect have said the same. So you see your mere existence has made me feel better. As for the girls, what can I say? They're absolutely wonderful.' He beamed at the mere thought of them.

Ethan relaxed a little. 'They are, aren't they? But you have other friends, surely?'

'There's no one else in Sarah's league. She was a mother/ aunt/sister all rolled into one.'

'I wish I'd met her. You speak of her so lovingly.'

'I wish you had too. I've only known Col for a few months, but he's helped fill the gap a little and been kind to a lonely old man. You're helping far more. I thought retirement would be marvellous, but it isn't. There's too much time to fill.'

'You're not enjoying being old, are you?'

'I wasn't. It's improved a lot lately.'

Ethan gave him a much warmer glance.

'And when we move to Mandurah, you can help me to keep an eye on Fleur and Portia as well, so that I can fulfil my promise to Sarah to look after them.' He added without thinking, 'Are you any good at going through historical documents? I'm not. And they have piles to sort out.'

To his surprise, his son's face lit up. 'History is a bit of a passion of mine, Dad. It counteracts the geekishness of my daytime job.'

'I should think your geekishness comes in very useful when you have a family to support. Anyway, those two women have been given the job of sorting out about two or three hundred years' worth of family documents, and clearly it's their own family as well as Sarah's. But they're not enjoying it all that much nor do they have a background knowledge of history against which to understand and judge the importance of some documents and photos. They've got one pile labelled "Needs expert help" and they're doggedly doing the best they can.'

He explained each woman's situation in more detail.

'That's an incredible inheritance to leave them.' Ethan sounded awestruck.

'Yes. Sarah was a very shrewd lady where money was concerned, and she did check out as far as she could that those two wouldn't waste her money. On the contrary, as far as I can tell they're still watching every penny they spend.'

'It doesn't hurt to be careful.'

'Yes, but though Sarah was assiduous in safeguarding her family's papers and photographs, she never did anything with them herself, didn't even attempt to sort them out. She said the likely human lifespan left to her was too short to spend time on jobs she disliked that much.'

'Do her heirs have any close family?'

'Fleur has two children, both nearly grown up now. Her ex sounds to be horribly selfish and a womaniser. Portia seems to have struggled through life for many years, first because the father she adored was ill and then because her widowed mother met a new guy and almost ignored her. Portia met someone and they moved in together for a while but broke up in less than a year. I'm not sure of the details of why, but on top of that, she's twice been made redundant in the past year.'

He frowned. 'I'm surprised she hasn't done much studying. She's not stupid or lazy but she didn't even try to go to university, was content to do a course giving basic clerical skills and leading only to a low-level office job. I think there's something she's hiding from me still, something that stops her studying.'

He shrugged. 'Anyway, when you come over to Western Australia, you can help me keep an eye on them both and if you love history and have some background in it, that'll be a big bonus for all of us.'

'Happy to do that.' Ethan reached out and squeezed his father's hand. 'Thanks for trusting me with the Blakemere family secrets.'

'I trust you absolutely but I'm not sure there will be any interesting secrets among those papers.'

They smiled at one another rather shyly.

Thomas could feel the warmth of that touch for ages afterwards. It made him feel that all was coming right with his world.

Chapter Twenty-One

Portia was feeling restless and tired of being indoors. She'd always thought better in the open air, so even needed to get away from her beloved studio for a while. She went to tell Fleur that she'd decided to go for a walk then do some grocery shopping but felt duty-bound to add, 'Do you want to come with me?'

'Not unless you need me. I've promised to help Col with some more clearing out of the small personal stuff. He says the old man who lived in that house must have been a real hoarder but Col doesn't want to throw away anything that might have intrinsic value. He's so impatient for settlement to happen, is absolutely dying to move in the minute all the legalities are sorted out. He has his things packed and ready in his flat.'

'I'm sure he'll be very happy there.' She was a bit fed up of hearing about Col and his new house, actually. 'All right then. I need some fresh air so I shall go for a long walk along the foreshore first then buy what's needed. What do you fancy for tea?'

'Anything I don't have to cook.'

'That's easy.'

By the time she got to the big shopping centre, Portia had walked briskly along the side of the estuary for a good half hour and was feeling as if she had shaken off the dust and boredom of sorting out documents. It had been an added stress trying not to let her dyslexia slow her down too much while they went through things. Fleur knew about it and was too kind to be scornful, but still, Portia didn't like to seem stupid.

Some of the nastier people at school had called her stupid, especially during her last two years there, which had been a truly miserable time. Oh, why was she thinking of that! It was long gone.

The pain of it wasn't long gone, though. Think of something else, she told herself, as she had many times before.

Cooking. That usually cheered her up and it brought an anticipatory smile to her face now. She was dying to stock their pantry properly and cook some of the dishes she'd learned from her mother, who was an excellent cook. Today, her main shopping focus, apart from getting something for tea, would be the basics that were still missing, some of her favourite spices, for a start.

And she wanted to try the different flours Fleur needed, like almond, cassava and coconut, plus she'd need yeast for some of bread mixtures in the wheat-free recipe book. She was intrigued at the thought of new culinary challenges.

It'd been hot outside by the time she finished her walk, so she waited till she got into the shopping centre to stop for a coffee and a salad sandwich in air-conditioned comfort. It was such a treat to be able to afford little breaks like this.

She found a seating area near the takeaway food stalls at one end of the concourse, choosing the part where shops took over from eateries. She enjoyed watching passers-by while she ate her snack. You couldn't draw figures accurately unless you did a lot of people-watching because even if you got the bodies correct, you still needed them to be doing credible activities.

The area had wooden benches and lovely big plants, real ones, not artificial. She finished eating then got out her list and added a couple of items to it. She'd have to—

She looked up, frowning. What was that sound? There it went again, a sort of whimper, as if some little creature were hurt. She turned round slowly, scanning the area, wondering if there was a lost puppy. Only it wasn't an animal at all but a small child, huddled between two of the large plants, sobbing. You'd not have seen the little girl if you were only walking past, or heard her either because of the general noise levels.

The child was clearly in distress and looked too young to be out in a big shopping centre on her own. Portia stared all round but couldn't see any adult who seemed to be searching for a lost offspring.

Would the little girl run away if a stranger approached her too closely? Portia edged slowly along the wooden bench towards her, stopping between each move and smiling.

Realising she was being watched with extreme wariness, she shuffled along one more time then sat still and tried speaking. 'My name's Portia. What's your name?'

That brought a stubborn expression to the little girl's face.

'Are you called Jenny?'

A shake of the head was at least some sort of answer.

'Patsy?'

Another shake of the head.

'Mooloo-wooloo-booloo?'

The child first stared then laughed at the stream of nonsense. 'That's not a name. I'm Mandy.'

'What a nice name! Where's your mummy?'

'Not got a mummy.'

'Oh. Where's your daddy, then?'

'In the shop.' She pointed towards a nearby supermarket.

'Shall we go and find him?'

Another frown, then a nod and a hopeful, 'Buy some sweeties?'

'We'll ask your daddy about sweeties. Come on, love.' She set off walking, not even trying to hold the child's hand. Her small companion came too but stayed a short distance to one side of her.

Suddenly there was a shout of 'Mandy!' and a man came running towards them from the checkout section of the supermarket.

'Daddy!' The child held out her arms to him and he scooped her up, holding her close and plonking a kiss on each cheek, clearly considering her precious.

'I found your daughter hiding behind one of those plants,' Portia said quickly because he was looking at her suspiciously. She pointed to them.

'The lady said to find you,' the child volunteered. 'Sweeties now?'

He'd been studying Portia as if trying to work out whether she was to be trusted, but at the child's words, he relaxed a little. 'I don't usually lose my daughter but she let go of the trolley when I wasn't looking and seemed to melt into thin air.' He was still holding her close and she was clinging to him.

'Sweeties?' she persisted.

'No. You were naughty to run away. No sweeties.'

Her face crumpled but she didn't cry and seemed to accept his words.

'They haven't got much common sense at that age, have they?' Portia said.

'Not when they're determined to have some sweeties. Her grandma must have bought them for her whenever they went shopping. I'll have to have a word with my mother-in-law about that. Thanks for keeping an eye on Mandy.'

'I didn't do anything but watch her from a distance. I was rather worried about such a small child being out on her own, especially as she was upset.'

'Look, let me pay for my shopping then buy you a coffee to show my appreciation.'

'There's no need. I'll leave you to it.'

But when she turned away, the child held out an arm to her and let out a sob, so Portia stood still. 'She needs to calm down. Why don't you pay for your shopping and I'll stay with her? Which café?'

'Thanks. We usually go to that one opposite. Um, I'm Ben, by the way.'

'Portia.' She waited for the usual joking comment about her name but it didn't come.

'Pleased to meet you.' He set the child down. 'Stay with the lady and do not move away. I'll buy you a fizzy water when I get back. How do you like your coffee, Portia?'

The child brightened up a little at that so Portia held out her hand and to her relief Mandy took it. They walked slowly across to the café. 'Let's find your daddy a seat. Would he like to sit on this bench or that one, do you think?'

Mandy studied them then pointed. 'This one.'

Good. The trick of giving a choice rather than asking whether she wanted to do something had worked, as it usually did with children that age. 'Let's try it.' Portia lifted the little girl up onto the bench and sat down beside her. Mandy immediately put a thumb in her mouth and leaned against her, sighing. Her forehead seemed rather hot. Was it from crying or was she slightly feverish?

Ben walked across and left his trolley near them, then queued up at the counter.

The child watched every move he took but also kept a firm hold of Portia's sleeve.

When he came back with the drinks, she waited till Mandy was engrossed in drinking through her straw to whisper, 'Does she seem feverish to you?'

He looked at the child and felt her forehead. 'Maybe a little. I'm not sure. Could be just from crying.'

'Give her a minute or two to calm down then see what you think.'

'You seem to know about children. Do you have some of your own?'

'I wish! No, I'm not married, but I've done a lot of babysitting to earn extra money.'

'Are you on holiday here?'

'Sort of. My cousin and I are staying at a relative's house.'

She'd decided not to tell people about her inheritance unless she had to, she still wasn't used to the thought of having so much money and not needing to work for a living.

What worried her was: the money might give her the chance to pursue her hobby, but it wouldn't bring her into contact with people and she needed that too. After her father died she'd rushed into a relationship with a man she now thought of as 'the oik'. She'd only realised after moving in that he was trying to use her as an unpaid servant. In fact, he'd proved to have very old-fashioned views about a woman's role, so that relationship hadn't lasted long. She wanted an equal partner or none at all.

She'd been very lonely for the past year or two, what with her mother going to live in another town and then being made redundant. She'd thought things would settle down after starting the new job but then had been made redundant for a second time.

Even with her inheritance, she might still do some babysitting just for the pleasure of it and to meet people. She loved being with little children particularly.

Ben's mobile phone rang just then and he said, 'Excuse me a moment. It might be my mother-in-law needing picking up. She usually looks after Mandy for me, even though I'm now divorced from her daughter, but she's been in hospital today having some tests.'

He looked at the contact info and said, 'Yes, it is her. Please excuse me a moment. Hi, Gwen.'

Portia concentrated on helping Mandy with her drink, but she couldn't avoid overhearing his voice and noticing how it changed tone. 'I'm sorry to hear that. No, don't worry, Gwen. I'll find someone else to look after Mandy. Do you want me to bring anything to the hospital for you?'

He listened, nodding. 'I'll leave it to your neighbour, then. No, no. It's all right, really it is. You can't delay these things and you've caught it early, thank goodness. You need to concentrate on getting better now. Oh, just a minute. Will you be up for visitors tomorrow? Ah. See you the day after, then.'

He ended the call and sat staring at the phone, shoulders sagging for all his cheerful words.

'She has to stay in hospital and have a minor op on her leg straight away. So she won't be able to look after Mandy for a while.' He rubbed his forehead. 'I'll have to take some time off work because I don't have a back-up carer at the moment.'

The words were out before Portia could stop herself. 'I could look after her for you, if you like. I enjoy being with children.'

'I can't ask you to do that. You don't even know me. And just as important, I don't know you.'

'You didn't ask. I offered.'

'But aren't you on holiday here with your relative?'

'No. I'm, er, helping my cousin to clear the relative's house. She died a few weeks ago and left it to us both.'

'Lucky you.'

'I'd rather have Cousin Sarah alive.'

'Of course you would. How old was she?'

'Ninety-five, almost ninety-six.'

'She had a good long life, then. That must comfort you.'

'Mmm.'

He hesitated then watched the child, sleeping peacefully now with her head on Portia's lap. 'Are you sure about looking after her?'

'Yes.'

'Do you have any character references I could take up here in Australia?'

That stumped her for a moment, then she remembered Thomas. 'Would a character reference from a retired lawyer help?'

'That'd be fine. I'd have to meet him, though. You understand, I must make sure I can trust you, for Mandy's sake.'

'Of course I understand. I'd be the same.'

'How about taking me to meet him now? You said he was retired.'

'Ah. He's over in the eastern states, helping his son who was injured in a car accident. I can phone him and get him to speak to you.' She saw him shake his head and said it before he could. 'No, that won't be enough, will it?'

Then she had an idea. 'There's Col as well. He owns a business in Mandurah and he's keeping an eye on me and Fleur till Thomas gets back. We're still getting used to living down under, you see. I can phone him and then take you round to see him.'

'That might work.'

She was lucky enough to catch Col and when she explained why Ben and his daughter wanted to see him, he exclaimed, 'What on earth made you offer to do that?' in a tone of such astonishment she hoped Ben hadn't heard what he'd said.

'I like children, actually. But Ben wants to meet you before he decides whether to let me look after Mandy. Which is only fair. I'm just, you know, doing him a favour.' It felt right to put something back into the world when Sarah had given her so much.

'Well, I'd definitely like to meet him before you go off alone with him. Bring him round to my new house. Fleur and I are here going through the pantry and kitchen today, clearing out stuff that's long expired. I reckon some of it should be given to museums, it's so old.'

She smiled involuntarily and when the call ended, she gave Ben Col's address and abandoned her shopping trip without a single regret. Mandy was such a little dear. Anyway, she could always go back to the shopping centre another day, couldn't she?

This felt like the first step she'd taken on her own in Australia, a sign that she was an independent woman, not a timid dependant, and had the ability to help other people.

Chapter Twenty-Two

As she waited for Ben outside the new house, Col and Fleur came out to join her, looking round for another car.

'Didn't he follow you?' Col asked.

'He'll be here in a minute, I'm sure.' And she was sure. There was something very solid and trustworthy about Ben, not to mention she liked the way he interacted with his child.

'What's his full name?' Fleur asked.

'Um—' Oh dear, she hadn't even asked that. 'I don't know, we only exchanged first names.'

Col and Fleur exchanged glances, then he said, 'Are you usually so impulsive about helping complete strangers?'

'No. But I love children and his daughter is such a dear little thing.'

The minutes ticked past and there was no sign of Ben.

'He might have been scared off. Let's go and wait inside.' Both Fleur and Col looked as if they didn't believe he would turn up.

'Very well.' Portia turned to follow them, then heard a car and stayed where she was. She hadn't even seen Ben's car, so wouldn't recognise it. But as soon as the vehicle got closer the driver waved and there was a child's seat in the back with a small hand waving from it. It had to be him. 'Here they are.'

The car drew up and Ben got out, turning to unfasten his daughter. 'Sorry to keep you waiting, but she had to do a wee-wee.'

Mandy stayed behind him, clinging on to the leg of his jeans and staring warily at Col and Fleur but smiling at Portia.

After everyone had been introduced and full names exchanged, Fleur said, 'Do come inside, Mr Peyton.'

Ben was staring at the house with a puzzled frown, but he picked Mandy up and followed them.

Col took them out on the patio, seeing his visitor's expression grow grimmer at the sight of the canal. When they were all seated, he said, 'Do you have any ID, Mr Peyton?'

'Yes, of course.' Ben got his wallet out and produced several forms of ID.

Portia saw Col relax a little as he checked them.

'I might ask you the same thing,' Ben said. 'Or at least, ask Portia.' He turned to her. 'Do you have some ID?'

'I've only got my UK driving licence here. I have my UK passport as well, of course, but I left that at our house.' She showed him the driving licence, which she hadn't bothered to take out of the transparent pocket in her purse yet.

'Can I ask where you're living?'

She pointed across the canal. 'In Dolphin Close, which is the next turn off this main canal.'

'The house your relative left you is in Dolphin Close!'

'Yes.'

'But you can't possibly need a job if you own half a house on the water. Dolphin Close is one of the best streets on the canals. Everyone knows that.'

'I don't need a job, nor did I say I did. But I do need something to do with my time, and I'd enjoy looking after Mandy.' She smiled down at the child, who had crept across to lean against her while her father was dealing with paperwork. She was now clutching the leg of Portia's jeans tightly.

Ben frowned at his daughter, then at Portia. 'Well, I'm still going to insist on paying you.'

'All right.'

'How much do you charge?'

'I haven't the faintest idea.'

He relaxed a little, smiling and shaking his head. 'Very practical. I'll find out the usual rates and pay you that. OK?'

Before she could answer, Col said, 'Let me see if I can find out now.' He fiddled with his phone, came up with a basic hourly rate for childminding and showed it to them.

'That sounds fair.' Ben looked at Portia questioningly. She nodded.

'Would you like to come and see where we live, Portia, then I can show you where all Mandy's things are. I'll have to ask you to come early tomorrow, I'm afraid. I start work at seven o'clock.'

'Fine by me. I'm an early riser anyway.'

'All right if we come with you?' Col still had that watchful look on his face.

Ben scowled at him. 'You're not very trusting, are you, Mr Jennings?'

'No. Not with people I've only just met, anyway.'

Ben shrugged. 'Very well. But I don't guarantee the house will be tidy. I'll even throw in a cup of coffee, though you might want to check it for poison before you drink it.'

Col relaxed a little and smiled. 'I doubt we'll need to go that far. I'll drive you there, Portia, Fleur.'

When the three of them got into the car, he didn't start it for a few moments. 'Are you sure about this, Portia?'

She relaxed. 'Yes. I really love children. I don't want to spend all day, every day sorting out papers.'

'And children seem to like you, too. I watched that little girl come to you of her own accord, even though she's only just met you.'

'I'm sure Ben's all right. He has a nice smile.'

Fleur nodded. 'I think he is too, but I'd still prefer it if we checked out his home situation.'

Ben lived in a neat town house in an upmarket development. And as they went round the parts of it that were relevant to looking after Mandy, the two men relaxed a little further with one another, thank goodness.

It was going to be all right, Portia decided. And she'd really enjoy looking after that delightful little girl for a few days. She did feel a bit guilty about deserting Fleur, but her guess was that Col would be there to fill the gap. The two of them were looking very much at ease with one another.

She didn't think she'd ever felt as at ease with any man of her age since she'd broken up with the oik. She and her cousin were both at ease with Thomas but that was different.

Anyhow, this job would only last for a few days, she was sure. Gwen was just having a minor operation.

As she was getting ready for bed that night, she smiled. It was good to be getting to know more people here in Australia, however she met them. She didn't want to date Ben, but she'd like to keep him as a friend, and keep in touch with Mandy.

She hadn't contacted her mother yet, and had better do it tonight. She'd forgiven the outburst of jealousy about the bequest, but just in case her mother was still huffy about it, she wouldn't phone but email. Really, she ought to have let her family know before now that things were going well.

She got out her phone. Better contact Cousin Josie too, though she might phone her. No, better not. Her mother would have another huff if she did that and only emailed her. She'd always had to tread a bit carefully with her mother about such details.

She spent nearly fifteen minutes on the email, checking and re-checking, hoping she hadn't made any spelling mistakes. Then she adapted it for Josie before switching off the phone and sliding down in bed.

It had been an eventful day and she was looking forward to spending a few days with Mandy. She was also quite proud of herself for offering to help. Better than being tongue-tied and later wishing she'd done it.

* * *

Portia enjoyed four days of looking after Mandy, had fun taking her for walks and playing little games with her, not to mention cooking tea for her and her father, using their slow cooker for casseroles to make it easy.

She refused to stay and eat with them for the evening meal because she felt guilty at leaving Fleur alone for so long. Since she hadn't been there to help go through the papers, her cousin left them alone as well. But at least she could still cook for the two of them.

At home, Fleur's lack of interest in cooking showed because she didn't seem able to produce anything but the most mundane of meals on the couple of occasions guilt made her insist on making tea. They were perfectly edible but not as healthy as Portia would have liked and from then on she insisted on doing it, because she could have done better standing on her head, as the saying went.

And yet, Fleur had some domestic skills that Portia lacked. She'd altered a couple of things for Sarah that only needed minor changes quickly and neatly, and promised to do the rest, so that Portia would have a decent wardrobe without having to spend a lot of money.

On the Friday morning, Ben said he could cope with his daughter over the weekend and since Gwen would be coming out of hospital on the Saturday morning, all being well, he'd not need Portia's help.

'I'm really grateful to you for stepping in, and I'll pay you the agreed amount tonight.'

He looked so determined to pay her she didn't try to stop him. She'd never had so much spare money in her life. The thought of it made her feel as if she were standing on a very comfortable rug.

When he gave her the money, he said uncertainly, 'I hope we can keep in touch. You feel like a sister almost, and Mandy is so fond of you.'

'I'd really like that. I've grown fond of her quickly, too.' She was glad he'd called her a sister because though she'd thought for a moment he was going to ask her for a date, and though she liked him she didn't find him attractive in that way.

She smiled as she drove home. Being able to help someone else had made her feel as if she were taller and stronger, somehow. It had seemed like a turning point.

Thomas phoned to say he would be bringing his son and granddaughters over to Western Australia on the following Tuesday, and they would all be staying in his house. He wondered if the cousins could find the time to buy in some fresh food for them and to check that there was nothing in the fridge needing to be thrown away.

After she'd put the phone down, Portia looked at Fleur and they both burst out laughing. 'That'll be the fourth house I've stocked up in the past week,' Portia said.

'You're brilliant at it. It'd take me twice as long and I'd still miss important things out.'

Portia treasured that compliment; she'd received so few in recent years.

'I'm looking forward to meeting Thomas's family, aren't you?' Fleur went on.

'Very much.' Portia hesitated, then confessed, 'I feel I have made more real friends in a few weeks here than I did during the last couple of years in England. Ben sent me a text to say Mandy wanted to send her love.'

'That's nice. You seem to have made good friends with those two.'

'I was terrified when I found I'd have to come to Australia. The thought of being alone in a foreign country! But I'm starting to think it's the best thing that's happened to me in a long time – and not because of the money, though that's wonderful too. How about you?'

'I'm enjoying the more leisurely way of living. I've worked so hard since my marriage broke up and perhaps now that James is nearly off my hands and Marie is settling into a relationship and just about coping with studying, I can focus on my own life for a change. I feel more energetic by the day. I don't know where my future will lead me, but I feel sure it'll be somewhere better than the past two years.'

'That's good.' Maybe it was also being with Col that was making her cousin feel good but Portia didn't say that. She'd been a little awed by Fleur at first. Her cousin had seemed such a competent person – well, except when it came to finding her way round a strange town.

And perhaps she wasn't confident when it came to men either. Col was showing every sign of being attracted to her but she seemed to be deliberately holding him at arm's length. Strange, that, when he was such a nice guy and the two of them got on so well.

As for the cooking, Portia smiled every time she thought of it. It was good to think she could do something so much better than her capable cousin, and it was fun, too, having the money to try all sorts of new recipes.

She could draw well too, and had a way with small children.

She stared across the room as it occurred to her that one of the benefits of going somewhere new was to see yourself more clearly, see your strengths as well as your weaknesses.

Had Sarah intended for that to happen? If so, Portia already felt grateful to her aunt for that push out of her shell and into a new life.

Chapter Twenty-Three

Thomas decided to fly back business class because it'd make things easier for Ethan. He didn't tell his son that until he'd booked and paid for their seats.

Ethan looked at him in dismay. 'I can manage without causing you extra expense. Our trip will only be slightly longer than your flight here, a bit over four hours instead of three and a half.'

'Why is it longer going that way?' Nicole asked at once. 'It's the same distance.'

'Prevailing winds will be against us.' Thomas turned to his son again. 'It'll be a lot easier for us all to travel business class, what with the wheelchair and everything. And we're allowed more luggage.'

Both girls beamed at him. 'We've never been business class before,' Liane said.

'Well, we haven't done much flying, have we?' Nicole said. 'Just up to Cairns on that school trip.'

'I hope you enjoy this new experience, then.' Thomas loved giving them treats. They'd been so good about looking after their father, they'd more than earned them, he felt. When he thought of the selfish, entitled youngsters you saw on TV sometimes, he was so proud of his newly discovered grandchildren.

Ethan was still looking unhappy, though.

Thomas watched him open his mouth and from his expression he was going to continue protesting. 'You're outvoted, Ethan. Get over it and enjoy the extra comfort. I know perfectly well that you're not taking advantage of me. It's not just you, anyway. I need the extra comfort too. When I'm old and even more decrepit, you can repay me by looking after me.'

'You're old now,' Nicole pointed out.

'Only in years.' He tapped his head. 'In here I'm still about thirty and my body's not doing badly for a man my age.'

The girls exchanged glances and rolls of the eyes that said they were not convinced about that.

He didn't allow himself to smile at their reaction, but he'd meant what he said. He knew they thought him ancient, but he was feeling younger by the day, enjoying their company hugely.

When they got off the plane in Perth, they followed the wheelchair, pushed by an attendant, and were swooshed through the landing formalities quickly. Then they were taken out to the public area on a trolley fitted with a special platform for the wheelchair at the back.

Ethan didn't say anything but his expression betrayed his feelings of humiliation at having to be moved about by others when it was over longer distances.

Thomas tried to look as if he hadn't noticed that and concentrated on getting everyone into the limo, letting Ethan get in on his own. His son moved slowly and stiffly, but could manage without help.

There was too much luggage to fit in the boot and the rest would be sent after them in a van, which the chauffeur of the new vehicle phoned for the minute he realised the problem.

Leaning back, Thomas enjoyed watching the girls' enjoyment of a further luxury ride and didn't pay much attention to the scenery. By the time they got to his home in Mandurah, however, he was feeling tired, he admitted to himself. You just didn't have the same energy at seventy-two as you'd had at forty-two, or even sixty-two, and it had been a busy few days.

Wonderfully busy.

As the chauffeur helped the others out of the vehicle, Thomas unlocked his front door and raised the roller door of the garage. Once Ethan was in the wheelchair, he was able to roll himself into the house and through it without encountering any steps.

That had all been incorporated in the design when Thomas had the house built for his final years, in case he was ever reduced to a wheelchair. He'd never expected it to be a much younger man who would need that, though, let alone that this man would be his son.

Even the girls fell silent as they followed their father and the size of the house registered with them. Seeing it through their eyes, Thomas felt a bit embarrassed, as if he were flaunting his wealth.

'There's a lift in the hall, but we're going through that door on the right first,' he called.

He turned to ask the chauffeur if he'd mind taking the luggage up in the lift and leaving it on the landing, then thanked him and slipped a nice tip into his hand. 'I'll be in touch with the company when we need taking anywhere, but I doubt we'll be going out again today.'

Once the luggage was upstairs and the chauffeur had left, Thomas went into the living room and found his three guests standing only a little way into the room. He gestured back to the hall. 'Now you've seen this place, which is where I spend most of my time, let's go upstairs. You two can choose your bedrooms and get your luggage out of your father's way. After that we'll come down and you can get to know the rest of the house and the outside.'

The girls chose to go up by the stairs, racing each other to the top, and the two men got into the lift. 'You really are rich, aren't you?' Ethan said quietly as they rose slowly upwards.

'I'd not call it rich – well-to-do is a better descriptor, maybe. But I didn't start off that way. I worked hard for my money, believe me. Too hard. I should have taken more time to smell the roses. Never mind that now. Come and see if this bedroom will suit you, Ethan.'

He led the way, with the others following, to the second bedroom at the front with its en suite bathroom. The girls said 'Wow!' and stood staring out at the wonderful water views.

'This is wonderful,' Ethan said, adding in a challenging voice, 'I can bring my luggage in from the landing myself.'

Thomas wasn't going to make an issue of it. 'OK.'

'This suite is perfect for you, Dad, with that walk-in shower.' Nicole gave her father a little pat on the shoulder. 'Where are we going to sleep, Pops?'

'I'll show you and we'll leave your dad to get his luggage.'

Thomas took the girls to the two rooms at the street side of the house, which had a shared bathroom between them, and flourished one hand. 'Voilà! Choose which one you each want, then take your luggage into them.'

He went back to join his son, rolling his remaining suitcase into the room. 'I don't know who's more tired, you or me, but the girls seem full of beans still. You're sure you'll be able to cope in this bathroom?'

Ethan rolled across to the bathroom with a small bag that presumably contained his toiletries. 'Yes, easily. And look, Dad, I'm sorry.'

'What for?'

'Being ungrateful. You were looking apprehensive, as if you were expecting me to sulk or something. It's myself I get angry at, taking so long to recover my mobility. I don't blame other people.' He gestured to the window. 'This is a beautiful house and I shall really enjoy the views.'

'It's always been beautiful to look out from but I'm hoping that you and the girls being here will make it feel more like a home with a family in it.' Damned if Thomas didn't get tears welling in his eyes as he said that special word.

As he blinked furiously to clear his blurry vision, he didn't see Ethan move towards him and get out of the wheelchair.

But he felt his son's arms go round him in a hug and clutched him in return. 'I'm being a foolish old man.'

'That's partly because I've been a foolish younger one, not appreciating your side of things.' Another hug, then he sat down in the wheelchair again. 'Let's get the girls in to admire the view again. They'll cheer us both up.'

He put his fingers to his lips and let out a piercing whistle and the two girls came running, bringing light and joy into the room with them. You could almost see it swirling round, Thomas thought.

They galloped to and fro like a pair of young colts, oohing and aahing at the fittings. But he noticed how carefully they set the cases on one of the armchairs and the little table, so that their father could easily unpack them.

They stood near the window, watching a boat chug past, then a couple of pelicans bounce along in its wake in an ungainly dance. Thomas didn't interrupt till the duo had bobbed past.

'I don't know about you guys, but I'm getting hungry now. Shall we go down and I'll show you the kitchen and the patio by the water? Portia and Fleur were going to get some food in, so we can grab a snack. If you're famished, later we can order in a takeaway for tea.'

The kitchen and its high-spec fittings had the girls speechless for a few moments, but only a few, and they were soon checking out the fancy gadgets, investigating the contents of the fridge, opening and shutting cupboard doors.

It was they who discovered the note from Fleur on the floor, probably wafted there by the doors opening and closing from the garage.

Portia made you a chicken casserole. It's in the fridge together with a bowl of salad and a crusty loaf. It can be used tomorrow if you're not hungry today.

We'll catch up with you soon.

Fleur and Portia

The girls found the casserole, had a quick taste and immediately voted to eat it for tea.

'We'll have some of that lovely crusty bread with jam on it to tide us over till then.'

Thomas winked at his son. 'We didn't think you'd be all that hungry yet.'

The two youngsters turned to protest, caught the twinkle in his eyes and laughed.

'Stop teasing, Pops. How can you not be hungry when someone leaves such lovely food? Fleur and Portia sound nice. Shall we be meeting them tomorrow?'

'Definitely.'

Ethan went up to his bedroom earlier than the others that night, assuring his father that he didn't need help and asking him to see that the girls didn't stay up too late. They didn't seem at all affected by the time differences.

'Don't wake me up, you two!' he ordered. 'If you want anything, ask Pops.'

On his own for the first time in ages, he got out of the wheelchair and limped slowly and painfully round the bedroom, using his walking stick and enjoying putting his clothes away in the huge walk-in wardrobe once he'd sorted them into piles.

The girls would have done this for him, but he'd wanted to do something for himself, even if it did use up the very last of his energy.

He treated himself to a shower, sitting on a special plastic stool, then put the bedroom light out, leaving only a bedside lamp. He turned to get into bed, then changed his mind and gave in to temptation. He limped across to stand staring out at the canal for a while. It was dark now and the lights from the other houses were reflected in the water, which looked so pretty.

He had intended to find a house for himself and the girls as soon as he was well enough, but seeing his father's emotion tonight was making him rethink that already. Thomas must have been very lonely indeed, even when his friend Sarah was alive.

Ethan had been lonely too since he lost his mother. How brave she'd been during her final illness! And how clever, summoning Thomas to their aid.

'Thanks, Mum,' he murmured, giving in to the temptation to look upwards as if speaking to her, as he did sometimes. He didn't know what he believed about an afterlife, but sometimes he could swear she was still hovering nearby.

He'd stay here for a while, he decided, in a wonderful house with a man who needed them emotionally. They'd benefit from his financial help too, but that was mattering less and less. That was what families were for, after all.

The sooner the final small operation could be arranged, the better. The first specialist had assured him that he'd achieve normal mobility again in the end, with some careful physio.

Smiling, he limped back to the bed and got into it, pulling out the book he'd been reading on the plane. He'd just have a few minutes' reading to relax himself into sleep, as he often did.

He woke later to wonder briefly where he was and why he'd left the bedside light on. The book lying on the floor near the bed reminded him.

After he'd used the bathroom, he peeped out of his bedroom and found a dark house sleeping peacefully around him.

Good. There were no problems to solve, no one to see him if he winced in pain, nothing to do but rest.

He got back into bed, not even attempting to read this time, but letting himself slide happily towards another sleep.

'Thanks, Dad,' he murmured.

Chapter Twenty-Four

The following morning the girls were up by seven o'clock, looking bright-eyed and ready to go.

Thomas helped them explore the contents of the fridge and they settled for fruit and scrambled eggs on toast for breakfast.

'What time does your father usually get up?'

'It depends on how he's feeling. He knows he can trust us to get our own breakfast and we had to get ourselves off to school sometimes and just poke our heads into his bedroom to say goodbye.'

Liane looked at him solemnly. 'He was quite bad at one time, but if he'd gone to the convalescent place, there would have been no one to look after us. Here, we'll have you, Popsie-Wopsie.' Her expression changed to a broad smile on the last words.

'You certainly will have me. But I shall be both strict and ferocious if you give me such silly names.'

They shrieked with laughter and each gave him a quick cuddle.

His heart just about melted with joy.

Half an hour later, the three of them were just finishing a leisurely breakfast when Thomas saw his son roll slowly into the living area from the lift, looking weary and rather pale. It seemed to him that Ethan was long overdue the second operation, a small tweak that would make a big difference now that the badly damaged areas of his leg bones had had time to heal. Constant pain would wear anyone down.

Nicole studied her father, then went across to plonk a kiss on his cheek.

'We're going to get fat, Dad, if Pops keeps feeding us so well.'

Ethan's smile was warm and he relaxed visibly as he pulled her back closer to return the kiss. 'Good.'

He turned to his father. 'I hope they haven't nattered you to death.'

'They have, but I've been very brave about it.'

'Can we go and sit by the water for a while, Dad?' Nicole nudged her sister, who nodded and scraped up her last mouthful.

'Of course. Do not fall in and no swimming in the canal, never ever, unless a grown-up is with you.'

'We know.' They were off.

'They're a credit to you,' Thomas said. 'Now, what can I get you for breakfast?

'Same as the girls would be fine, if you don't mind. I'm actually hungry this morning.'

He sounded so surprised that Thomas shot a quick glance at him. 'Good. And afterwards we'll find out how soon we can get you an appointment to see the specialist. The sooner an operation can be arranged, the better. You have your referral from your GP to hand?'

'Of course. But shouldn't we all take the time to settle in together before I do anything about that?'

'No. Your full recovery is top priority, as I'm sure the girls will agree. I'm here to look after them and we're already getting on well. Besides, we're three to one when it comes to important decisions like that so you'll be outvoted.' He saw the moment Ethan gave in.

He got breakfast for both of them, not realising he was humming till his voice echoed more loudly in the walk-in pantry.

Like his son, he wasn't usually hungry in the mornings but today was different – in so many delightful ways.

When Marie got home late one evening, Cody was sitting in the living area, looking solemn and rather weary. He stared across at her as she came in but made no attempt to get up and greet her in any way.

She dropped her bag near the door and went across to him, intending to kiss him.

'Don't!' He held up his hand to prevent her from coming any closer.

She stopped, puzzled.

'You were supposed to be cooking tea tonight, remember? It was your turn to buy the food as well. It's now nine o'clock and you don't seem to have brought any shopping home.' He pretended to look round. 'Or am I missing something?'

'No. Sorry. I forgot. I met some friends.'

'What about the shopping? Couldn't you have done it on the way home afterwards?'

She hesitated but could think of no way to soften the words. 'I didn't have any money left by then. I had to borrow my bus fare home, even.'

He continued to stare coldly. 'Spent it all at the pub?'

She wriggled uncomfortably. That was exactly what had happened. She hadn't meant to have more than a half of shandy but she'd been having such a good time that she'd bought a few more drinks to keep up with the others.

'Any housekeeping money left at all?'

She shook her head.

'It's not the first time you've spent my share of the food money on booze.' He took a deep breath and said slowly, 'This isn't working, Marie. You and me, I mean. You're a gorgeous-looking woman but you need a rich man to look after you and servants to pick up after you. I have to work part-time to see myself through a degree and prepare for my future career. I can't afford you.'

'I'm sorry, Cody. I won't do it again.'

'You won't get the chance. Getting a good degree matters a lot to me because my whole future depends on it. You're probably going to drop out of university. Studying is definitely not your thing. I should have listened to my head when I hooked up with you, not my . . .' He patted his groin.

'Don't say it's not working, Cody. I'll do better and—'

'I'm sure you mean to but you won't carry through. You promised that last time we spoke about our situation and you didn't even manage to stay tidy or do your share of the housework for a whole day. That's how much your promises are worth. I can't go on like this so I'd be grateful if you'd find somewhere else to live and move out as quickly as you can.'

He stood up in one of the graceful, athletic movements she loved to watch.

'I'm going to stay with my friend Giles for two days. When I come back, the day after tomorrow, I expect you and your possessions to be gone and the flat to be left tidy. If you are still here, I will literally throw you and everything you own out on the street. Do I make myself clear?'

She could only stare at him, feeling numb and helpless. She had never seen him look so grim. No other man had ever spoken to her like that.

'That's settled, then.' He stood up and went across to the door, picking up a backpack she hadn't noticed when she came in.

She turned round, staggering a little. 'Cody, don't go!'

But she was talking to herself. He'd left the flat quickly without a single backward glance.

She began to cry and somehow couldn't stop. She had no money left, had been going to ask him for a loan, so how could she move out? Besides, there was nowhere else to go, even if she had been able to afford to rent share somewhere else.

In the end the only thing she could think of doing was calling her father. As she sobbed into the phone, not managing to stop crying for more than a moment or two, let alone make much sense, her father said abruptly, 'Remind me of your address . . . Right. I'll pick you and your things up in about two hours. Get everything packed and be ready to leave.'

When she ended the call, she continued to sob but stumbled round the flat, shoving things into her suitcase anyhow.

What choice did she have but to leave? Cody didn't love her any more and this was his flat. Had he ever loved her? Or had it just been for the sex? What did that matter now? Her whole life was in tatters.

It wasn't just Cody. She couldn't do this university stuff any longer either, hated it here, was in trouble with all her tutors for not handing in assignments. She should never have let her mother persuade her to enrol and how she'd got through the previous year's exams, she couldn't think.

She stopped to grab some tissues and wipe her eyes and nose, frowning. Or had it been her father who'd insisted she go to uni? No, it couldn't have been him. He'd never have been so cruel to her.

She couldn't think what to do after she left here. There was nothing, absolutely nothing she liked except clothes and dressing up and having fun.

If her father wouldn't help her to find some way of scraping a living, she'd throw herself off the nearest cliff.

All she knew was, she was never, never going near a university or any other sort of studying again as long as she lived, not if she had any choice.

Only – her father didn't always give you a choice about what you did.

More tears flowed as she waited for him.

* * *

Terry got out of his car and scowled at the shabby block of flats. He rang the doorbell and his daughter's voice came over a speaker that was fizzing slightly.

'Come up, Dad. Second floor, our door's to the right.'

The outer door of the building opened with a small clunk and closed quickly behind him as he went inside. He got into a lift, which laboured its way up in a series of jerks and deposited him on a filthy landing with rubbish piled in one corner.

When Marie opened the door of the flat, he was shocked at the sight of her. Women cried, they all seemed to do it from time to time, but his usually beautiful daughter was an utter wreck and looked as if she'd been bawling for weeks. Her eyes were puffy and red, her hair was damp and matted round her face, and there were unpleasant-looking, snotty little smears of make-up here and there near her hairline.

She flung herself at him before he even had a chance to get into the flat so he had to nudge them both forward and kick the door shut behind him.

'Shh, now. Shh. I'm here. We'll sort it all out. Come and sit down.'

As she sobbed out her tale, he looked round at the mess, shocked. She'd always been untidy but if this was how she looked after herself without her mother to nag her, she'd be terrible to live with. He couldn't have put up with it. This Cody guy must have been well and truly smitten for her to have lasted this long. No wonder he was kicking her out.

Terry was furious that Fleur was ten thousand miles away in Australia and there was only him to sort things out. She was the one who'd had experience handling their children, not him. She hadn't been legally obliged to go to Australia, could have got the money without doing that, damn her.

But the way Marie was looking and talking frightened him so he didn't dare leave her to deal with the situation herself. 'Tell me exactly what happened.'

When she didn't manage to put two sensible words together, he gave her a little shake. 'Stop that. Stop it right now! How can I help you if you won't control yourself enough to tell me about it?'

It took her a few minutes to do that.

'All right. I see. Well, I see enough. You've been a fool, an utter fool. Now Cody doesn't love you and it's over. I'd not love you if you spent the housekeeping money on booze, either. You can come back to my place, but it's only temporary.'

'Th-thank you.'

'We'll have to sort something else out for you. You're obviously not suited to university life.'

'I hate it.'

'People don't always get the choice of doing something they like, Marie, not if they want to eat.' But he could see his words weren't sinking in. 'Before we leave, we need to go round this place and check that you've packed every single thing you own.'

'I don't care.'

'Well, I do. Your mother and I don't give you money for your clothes and books, only for you to scatter them about behind you.'

'I'm not going to need the books again, am I? I can't do studying. I don't care what anyone says, I can't!'

'We can sell them. Even a small amount of money is better than none.'

She looked at him so bleakly, he wondered if she was taking in what he was telling her. Perhaps she was having a nervous breakdown. Just what he needed, with a big job coming up at work, one he'd worked hard to put himself in line for.

'We'll talk about your future later, Marie. At present we have to clear your things out of this flat. I'll walk round with you and we'll check every single drawer and cupboard.'

She opened her mouth to protest and he snapped, 'Do as you're damned well told!'

They filled a big rubbish bin liner with other oddments, including a lot of dirty clothes. It was disgusting. Her mother would never have let her leave things lying around like that. He had a sudden memory from just before he and Fleur broke up. He'd laughed off his wife's plea to him to help her control Marie's untidiness and carelessness about possessions. Now he felt guilty about that. He hadn't realised how bad their daughter really was.

Water under the bridge now, but he'd make sure a few lessons were taught. He wasn't going to spend the rest of the year rushing round the country to rescue his daughter while Fleur lived the good life in Australia.

He glanced sideways at Marie and she looked so hopeless, so young and afraid, he had to pull her into his arms and give her a quick hug. 'Come on, you. Let's get out of here.'

She began sobbing again as they left the flat. 'Cody didn't love me. He kept saying he did, but he didn't. Mum doesn't love me either. She did nothing but shout at me or complain. No one loves me except for you, Dad. If you don't help me, I'll kill myself.'

'Don't you dare! And I might love you but I don't love living in filth and chaos, either. Normal people don't.'

The trouble was he believed her final threat, and those dreadful words lodged the burden of dealing with her even more firmly in his court. He'd never seen anyone as distraught.

To his amazement Marie fell asleep in the car on the way back and he had to shake her awake when they got there.

'Come on, sleepyhead. Help me get your things inside the flat.' And let's do it quickly, he added mentally, not wanting anyone to see this collection of boxes and bags that looked more like rubbish on its way out to the tip than the possessions of a man noted for his stylishness.

Chapter Twenty-Five

Fleur and Portia laboured over another box of miscellaneous papers, each trying valiantly not to show her frustration as some of the faded handwriting defied their attempts even to work out who'd written or signed them, let alone what the contents meant. The online references and translations weren't much help, even on the rare occasions they could figure anything out.

As the morning drew to a close, Portia picked up the next folder, sneezed mightily and slapped it down again. 'That's it. I can't face another one today.'

Fleur followed suit. 'Me neither. The first stage of this job seems to be going on for ever, doesn't it? But look.' She gestured to one half of the room. 'We have made progress.'

'I suppose so. But there's still a long way to go. What on earth shall we do with them afterwards, anyway?'

'Who knows? Thomas may have some ideas. We just have to do our best. There's no exam to pass.'

'We must hope he will have suggestions.' But when Portia picked up an elegantly written document that appealed to her visually, she was betrayed into stroking it with one fingertip. 'People took such care with some of these. Look at how beautiful this one is. Maybe we can find a museum that would like them.'

'Good idea. But maybe we ought to feed our faces now and worry about that in a few months' time. I'm absolutely famished.'

As they walked into the kitchen, Portia said, 'I have a craving for chocolate cake and that recipe for a gluten-free one that I found in your cookbook sounds absolutely yummy. We have all the ingredients. Shall I make one?'

'Ooh, yes please. And let's phone Thomas to see if he and his guests would like to come round for a sundowner and sample it.'

'Good idea. You phone them, though.' Portia grimaced and waved one hand. 'You're much better at that sort of thing than I am.'

'You're getting better at interacting with people.'

'I am? Really?'

'Yes, really. I don't lie to you. Now, you put the kettle on while I contact Thomas.' Fleur picked up the phone.

Her call was answered immediately and when she explained, Thomas accepted her invitation straight away.

Afterwards she hesitated, not ending the call. 'Shall I invite Col as well, do you think, Thomas?'

'If you have enough cake to go round, yes, do. He used to enjoy our sundowners at Sarah's house. It'll bring back happy memories for us both. It's nearly time for him to exchange contracts and move into his new house, isn't it?'

'Yes. He was going to spend the morning in the office today, though, clearing the decks for action.'

She phoned Col at work. 'Oh, hi. I did guess correctly about where you'd be, then.'

Portia watched her cousin's face light up and the conversation went on for longer than you'd have thought necessary for a simple invitation to come round for drinks.

She got on with preparing the lunch but the sight of Fleur's smiles from the far side of the room as her cousin continued chatting, and especially the sound of gentle gurgles of laughter, made her wish she had someone she could talk to that easily.

That reminded her of how she'd met Ben and Mandy for a walk in the park the previous day. Only it had been mainly Mandy she'd dealt with because he'd received an important business call and stepped to one side.

He'd apologised afterwards and she didn't mind because she was fond of the child, but she was beginning to wish she had a relationship with someone.

When Fleur re-joined her and apologised for spending so long on the phone, she shrugged. 'You don't need my permission to chat to friends.'

'But I've kept you waiting for lunch. You should have started yours without me.'

'It's no biggie. Is Col coming tonight?'

'What? Oh yes, of course. Just think, we'll have five guests and a few weeks ago we knew no one here. I wonder what Thomas's son is like. He's in a wheelchair, isn't he, but it's only temporary.'

She picked up a scruffy-looking book of names that they'd been using intermittently. 'Ethan isn't a name I've come across much. I can't help wondering where it's from.'

She flipped through the pages. 'Ah. It's from the Old Testament. And it's quite popular these days.'

'Mine's from The Merchant of Venice and it's not popular. I wish I'd been given a more ordinary name. Yours is pretty, but what was Mum thinking of to call me after a Shakespeare heroine?' She grimaced.

'I think it's rather nice to have a name that's a bit different. You could always change it officially if it upsets you.'

Her cousin scowled. 'Don't think I haven't thought about that, but I'd never dare. Mum would throw a hissy fit.'

'Then you'll just have to put up with it. I don't think other people care as much as you do, though.'

Thomas told his son that he'd phone the specialist's rooms in case there were any local details that needed to be understood. In reality, he wanted to see whether there was any way he could get an early appointment. But however much he cajoled the receptionist, offering to pay extra, he couldn't get an appointment for his son till the following month.

'Please bear us in mind if there are any cancellations,' he said as an afterthought. 'We can come in within half an hour maximum because we won't be going anywhere outside Mandurah while he's still in a wheelchair. And he's already been diagnosed. Shall I get him to email you the details from his former specialist and GP over east straight away? Can do. Thank you for your help.'

He sighed as he put the phone down. He could see how his son was fretting at the way the final step towards full recovery had been delayed. He also saw how watchful his granddaughters were about their father's everyday needs. They were very mature for their age.

Then he shook off the momentary sadness and went to find the others. 'Who fancies a quick drive round the town so that I can show you what the main tourist area near the estuary is like?'

All three of them did. They'd been wandering round the house like three caged but very polite tigers, poor things.

'Who phoned earlier?' Nicole asked.

'Good heavens, I nearly forgot to tell you. It was Fleur. She's invited us round for a sundowner tonight. They're living in Sarah's house on the opposite side of the canal.' He pointed. 'It's the one with the blue corrugated iron roof.'

'If the evening is just for grown-ups, we can stay home and watch TV or something. We're old enough not to do anything stupid,' Nicole offered.

'The invitation was for all of us.'

'We're invited too? Oh, good. I like your friends already.'

'So do I. Besides, I want to show you two off. I'd better warn you that Portia may seem a bit stand-offish, only she's not, she's rather shy. She's baking a gluten-free chocolate cake for Fleur and they'd appreciate us testing it for them.'

'There was a girl at school who was coeliac and she couldn't eat all sorts of things. The stuff she called bread wasn't like the real thing, so I bet it won't be a very nice cake.'

'You'll have to wait and see, won't you? And whatever it's like—'

'We'll eat it and be polite,' they chorused. They often said the same thing at the same time.

* * *

The drive round the central area of the town went well, especially when Thomas insisted on stopping to buy them all ice creams from his favourite kiosk and they sat overlooking the water as they ate them.

When they passed a second-hand bookshop, Nicole yelled, 'Stop!'

Thomas quickly checked his rear-view mirror and braked hard. 'What's wrong?'

'There's a bookshop. Could we buy a book or two, Dad? It's second-hand stuff, so it won't be expensive.'

'Good idea. I can always use more books.' Thomas managed to get parking so close to the door that Ethan could use his crutches to hobble inside.

Nicole soon found some books. 'What do you think, Pops? Which one should I choose?'

'We'll buy them both, and any others you want,' Thomas said. 'What's more, I'd like to borrow that one afterwards. I've been intending to read it.'

When his son gave her a stern look, Thomas added, 'Don't stop me treating them, Ethan. I have to make up for years of not being able to buy you all presents, so you should all get any books you fancy.'

Both girls cheered and went off to find more of their favourites.

He grinned at his son. 'What can I say? I'm a bookaholic from way back.'

'Me too.'

'Go and get some for yourself, then.'

In the end he bought them an armful of books each, and the same for himself.

'You're spoiling us,' Ethan whispered after he lost the argument with Thomas as to who was going to pay for the books he'd chosen.

'Yes. Isn't it fun? Enjoy.'

'I will.' Ethan chose another book on the way to the checkout and gave it to Liane, who was carrying his books for him.

It only took five minutes to get home again. After their late lunch, Ethan gave in to the need for a rest, and the girls each chose one of their new books and said they'd go outside to read them.

Thomas noticed that Nicole had chosen a popular science book while Liane had a book about the history of fashion.

'Are you into fashion?' he asked her.

'Not necessarily, but I like reading about the past. It's so interesting to see the shapes fine ladies have crammed their bodies into. No wonder they fainted if they laced their waists down to nineteen inches, old measurement.'

As they went outside to the flyscreened area of the patio to sprawl on sun loungers and read, he did a quick calculation in his head and translated that into about forty-eight centimetres, shaping his hands to that size and shuddering at the thought of an adult human's waist squashed into a corset that small. He didn't understand fashion. He bought his clothes for comfort and had never wanted to change what he was wearing simply to look like everyone else.

Women's fashions could be very silly, if you asked him. He looked at some of them in amazement. They might not crush their waists nowadays but they still did all sorts of other daft things to their bodies. Not that anyone ever did ask him. He was an older man – what did he know?

But he couldn't help noticing jeans that were ripped across the knees when new – the manufacturers must be laughing all the way to the bank – and tops with holes at the shoulders. He'd gaped the first time he'd seen one but they'd stayed in fashion for a while.

Chapter Twenty-Six

When it came time to get ready for their outing, Thomas was rather touched by the effort the two girls made to dress smartly, even checking with him as to whether what they were thinking of wearing would be suitable. He knew even less about what girls that age wore than about women's fashions, so he just said, 'Your outfits look nice to me. Not like some of the silly things I see on the TV sometimes.'

'Gran wouldn't have let us choose silly things.'

He watched tears well in their eyes at the thought of Hilary. She had been greatly loved, anyone could see, and had left him a wonderful legacy.

He turned to his son. 'It's only about a hundred and fifty yards along the street to Sarah's house. Will your wheelchair manage that and back, Ethan? Or should we go by car?'

'It'll manage it easily, but it's not all that speedy.'

'We can stroll round slowly. I shall enjoy that.' He lowered his voice to add with a grin, 'I'm looking forward to the sundowner. I never know what those two girls are going to say next. They make me see the world differently sometimes. It's brilliant.'

'I'm glad you're enjoying their company.'

'To put it mildly.'

'They're enjoying yours too.'

They arrived just after four o'clock and Col's car was already there.

Thomas told Ethan to wait near the front of the garage, then rang the doorbell further along. He knew that Sarah's house, like his, had wheelchair access through the garage.

Fleur answered, beaming at the sight of him.

'Let's get inside before we bother about introductions,' he said quickly.

'I'll just open the garage door for him. How silly of me not to think of that.' She gave everyone a quick smile and went into the garage as the door rolled up, calling, 'I think you can get your wheelchair in between the cars, Ethan. If not, I'll move one of them.'

He moved forward and executed a neat couple of turns into the house, stopping just inside for a moment when he saw that it was even bigger than his father's house. Thomas gestured to his family. 'This is my son, Ethan, temporarily on wheels, and my granddaughters, Nicole and Liane.' He turned to his family and gestured to their hosts. 'Fleur and Portia, Col.'

'I thought we'd go and sit outside,' Fleur said.

Everyone nodded and followed her out to the patio but Portia detoured to fetch a trolley with some glasses on it. She took a jug of fresh lemonade and a bottle of wine out of the fridge, then hesitated about putting the bottle onto the edge of the heavily laden trolley.

Ethan followed her across in his chair and said quietly, 'I can carry the wine for you.'

'Oh, great! Thanks.'

They smiled at one another and didn't move on for a few seconds as the smiled lingered.

The girls shared quick glances and mouthed, 'Wow!' at the size of the great room, then walked out to the patio.

Portia made sure that everyone had a drink, then turned round to find that the only free seat was next to where Ethan had parked his wheelchair. That pleased her because he had such a kind smile she didn't feel shy with him. They were soon chatting about how beautiful it was here on the canals.

'I had a grotty little one-room flatlet in the UK,' she confided. 'It was all I could afford.'

'We had to move to a cramped town house in Melbourne to be near one particular hospital.'

'For your operations?'

'And because my mother had cancer. They had a specialist cancer unit there. She died about three months ago.'

'Oh, I'm so sorry. That must have been awful for you.'

'Yes. It was made much worse by the drunken idiot who did this to me a few months before that.' He slapped the wheelchair and glared down at it.

'Troubles always seem to come along in groups.'

'Like when you're waiting for buses.'

She smiled. 'It was like that in the UK but there don't seem to be many buses here. The relative who left us this house kindly provided cars for us. I'm still not used to living in such luxury.'

'I feel the same about my father's house. It's not quite as big as this one, but bigger than anything I've ever been able to afford.'

They chatted easily, exploring each other's situations, as strangers do when meeting someone they like. Only, speaking so easily as this wasn't usual for Portia. Just imagine! She hadn't been stuck for words once.

She turned to look across the table again and risked saying what she'd been thinking. 'Your daughters have wonderfully vivid faces, alike and yet different. Do you think they'd let me sketch them? I've never done twins before.'

'Are you an artist?'

She started to say no, then changed her mind. Only last night, after talking to Fleur, she'd vowed not to downplay her skills and she wasn't going to fail the first time the subject cropped up. She knew she didn't do badly when she drew things. 'I love drawing and painting. I don't think I'll call myself a proper artist, though, not till I've started to earn money from my efforts. I've got plenty of time now to improve my skills.'

'That must please you.'

'Yes. Nothing else makes me as happy as drawing and painting.'

'Well, I think my two would be thrilled to pieces to have you sketch them. I'll mention it to them when we get home again and let you know, shall I? I doubt I'll get a word in while they're chatting to Col and Thomas.' He took out his phone. 'Could I have your number?'

She gave it to him and suddenly realised she'd talked openly to him about her sketching and stared at him, mouth half open.

'Is something wrong?' he asked.

'I don't usually talk to strangers about my artistic efforts. But you're so easy to chat to.'

'So are you. I don't usually talk to people about my mother's illness, either.'

They smiled at one another, then as Thomas asked her something just then, they turned to talk to the others. But the pleasant feeling of chatting to Ethan and realising he was truly interested in what she had to say had made Portia feel safer in chatting to any of these guests.

The twins listened quietly to the polite conversation for a while before plucking up the courage to join in. Liane asked permission to refill her glass with lemonade and went to speak to Portia afterwards.

When she revealed that she'd overheard Portia talking about sketching and art, something she loved too, the two of them began to exchange views about which art medium they preferred.

They got on so well that Liane went back to the kitchen with Portia to bring out the food, still asking questions.

'I haven't got my studio set up properly yet, but you're welcome to visit once it's ready,' she told Liane. 'I'll even let you try out my fancy new easel.'

'Really? Oh, I shall enjoy that. And it's only a short walk away from Pops' house so I could come on my own.'

The finger foods were enjoyed and praised but it was the chocolate cake that won all hearts and every crumb vanished.

'We're eating you out of house and home,' Thomas said apologetically.

Their two hosts beamed at him and Fleur said, 'Portia's the cook.'

Her cousin blushed. 'I enjoy feeding people.'

'What did you use instead of flour?' Nicole asked as she helped clear up.

'Almond meal. I'll give you the recipe if you like. Are you into cooking?'

'I am, rather. Liane and I have had to take over making meals while Dad's been incapacitated. She does it because it's necessary but I enjoy being creative about food when I have time.'

'I've just started learning about gluten-free cookery for Fleur. It's very interesting.' And the two of them were off into a lively exchange about the necessary differences in what you put into that sort of food, which ended with them going across to the corner bookcase to pull out the two new cookery books that had now been acquired.

That made three people she'd chatted to easily today, Portia thought in wonder. And before that there had been Ben.

After their guests had left, Fleur grinned at her cousin. 'I think you're going to be very popular if you keep producing brilliant cakes like that.'

'I'll make you another one tomorrow.'

'Yes, please. And if I can put a few pieces in the freezer this time, I'll have my first emergency stash started.'

'Do you do that a lot, freeze stuff I mean, and keep emergency stashes of safe items?'

'Yes. I usually cook my food in big batches. People are very kind, well, most of them are, but I can't expect them to give up things they've eaten all their lives because it upsets me, so give me a week or so and you'll find I can usually pull something out of the freezer when you lot want to eat normally.'

Once they'd finished clearing up, Fleur said, 'There's another bit of good news from today. It turns out Ethan is into history and has offered to come round and help us look through some of those old documents. He says he gets bored sitting in that wheelchair all day.'

'Brilliant.'

As they ate a light supper sitting out by the canal, Portia said suddenly, 'I was terrified when I found I had to come to Australia; now I'm worrying about what I'll do with myself after this year is over. I have no one to go back to, because Mum's gone off with her new guy. I can stay with them temporarily but I'll have no place to live and won't know where to settle.'

'Why go back, then? You could always stay here. You were born in Australia like me so there would be no difficulty about visas.'

There was no answer for a few moments as Portia looked at her in shock. Then she said slowly, 'I could stay here, couldn't I? Are you thinking about doing that?'

'Unfortunately I can't. I'd like to but I shall have to go back because my children are in the UK. I know they're both just about grown up but Marie especially sometimes needs help. James is very capable, but I do like to see him regularly. But you could stay if you wanted.'

Portia wasn't sure she would dare do that on her own.

Fleur seemed to guess what she was thinking. 'No need to decide anything for ages yet. Our year's only just beginning. Isn't it wonderful to have options and possibilities, though?'

It was also wonderful, Fleur thought but didn't say it, to see Portia blossoming and looking happier than at any other time since they'd met.

Chapter Twenty-Seven

The first morning of his daughter's visit, Terry got up later than usual after his disturbed night. There was no sign of Marie so he knocked on her bedroom door, peered inside and let out a growl of annoyance.

As he started moving across to wake her, he felt something soft beneath his feet and saw to his disgust that she'd dropped a trail of dirty clothes on her way to bed, leaving them crumpled on the floor wherever they'd fallen. She was still sleeping peacefully though he'd made no attempt to be quiet, so he shook her shoulder gently.

'Go 'way,' she mumbled and rolled away from him.

'Wake up, Marie!'

She half-turned her head and opened her eyes but didn't seem to be focusing very well. 'Tired. Go 'way an' let me sleep, Dad. I'm not going into classes today.'

Well, that attitude was going to stop, even though he thought she should quit university with her record of near-fails and find something else to do. He shook her harder, yelling, 'Wake – up – Marie!'

This time she jerked upright, staring at him in shock. 'What's the matter?'

'It's time to get up.'

'Oh, is that all? No need. Didn't you hear what I said last night? I'm not going to uni any more.'

'That's nothing to do with it. I've allowed us both a late start today, but normally you'll get up at the same time as I do, which is seven o'clock.'

'I'm not even half awake this early. I'm absolutely exhausted, Dad, I've been stressed out.' She tried to roll away from him but he dragged her back and pulled her to a sitting position.

'You're hungover, more like, but you need to understand one thing, Marie: if you want my help, you'll do things my way. You didn't lie in bed half the day when your mother and I were still together and I'm not having it now.'

She stared at him in dismay. 'No, because she pulled the covers off me. But there's no need to get up early now.'

'Oh, but there is a need. You have a big wash day ahead of you today, for a start.' He followed his ex's example and whipped the covers off the bed, hoping he'd not embarrass them both. To his relief Marie was still wearing her underwear from the previous day.

She shrieked loudly and tried to grab the covers back, but he threw them on the floor, staring at her face in further disgust. 'I thought you were going to grab a shower last night before you went to bed.'

'It was past one o'clock when we got here and I was too tired to think straight.'

'You were also drunk, not to mention sweaty, with smears of make-up on your face – some of which is now on my expensive bedclothes. Get up this minute and clean yourself!'

'Just another hour's sleep? I'm always slow to wake up, Dad, you know I am,' she pleaded.

He pushed his face close to hers and said loudly and slowly, 'I shan't say this again: if you wish to stay here, you will live to my timetable and rules. If you don't do that, you can leave immediately.' He pulled her up without warning, making her squeak in shock. 'Get a quick shower and then come down for breakfast. And don't put any more of that cheap gunk on your face.'

She looked at him warily and must have seen how angry he was because she asked, 'Where's the bathroom? I've never stayed the night in this flat of yours before so I've only ever used the downstairs cloakroom. It's very posh to have a two-storey flat.'

'Your en suite is through that door. And before you come down to join me, hang the towels up neatly and bring the first load of dirty clothes down with you to be washed. I expect there will be several loads, because nearly everything I saw when we were packing your stuff needed washing.'

She scowled at him, opened her mouth to answer back, then thought better of it. But her sulky expression would have suited a ten-year-old and looked ridiculous on a young woman's face.

She could look beautiful, he knew, and make him proud of her, but at the moment she looked like an unwashed slut and he hated to see it.

He paused at the door to add in his sternest voice, 'You are not allowed into my bedroom at any time.'

She looked at him, warily, and nodded.

When she came down to join him she was empty-handed.

'We need to put your first load of washing on before you eat.'

'Can't I do that afterwards? I didn't eat anything last night and I'm ravenous now.'

'Get the first load of washing on first. I'll wait for you in the laundry and show you how my machine works. It's through there.' He pointed.

'I know how to use a washing machine.'

'I'd like to make sure of that.'

She came down clutching an armful of miscellaneous clothes.

'You didn't even try to sort them out, did you? Light-coloured underwear and flimsies first. Go back and get all your dirty clothes and we'll do this properly. And hurry up. I want my breakfast.'

She scowled at him but went back up to her bedroom. It took her only a couple of minutes to gather a pile of clothes but then he made her sort them out into loads of similar washing before giving her a lesson on which of the fancy machine's cycles to use for the first load. Only then did he allow her into the kitchen.

He had set out a healthy breakfast, fruit for starters, and was intending to scramble some eggs with one piece of wholemeal toast.

'Thanks, Dad, but I only have toast and jam for breakfast.'

'While you're here you'll be eating healthily. Your skin looks puffy and unhealthy, so you'll not only eat properly but do some exercise each day.'

Her mouth dropped open in shock and their eyes met in what might have been a challenge, but he saw how quickly she thought better of it. She ate the food he put in front of her, pushing it to and fro on the plate and trying to leave quite a lot of it.

'Eat it up. Your skin needs the vitamins.'

After she'd finished eating, she got up and left her dishes on the table.

This was ludicrous, like training a young child. 'Come back. The dishwasher is over there, Marie. Scrape your leftover bits into the bin first. All my household equipment is high-end and I don't want it misused.'

And so it went on for the rest of the day. He was exhausted by the time she said she was going up to bed, but he'd made her toe the line and do every single thing properly.

What had Fleur been thinking of to let Marie get so slack and lazy? Or had their daughter only changed after she went to uni? If so, it was another reason for him to regret insisting she go on to tertiary education, even if it was only for a Mickey Mouse degree.

'We'll discuss your future once you've learned to look after yourself properly,' he said. 'I want you up by seven o'clock tomorrow morning, so set your phone to wake you. We'll be starting the day with a brisk walk.'

He heard her crying after she went into her bedroom and that upset him. But it'd upset him even more to have his daughter turn into a slob who couldn't even tidy up after herself. He wasn't going to let her end up on the street, whatever it took. She was going to get a job and earn her living like the rest of the world had to.

He raised his glass of cognac and apologised mentally to his ex. He hadn't realised how lazy Marie had become, should have done more to help Fleur with the girl. And he admitted to himself that she wasn't very bright.

He sat thinking out the general situation in his family and with his ex. He was still astonished that Fleur was rich and he was looking into her finances, just in case there was some way of getting a share.

It had been quite easy to get information about this Sarah Blakemere, who had apparently been quite well known and active in Australian business circles even into her seventies. He'd also found out how much houses like the one his ex had inherited had sold for recently. It galled him to think that if he'd stuck with Fleur for two or three years longer he'd have been entitled to a share of her inheritance when they split up.

You couldn't change the past but he was beginning to wonder whether he could use Marie's predicament to slip back into Fleur's bed, so to speak. It was worth a try. He wasn't going to rush into it, but he might make a few tentative plans.

He grinned as he realised the best way to get hold of some of that money was probably through their daughter and Marie had just tumbled into his hands like a ripe juicy peach. At the very least, Fleur would have to help support her till she got her act together.

He didn't think James would be any help with Terry getting back into his mother's good books. He and his son hadn't got on for years but at least, give the lad his due, James sounded to have developed valuable skills and to be set for a successful career in antiques restoration.

Hmm. After he went to bed he lay smiling in the darkness. He enjoyed challenges, which was why he was so good at his job.

He didn't exactly need his wife's money, because he was doing rather well for himself, which was a good thing given his expensive hobbies, but it'd be fun to try to get hold of some of it anyway.

Chapter Twenty-Eight

The evening before Col moved, Fleur came home from helping him, looking relaxed and cheerful.

'I shan't be able to do any paper-sorting tomorrow because I've promised to help Col put the final touches on the new house once his own bits and pieces of furniture have been moved in.'

'I thought everything was done,' Portia said.

'It could have been but the lawyers insisted he leave all his own possessions in his old home until the legalities were complete. How silly when they'd allowed him to clear out the house and rearrange the furniture! But you know how fussy lawyers can be.'

'Well, I'll take the morning off paper-sorting too. I thought I'd make a casserole as a housewarming present for him and one for us, too. What do you think?'

'Great idea. He said to tell you he's going to have everyone round for a sundowner in a week or two and of course you're invited.'

'That'll be nice.'

'He's going to invite a few people he knows from the Small Business Breakfast Group too, and get it professionally catered for.'

'That sounds lovely. So we'll be meeting some more new people.'

Fleur saw the wary expression return to Portia's face and said quickly, 'I'll help you sort out what to wear and you're getting better and better at small talk, so you'll be all right. Anyway, I doubt Col will be inviting anyone who isn't nice to know. If in doubt, paste a smile on your face and nod at something they say. It sends out the right message.'

Her cousin's voice was gruff. 'Thanks. I'll remember that trick.'

Thomas picked up the phone.

'Mr Norcott?'

'Yes.'

'I'm calling from Mr Snawley's rooms. You said you might be able to get here quickly if we had a cancellation. We have one coming up in half an hour. How long will it take you to get here?'

'We can come straight away. It'll only take us about fifteen minutes.'

'Good. Then come in as quickly as you can. There will be a few forms to fill in and one or two final tests.'

He beckoned to Ethan, who had been sitting watching the news on TV but had turned to look across at him when the phone rang. 'Your new surgeon has a cancellation. We have to go to his rooms straight away. Do you need to get anything?'

'No. I'm good to go. But Liane's gone out for a walk round the streets.'

'I'll deal with that. You get yourself into the car and I'll see to the wheelchair.'

He picked up the phone again. 'Portia? Ethan's got a cancellation at the surgeon's but Liane is out for a walk. Could you possibly come round and stay with the girls while we're out?'

She didn't hesitate. 'Yes, of course.'

When Portia got there, Nicole answered the door, jigging about and looking excited, so she locked her car and went into the house.

'It's good news, isn't it? Dad's positively twitching to get out of that wheelchair. He says he's going to hurl it off the nearest cliff when he doesn't need it any longer.'

'That's excellent news, the appointment I mean, not wanting to hurl a wheelchair off a cliff. You don't look exactly happy, though.'

'Well, all operations are a bit risky, aren't they? Even minor ones. I'm glad for him but worried too. Dad's not young.'

Portia managed not to smile at this. 'He's not exactly old, either, still in his thirties like me and I don't consider myself old. All life is risky, so you're allowed to worry a bit but don't let it run away with you. He survived the major operations, after all, and there is only this minor one left. Anyway, he's only going in to see the surgeon today; they're not doing any procedures.'

Nicole let out her breath in a whoosh. 'Yes, of course. I'm being silly. It's just that Dad has had a horrible year and I love him so much.'

'Of course you do. He'll be over the moon to get the final stages sorted out, won't he?'

'Yes, of course.'

There was the sound of a key in the front door and Liane came in. 'Oh, hello, Portia.' She looked from one to the other, her smile fading. 'Is something wrong?'

'Not wrong,' Portia said firmly. 'It's just that there was a cancellation at the surgeon's and your grandfather has whipped your father off to see him.'

She looked from one to the other and added with a smile, 'They asked me to come round and babysit you two.'

As she'd hoped, that distracted them and they both spoke at once, oozing indignation. 'Babysit! We're too old to need that.'

'Gotcha!' She smiled at them. 'Lighten up, girls. He's only seeing Mr Snawley today, no knives involved.'

They looked so worried still that she walked across and put one arm round each of them. 'You should be glad for him.'

'We are. But we don't like him having operations.'

'Well, you can come to me or I'll come to you whenever it happens and we'll wait it out together.'

They both hugged her at once.

'I'm glad you're a neighbour,' Nicole said gruffly. 'We didn't have any nice neighbours before.'

'And you've got a grandfather here as well, so you're way ahead this time for when your father has to go into hospital.'

But they stayed in the shelter of her arms for a while and it felt so good she didn't attempt to move away.

Maybe Fleur was right about her fitting in better in Australia than she had done in England. It wasn't that she didn't get on with her mother, but they weren't close.

'Would you mind if I adopted you as honorary nieces?' she asked softly. 'I haven't got any and I always wished I had. Would that be all right?'

'Perfect,' Liane said in a muffled voice.

'Perfick,' Nicole said. 'I like that way of saying it better, like they did in that TV series.'

'Perfick it is, then.'

'OK, Auntie!'

She should count her blessings, Portia thought later. She was still in touch with Ben and Mandy, and now she'd adopted two nieces.

But she admitted to herself that she envied Fleur her growing closeness to Col, and was ready for something similar. She gave a wry smile. Not like Ben, though, who continued to act in a brotherly way. Strange how the two of them were not attracted to one another romantically.

It was hours before the two men came home, and Ethan had a strange, half-shocked look on his face.

'What's wrong, Dad?' Nicole asked at once.

'Nothing's wrong, but I'm going in for the operation in two days' time. The woman whose cancellation I took can't make it, so I'll soon be on the operating table, hopefully for the final time.'

'Wow. No wonder you look like a stunned mullet.'

'What does a stunned mullet look like?' Thomas asked. 'I've always meant to find out.'

Portia grabbed the pad from the kitchen surface and sketched quickly, then held it out for them to see.

They burst out laughing because the fish she'd drawn somehow had a look of Ethan as well as a look of shock.

'You're good,' he said. 'Can I keep this?'

'It's only a scribble.'

'But it's fun and I'm going to have it framed.' He fumbled in his pocket and pulled out his wallet, removing a ten-dollar note and holding it out to her. 'Here you are.'

'What's this for?'

'You said you couldn't call yourself an artist till you got paid for your work. I have the honour of being the first to pay you. Go on! Take it!'

Bemused, she let him press the money into her hand. 'Well, OK then.'

He kept hold of her hand, smiling warmly at her. 'Say after me: I am an artist.'

She gave him a rueful smile. 'I am an artist.'

Nicole pointed to the drawing. 'Well, duh! That's obvious.'

Portia felt happiness run through her and decided to keep the money. She might even get it framed.

He gave her a little nod. He understood her better than anyone she'd ever met, probably because he'd spent so long in a wheelchair watching people. And because he was a very kind man, like his father in that.

'It's a good thing I still have the pyjamas from my last hospital visit.' He grimaced. 'They're very conservative and all-concealing.'

'You called them passion-killers last time you wore them,' Nicole pointed out.

Ethan went slightly pink, Portia couldn't hold back a snigger and Thomas roared with laughter.

Chapter Twenty-Nine

The following day, Fleur woke early and couldn't get back to sleep, so in the end she left their house just before seven in the morning and went round to Col's new house to wait for the main event. She felt excited for Col and was sure that the few special pieces of furniture he'd shown her in his flat would fit into his new home beautifully.

She used the key he'd given her to get into the house and first put the food she'd brought for lunch in the fridge, together with a bottle of fizzy wine.

She'd bought a bouquet of flowers the previous day and now put them in a pretty vase they'd found here when clearing the place out. The colours of the flowers ranged from palest pink to soft rose red, and they looked gorgeous standing in the middle of the previous owner's gleaming mahogany dining table, which Col had decided to keep.

She'd have kept the table too. There was something special about Victorian dining tables, she always felt. She could imagine this one at Christmas, set out with a

Dickensian-style feast. Only, would she still be here in Australia then? And anyway, she wasn't a good enough cook to provide such a feast. They needed Portia for that.

She walked round, feeling restless, checking the various rooms. She was early and Col wouldn't be here for ages yet because he had to make sure that all his chosen furniture was loaded into the removal van and then he'd quickly tidy up the flat he'd been renting.

It would be her job to let the removal men in and tell them where to put the various pieces. It wouldn't take long to load and unload them, though.

She continued to move from one room to the other, feeling restless. She'd enjoyed helping Col sort out the new house but what would she do with herself after today? She'd miss being with him, miss being here too. It was such a warm, welcoming house.

That was the exact moment when it hit her why she enjoyed his company so much and how amazingly comfortable they had been with one another from the start.

She hadn't realised – hadn't let herself realise until now, she amended mentally – that she'd fallen in love with him. She might have vowed never to marry or live with a man again, but when you met someone you were attracted to, your body and emotions took over from your reason.

Besides, Col wasn't like Terry. She was utterly certain of that. He was kind, even-tempered and not money-hungry. Nor did he have those odd changes of mood that had been increasingly hard to live with.

She had another sudden thought. She had much more

money than Col now. Would that come between them if, well, something started to happen?

She let out an exasperated grunt. Why was she thinking like that? Col hadn't given any sign of wanting more than friendship from her. They were not 'together' in that sense. Her feelings were just in her own mind.

Oh, heavens! She hoped he didn't feel she was forcing herself on him?

No, of course he didn't.

Did he?

Oh, what did she know?

It was a relief when the movers turned up with the furniture and oddments, and she had to give them her attention.

It wasn't a relief when Col turned up shortly afterwards because she didn't know how to face him and could feel herself blushing.

Ethan watched Portia calming his daughters down, teasing Thomas and making everyone a cup of tea. She'd even made some scones in case they were hungry.

She was so capable about the practical side of life, just not so capable with her personal interactions with strangers. And if talk got at all personal, she tended to clam up.

She had other talents, though. He smiled at the memory of her 'stunned mullet' drawing. He was definitely going to have that framed. And when he got better from the operation, he was going to get to know her much better, to find out if they'd suit long term. Would she be interested? He hoped so.

'Dad!'

He turned to Liane. 'Yes, love.'

'Portia's spoken to you twice. You were miles away. She wants to know if you'd like a scone.'

He looked across the kitchen. 'Sorry, Portia. I was just thinking about what I have to do before I go into hospital.' He couldn't help grimacing. He'd had more than his fill of hospitals during the past year. 'What did you want?'

'I was wondering if it'd help – I could – you know, come in and cook for everyone while you're away.' She glanced at Thomas and then at the girls.

'We can't ask you to do that,' Ethan exclaimed involuntarily. He so hated having to depend on others.

'We didn't ask her,' Nicole pointed out. 'She offered.' She grinned at Portia. 'Never mind Dad and Pops, I'd like to accept on everyone's behalf. Your cooking is magic, and we'll be in and out, visiting Dad. Oh! You didn't say how long it'd be this time, Dad.'

'Only three days in hospital and then two days in a rehab centre learning some exercises and working out an ongoing recovery programme.' He looked at his father. 'Do you want to cook or shall we accept Portia's kind offer?'

Thomas shuddered. 'I'm the plainest of plain cooks, so I'd be extremely grateful if Portia could come in, at least a couple of times.'

'That's agreed, then. But once I'm properly mobile, I'm going to insist on taking everyone out for a meal to celebrate, Portia included.'

'That'd be nice,' she said quietly. 'I'll get the girls to tell me about what sort of things you all enjoy eating. Just leave it to us.'

'I enjoy anything I don't have to cook,' Thomas said at once.

'We're the same,' Liane said.

Ethan gave them a stern look. 'Just one thing. If you're doing the cooking, the girls will do all the clearing up.'

'Don't worry, Dad. We're quite used to that.' Liane linked her arm in her sister's. 'Behold, the champion housekeeping team.'

They flourished their free arms and took a well-synchronised bow, which made everyone chuckle.

They were such lovely girls, Portia thought. A wonderful family, already including Thomas even though he hadn't been part of them for long. Oh dear, she liked them too much, far too much. She had to remember that they weren't her family.

She wished they were, all of them, even Thomas, who'd overawed her at first.

As for Ethan, he was so easy to chat to. She hoped he'd become a good friend. She didn't let herself think further than that. She had learned the hard way not to be too optimistic about men.

Thomas drove Ethan to the hospital the next day, stayed with him through the preliminary interviews, then left him settling into a very nice private room. There were to be a series of minor tests, though the specialist had said Ethan seemed to be making excellent progress, as the X-rays showed, and he didn't foresee any problems now that the rest of Ethan's leg bones had healed fully.

Portia had driven round to stay with the girls while Thomas was out. Both of them had protested loudly that they didn't need a babysitter, but Thomas watched them greet her and it seemed to him that they welcomed her company.

So did Ethan. Well, Thomas thought he did. His son was a bit harder to read.

Maybe there was hope there for two people who both needed someone to love – well, they did if Thomas was any judge. And if a further grandchild or two resulted, he'd be over the moon. Or was he being ridiculously optimistic? He hoped not. Poor Portia had no one at all. He was old enough to know a sudden exit from this life might happen out of the blue and he really wanted to leave his son with a partner.

His own life had been so much better since this unexpected family had popped up out of nowhere that he hoped to follow Sarah's example and perhaps succeed where she had failed and reach the century mark. Why not? He felt to be in good health for his age.

Ethan was glad when the series of tests and X-rays was over. It hadn't been painful in any way, which they said was a good sign. You could hardly complain about it being boring when the result of all this waiting around would be the ability to walk normally again.

He could have walked about more and used the wheelchair less but had been strictly forbidden to do so until long-term healing of the several broken bones had taken place and been confirmed.

He looked up as a nurse peeped into his room.

'Feeling all right for a visitor, Mr Smith?'

'Yes please.'

He watched the door, wondering who it could be, and when Portia came in with that tentative look on her face, carrying a transparent container, he beamed at her.

The nurse was still waiting.

'I know you won't be allowed to eat this tonight but I thought a few home-made choc chip cookies might be welcome tomorrow.' She gestured to the nurse. 'They'll be taken away after you've seen them.'

He peeped into the container, inhaling the wonderful smell, then the nurse said, 'Sorry. Daren't leave something so delicious within reach. I'll bring them back tomorrow afternoon once you're fully over the anaesthetic.'

'I don't want to intrude—' Portia began.

'The tests are over now, so if you've time to stay for a while, I'd really welcome some company. I told Thomas and the girls not to come visiting tonight because no one could tell me how long the tests would take.'

'I left them some cookies too. They've already tested them for you.' She came across and sat on the chair next to the bed.

As they chatted quietly of this and that, he took a deep breath and risked saying, 'After I'm out of hospital I'd like to get to know you better. Would that be all right with you?'

She looked surprised. 'Does that mean what I think it does?'

'It means I'd like to get to know you better. Nothing more, nothing less. The usual possibilities but no promises.'

'That suits me far better than someone who makes promises then only wants a cook-housekeeper.'

'Is that what your last guy was like?'

'Yes.'

'Some men are still living in the dark ages. But I can promise you that I'm looking for a friend and partner, not a cook-housekeeper. I can manage a house perfectly well on my own, though I'm not in your league for cooking.'

They smiled at one another, then he added, 'The girls like you. That's very important to me and, actually, they're excellent judges of character so it's a good sign.'

'They're fun to be with.'

He leaned back. 'I shall think about you as they put me under.'

'That seems like a compliment.'

'It is.'

The surgeon's assistant popped her head round the door just then. 'Your tests were all fine and we're putting you first on the list tomorrow. Means an early start, I'm afraid.'

'The earlier the better.'

'Rotten luck, your accident.' She gave Portia a vague smile and left with a 'See you tomorrow'.

He clasped Portia's hand and gave it a squeeze. 'I've waited months for this operation.'

He didn't seem to notice that he'd kept hold of her hand. She liked the firm feel of his, the warmth on hers, was sorry when a nurse came in to say she'd have to leave now and let Mr Smith get an early night.

Portia beamed all the way home.

When she got back she noticed that Fleur seemed in a good mood too, but they didn't discuss how they were feeling.

Chapter Thirty

Terry's phone rang just as he was about to leave the office early. When he picked it up he heard the CEO's voice.

'Could you come up and see me, Davies? Something's cropped up.'

'Sure. Straight away?'

'Yes, please.'

When Terry went in, Mal Lammeter offered him a glass of wine, which augured well, he thought. 'Just a half. I'm driving. Thank you.'

'I'll get straight to the point. Cater in Australia has had a heart attack and he was in the middle of an important restructure. Would you go out for a few weeks and finish the job?'

Terry managed not to beam at him, then he remembered. 'Damn! I'd really enjoy that, but there's one small problem. My daughter has just had a nervous breakdown and had to pull out of uni. She's rather fragile and I don't like to leave her on her own.'

'Take her with you, then. It'll distract her and probably help defuse any hostility you might meet from Cater's second-in-command.'

'Is he not up to making the changes?'

'She will make a fine senior executive one day, but she's inexperienced, only just been promoted into the job.'

'Whereabouts in Australia? Sydney?'

'No. Perth, Western Australia. I gather you worked there twenty years ago?'

'Yes. It's a great place.'

'Bit too remote for me. I'm more of a big city guy.'

'Yeah. Me too.'

He hid a smile as Lammeter continued to chat, living up to his reputation by telling him all about the latest musical he and his wife had been to see. It was hard to pretend an interest.

When Terry got home he found Marie slumped in front of the TV, but at least the house was tidy – well, fairly tidy.

'Have a nice, restful day, did you?'

She looked at him warily. 'Yes. I needed a rest.'

'Switch the TV off. I've got some exciting news for you.'

As he told her about his new assignment, she began to look worried. 'What happens to me?'

'I don't trust you to behave sensibly if I leave you on your own so I've arranged to take you with me. You can stay with your mother while we're there and if I can, I'll con a bed out of her for myself, too. Several weeks in a hotel would not be fun.'

Marie's mouth fell open in shock, then she began to smile. 'That's wonderful, Dad. Thank you so much. And it'll be summer there, so it'll be a real holiday.'

'Well, we're going in a couple of days' time, so I'll need to take you shopping. We can start straight away. I came home early on purpose.'

She frowned at him. 'What do we need to go shopping for?'

'Clothes.'

'I've got quite a few clothes.'

'I'll need you to be wearing smart clothes, not punky rubbish like that.' He jabbed a finger at her.

'This was all the fashion at uni and people admired the clothes I made myself.'

'You're not going back to uni, remember. So we'll need to buy quite a few clothes that are much smarter. I saw yours when we washed them. Utter rubbish. Don't forget you're going there as my daughter and you'll be mixing with moneyed people. Do you want to look like a beggar?'

An eager look slowly replaced her worried one. 'No. Maybe afterwards they'll help me get a job.'

'We can hope. In the meantime your skin is already looking healthier. Did you eat that salad for lunch?'

'I didn't have much choice. That's all you seem to have in, salads and fruit and veggies.'

'Unlike many men my age, I'd not be happy to develop a paunch.' He patted his stomach. He was rather proud of how he'd kept his body trim and youthful, and women still considered him good-looking. 'At your age, you should be revelling in your looks. You could look quite special if you made more effort. Which reminds me, I've got you an appointment to have your hair re-styled tomorrow at Maxsey's.'

'Really! All the stars go there.'

'Well, I happen to know the owner, so you're in luck. I go there too.'

Marie beamed at him and when she came out of the salon, he saw the first signs of a daughter he could be proud of, sparkling eyes, skin flushed with excitement and a very flattering hairstyle.

He was regarding her transformation as a project, something a bit different. You could get rather bored with doing the same old business stuff time after time. He was good at it, no doubt. But he needed stimulus, change, variety – sometimes had to find them in other ways than through work.

Terry enjoyed the flight to Australia. Business class was comfortable, the service excellent and he'd long ago learned not to fret at spending such a long time in the air. It had been years since he'd visited Australia and he was looking forward to seeing how it had changed over the years.

Marie was travelling economy class, had pulled a face at that.

'You have to earn your way into business class by what you do with your life,' he told her.

'But I don't have any skills that will ever earn a lot of money like you do.'

'No, but you could have real beauty if you'd put a bit more effort into it. Looking good never hurts a woman. There are always rich, older men looking for wives. Few younger men have much money.'

She scowled and opened her mouth to reply, then caught his gaze and closed it again.

After the flight ended, he met her at the luggage carousel, as arranged, then they left the airport in the car that had been waiting for him. It took them to a good hotel, where the company had booked him a room.

Marie frowned as the receptionist gave him the key card and then turned to the next customer. She tugged her father's sleeve. 'What about me? Where am I going to sleep?'

'I thought I'd take you to your mother's and ask her to put you up.'

'Oh, no! I'd much rather stay with you.'

'And I have plans that might be furthered by you staying with her. Look, we can't talk here in the lobby. Come up to my suite and we'll work out the best way to do this. We don't want to give your mother any chance to refuse to put you up.'

Even so, Marie was still scowling as he sat down with her. He'd have to train her to conceal her feelings better.

'Tactics are going to be crucial. You must pretend you missed her,' he began.

Marie heaved a sigh and wondered whether to confess that she'd not even answered her mother's recent emails. Given what he was planning, she thought he might be angry about it so kept quiet. She knew she wouldn't get the help she needed by offending him.

What did she really want to do with her life, though? She hadn't the faintest idea. Just not spend time among dull books, and she loathed writing essays. At least she was here in Australia with the sun shining brightly, not rain lashing at the windows.

'And no more of those childish sighs,' he added. 'You're a grown woman now and should act like it.'

'All right, Dad. I'll do my best.' She held her breath but he seemed to believe her. She wasn't sure what she could manage, though. Her mother always seemed to see straight through her if she lied about anything.

'Let's get something to eat, then we'll drive down to Mandurah and see if we can catch your mother at home. It's about an hour's drive away. I think it'll be easier if we just turn up. Well, we're not supposed to know her phone number, so it'd look strange if we phoned her.'

Marie didn't let herself sigh but she wanted to. Life would be boring with her mother, who always worked long hours. Then she frowned, wondering how her mother spent her time now she didn't have to work for a living. Perhaps she lived a life of leisure. No, Marie couldn't see that. Her mother liked to be busy.

Ethan came home after a few days, as he had left, with a wheelchair as his main means of moving around.

Portia grabbed Nicole as she would have thrown herself at her father. 'Careful!'

He smiled at her over his daughter's head. 'Thanks. No sudden movements, kids. Let me move myself slowly and carefully and gradually build up what I do on my own two feet. I don't want any setbacks.'

As he proudly displayed his new ability to walk straight, Portia was surprised to see that he was taller than her, at least six foot.

He looked at her across the others' heads and it felt as if he was speaking just to her. 'I can increase my walking time by an hour a day, split into two half hours. After a week of that, I can go cautiously into walking all the time, only using the crutches or wheelchair when I feel it's a bit of a strain walking.'

'That's great. I'm really glad for you.' Portia picked up her shoulder bag. 'I'll leave you to it for today. I've left a beef and veggie crock pot simmering for tonight, but if you like I'll come and cook for you tomorrow as well.'

'Don't go! Stay for tea!' Both Ethan and Thomas spoke together.

'My father's been telling me how much cooking you've done for them, and I think you should stay and share this meal with us.'

'Not tonight, if you don't mind. I'm neglecting Fleur.'

He smiled ruefully. 'Another time, then. I was hoping to have a sundowner in a day or two to celebrate, but I think I'll give it at least a week, then I'll be able to stand up for the best part of the time. Will you explain to Fleur and ask her to tell Col?'

But once again, it felt to Portia that he was speaking to her more than anyone else, smiling at her as if they were alone in the room.

Then he suddenly seemed to realise what he was doing and as she hastily nodded farewell and left, he turned to his daughters. 'Let's go out and sit by the water.'

'Are you up to a drink of wine yet?' Thomas asked.

'Better not. I want to be as sure-footed as possible.'

As the days passed, Ethan made progress by leaps and bounds – and Portia continued to come in and prepare meals for them, often sitting to chat to him while the girls were occupied elsewhere.

He saw his father watching them, but Thomas didn't interfere or even comment. Which was a relief, Ethan thought, because if he and Portia were to get together, they'd do things better in their own time and at their own pace.

Since Portia seemed to be spending a large part of the day round at Thomas's house, and had twice gone to meet Mandy and her father in the park, Fleur wouldn't pass an opportunity to spend time with Col. His business was going through a quiet patch and he wasn't needed a lot of the time, so they played tourists, with him showing her the area around Mandurah.

'I could make more money from my business if I put a greater effort in,' he said one day. 'But I have more than enough to live on, because thanks to Sarah's gift of a winning Lotto ticket, I don't have a mortgage.'

'She was a delightful person when I was a child. I wish I'd known her as an adult. I hope I'm remembered as fondly as you speak about her after I've shuffled off this mortal coil.'

'I'm sure you will be.'

She shook her head. 'I've done nothing of note with my life.'

'Except for raising two children.'

'One of whom doesn't care enough about me to stay in touch. I don't even know what she's doing with herself, or planning to do. It was James who told me Marie had given up university and gone to stay with her father, but I can't see Terry subsidising her for long. He's never been the patient sort and she'd try anyone's patience.'

'There's nothing you can do to help her if she won't reply to your emails and texts.'

'I tell myself that but I can't help worrying about her.'

'Come round tonight for tea and I'll cook us a barbecue and worry with you.'

'I'd love to. It's usually the woman who cooks for the man, but not me. I don't ruin food, but what I produce is plain and ordinary. You, on the other hand, produce delicious meals.'

'So come round and enjoy one.'

She looked at him and neither of them put anything about their relationship into words, but she felt they were getting closer to it and even the way they looked at one another was changing.

It suited her to take things slowly, though, after years of being married to Terry and his sudden needs to do this, find that or chase after the other. If anything came of her and Col, she wanted to be certain of a more peaceful and co-operative relationship, one in which they could both continue to grow.

She'd had some very unfulfilled years towards the end of her marriage and afterwards, when she was working so hard to support herself and her children.

She realised Col was waiting patiently for her response. 'I'll be happy to come round. I'll bring a bottle of wine. Sarah had a very extensive wine collection. She must have understood them better than I do.'

'Better than I do too. I enjoy the sociability that accompanies sharing a bottle of wine but a couple of glasses are enough.'

Chapter Thirty-One

The following day Fleur had just finished reading the newspapers online and was trying to persuade herself to do some more sorting out of papers without Portia's help when the doorbell rang. 'Oh, bother!'

Since Portia had gone off to the supermarket to supply both them and Thomas's family with fruit and vegetables, she got up to answer it, stopping dead in shock with the door half open when she saw her ex standing there.

'What the hell are you doing here, Terry?'

'That's a nice, friendly greeting.'

'I don't feel friendly towards you and never shall again.'

Only then did Marie move into her line of vision and Fleur was lost for words. All she was certain of was that she didn't want him even setting foot over the threshold and there was some trickery brewing.

'Don't we get invited in, Mum?' Marie asked.

'You are welcome to come in, but your father isn't. Not now, not any time.'

Terry gave her one of his wolfish smiles. 'Then I'll go and get Marie's luggage and you can phone me when you're ready to discuss the emergency.'

'What emergency?'

His eyes flickered towards their daughter.

He'd done it, damn him, found a way to get in. She looked beyond him and saw a taxi waiting. 'You'd better tell him to stay. I'll give you ten minutes max to explain.'

As he went to the car, spoke to the driver and brought some luggage to the house, Fleur admitted to herself that she couldn't very well refuse to let her daughter stay. But she'd make sure both of them realised that she'd changed.

She led the way into the living area and pointed to the chairs. 'Hurry up and explain.'

'Our daughter came close to a complete nervous breakdown just before I was suddenly asked to come to Western Australia to sort out an emergency. I didn't dare leave her alone in the UK so had to bring her with me.'

'Wasn't there a counselling service at her university?'

Marie scowled at them both. 'I left, couldn't stand it there any longer. And nothing anyone says or does will make me go back. I am not, repeat double not, interested in rubbishy old books. Only, I didn't have any money or anywhere to live because Cody had chucked me out.'

Fleur could see tears in Marie's eyes as she said this and remembered the young couple glowing with love who'd visited her to collect Marie's belongings. 'I'm sorry it didn't work out with him.'

'So am I.'

Terry smiled. 'There you are then. Since I'll be working long hours, I'll have to leave Marie with you.'

With an effort, Fleur kept her voice steady. 'I'll keep her for as long as she's polite and co-operative and if she isn't, I'm bringing her back to you and dumping her at your office.' She gave Marie a hard look and added, 'I mean that.'

'Well, before we get to that stage, you and I had better get together to work something out for her. She can't just sit around all day doing nothing, can she? And since she refuses to go back to university, we'll have to find her some sort of job or training.'

Fleur opened her mouth to protest and he held up one hand to stop her. Oh, she remembered that gesture all too well, damn him.

'If you give me your phone number, I'll arrange a half day off as soon as I can and come back here to discuss it. Within a couple of days max.'

'Very well.'

He turned to their daughter. 'Chin up, Marie! And mind your manners.'

She scowled at them both impartially and Fleur's heart sank. She knew that look. It meant emotional storms were looming, probably because Marie hadn't wanted to come to her. Had she even wanted to come to Australia? She might have been born here but they'd left it when she was still a baby.

Fleur knew one thing: Terry wouldn't have brought their daughter to Australia unless it fitted into his plans. What could he want with her, though? They'd split up several years ago. It could only be the money. He wanted to find some way of getting at her and her money. Did he think she was too stupid to realise that, or expect her to fall for his charms again?

Could be. He was conceited enough. The old Fleur might have been weak; the new Fleur was growing stronger all the time. Thank you, Cousin Sarah.

Terry was definitely overly arrogant about his ability to manipulate 'the weaker sex'. It had taken her a while after they split up and she started dating other men to realise that Terry was actually old-fashioned enough to think of women in that way. The men she'd met here seemed to be far more 'liberated' in that sense and had treated her as an equal.

Col didn't treat any woman as unequal because he didn't see them that way. He was kind and courteous, fun too, treading lightly through life. Terry was looking a lot thinner, a bit haggard. Had he been burning the candle at both ends socially, or had he been unwell?

'Is that all?' she asked.

'For now.' Terry stood up and she walked to the door with him.

He stopped to say, 'I really am concerned about Marie's mental health. And we're still both her parents.'

She shrugged.

He looked at her, head on one side, then shook his head as if she was in the wrong and went back to the taxi.

She waited to watch it drive away. He waved to her. She didn't wave back, tried to keep her face expressionless. What had she ever seen in him apart from good looks? Whatever it was, any attraction to him had long vanished.

She locked the door carefully, then went to find her daughter, who was now standing by the big wall of windows, staring out at the canal. 'Let's get your luggage and take it up in the lift.'

'There's a lift here?'

'Yes. The house belonged to a very old woman. The lift comes in useful for taking stuff up and down.'

Marie picked up her bags. 'I can manage this, thanks.'

'OK. New outfit? Not your usual style.'

'Definitely not. Dad didn't like how I dressed and now I'm not a student, I can see that I shall need to change how I look, but I'm not into stuff like this. Only I had no choice. You know what he's like. He's not bought me much. I think he's hoping you'll share the costs by buying me a few more clothes.'

As the lift came to a halt, Fleur let out a derisive snort. 'We'll see about that.'

Another scowl greeted this. 'You two usually go halves. I really don't have enough clothes to manage. He wouldn't let me bring anything but my old underwear.'

'I'm not buying clothes like that thing you're wearing at the moment for someone your age. They're not suitable.'

'Well, that's something we agree about anyway. Dad chose them.'

'I could take you to the nearest big store and buy a few casual clothes.'

'Really? Thanks. That'd be a big help.'

Her daughter actually sounded genuine about that, Fleur thought as she pushed the lift door open. 'This way.'

Marie looked at the landing window and saw that

they were going towards the street side. 'Is there a room overlooking the canals? I'd love to look out on the water.'

'No. Portia has the other room and the third room was Sarah's. We haven't finished clearing it out. Besides, you won't be staying long, believe me.'

'Who's this Portia exactly? Why did she inherit?'

'She's a cousin of mine, has as much right to it as I do.'

'Is she old like you?'

'No, she's a decade younger. Our fathers quarrelled so I never met her before, but I like her. She's rather shy, so I'd be grateful if you'd tread carefully.'

'I'll do my best. People have trodden all over me lately and I don't want to do that to anyone.'

'Good.' Fleur indicated the three doors at the rear. 'Choose any of these bedrooms. Once you've unpacked, come and join me downstairs. And by the way, I'll know if you go into any of the front bedrooms, so don't even try.'

'How would you know?'

'We have a separate security system for each of those rooms. Hurry up and choose.'

Marie shrugged and went into the nearest room. 'This one will do.'

'Right then, I'll leave you to it.'

After Marie went down, she had something to eat and found herself yawning.

'Didn't you sleep on the plane?'

'Just dozed a little. Dad flew business class but I didn't.' Another yawn took her by surprise. 'Would you mind if I went up for a nap?'

'Not at all. But we're all going out for tea, and you'll be included once I let them know about your arrival in Mandurah, so I'll wake you if you sleep too long.'

'Who are you going to see?'

'Col, who was a friend of Cousin Sarah's. I've been helping him move house and this is a bit of a house-warming. Some others will be there too. Thomas is the lawyer who's handling Cousin Sarah's estate and his son, Ethan, is staying with him. He's just had some major surgery after a car crash. And there are Ethan's twin daughters too. They're twelve.'

Marie pulled a face. 'Children, then.'

'They seem more like adults, actually. They've had to grow up fast. Their mother isn't around; their grandmother, who was once married to Thomas, brought them up, but died recently and they've had to care for their father. Portia's been helping them with the meals. She's a brilliant cook.'

'This Col person is your friend, not mine. Why would he invite me?'

'Out of sheer courtesy.'

'Oh, right. Nice of him. I'll get a quick drink of water then go and have a lie down.'

When she was on her own, Fleur stood for a moment looking out at the water, pressing both hands to the sides of her head in a vain effort to calm herself down. She still felt angry at Terry and concerned about what he wanted.

She went into her partly furnished office and picked up her phone. 'Col? You'll never guess what's happened . . .'

* * *

Col listened to Fleur's explanations, then said, 'Strange thing to bring your daughter all the way to Australia on a business trip.'

'That's what I thought. Terry's no altruist, believe me, so he must have some ulterior motive. Probably money.'

'Ah. Well, you're not stupid enough to give him yours. Why don't you bring Marie round to my place tonight, share the load a little.'

'I thought you'd ask her so I already told her we'd be going out. You don't mind?'

'You knew I wouldn't.'

'Yes, I did. I'm sorry to have to do it to you. I doubt you'll enjoy her company.'

'I'll enjoy seeing you and the others, though. I always do.'

He ended the call, then sat down looking out at the water, thinking hard. He agreed with Fleur. It seemed fishy to him as well that her ex would suddenly turn up with their daughter in tow, after not keeping in touch.

Once he'd met the chap, he'd be able to judge what he was like for himself, but in his experience, manipulative sharks didn't suddenly turn into caring parents. Nor did selfish brat daughters who preferred their fathers come running to their mothers for help.

Well, if Fleur needed anything, he would do whatever he could to help her. He hated to think of anyone taking advantage of her.

Portia came home to change her clothes after an afternoon spent with Thomas and his family, and Marie was interested to meet her. She seemed an awkward sort of person but pleasant enough.

Marie's mother took one look at her blouse and suggested she change into a more casual top.

'I only have two T-shirts and they both need washing. He threw my other stuff away but I pulled those two out at the last minute.'

'Has he gone mad?'

'He seems more bossy than he used to be.'

'Well, I can lend you something. We're still about the same size.'

'That'd be a big help.'

'The jeans are OK. I've got a new T-shirt that'll look right. Come and try it on.'

She did that, because her father had made it very clear that she was to stay meek and mild. Her job was to observe and pass any information on to him. But her mother had been very helpful, kind even. People could be so puzzling.

When she saw her mother's bedroom, Marie couldn't help feeling jealous. It was so beautiful and luxurious.

'Here. Try this on.'

The T-shirt might be casual but it was of good quality and she couldn't help stroking it. 'Thanks. It's lovely.'

'You can keep it.'

As they got into the car, Marie wondered what her father would say if there was no information to pass on about the group.

She was surprised at how well they all seemed to get on. Her mother hadn't had a lot of time for making friends and socialising over the past few years, but she relaxed and joked with these people as if she'd known them for years.

They were all polite but Marie felt very much the odd one out. And her mother was right: the twins were indeed mature for their age. They kept an eye on their father and so did Portia.

Thomas seemed to be keeping an eye on everyone and even made an effort to chat to her. To her surprise she found him kind and interesting to talk to.

It wasn't till Col took the barbecued meat into the kitchen to put it on a warmed serving plate and her mother went with him to get something out of the oven that Marie began to wonder if the two of them were getting together. Only they didn't touch one another or steal kisses or anything so she wasn't sure. But the way they looked at one another either meant they were old friends, which she knew they weren't, or else they were getting together.

Surely a woman who'd been married to Terry Davies wouldn't go for such a quiet, ordinary-looking man as Col Jennings?

Perhaps she was too jetlagged to judge the situation properly. She was still finding it hard to stay awake. It wasn't just travel stress. She was really upset about Cody dropping her. She'd hoped for more.

But she could see now that he'd not been interested in going out much and was a hard worker.

She should have taken more care, only she'd been enjoying life away from her parents. Her father had kept an eye on her even after he and her mother split up and had pulled her up short a couple of times, to her surprise.

She simply couldn't work out where things were heading. Oh, who knew anything? Her mind was a lot clearer now she'd had a few days off the booze. She hadn't realised the difference it made. If she wanted to work out a new life, she'd better keep away from booze.

Terry surprised the office staff in Perth by turning up that same afternoon. It all seemed to be running smoothly and even though the second-in-command was a woman, she seemed to be efficient.

The main reason head office had thought it necessary to send him down under wasn't to run the office but to land a big contract that was currently pending with a Japanese company. That'd mean going up north and socialising with them.

He was a bit jetlagged, so didn't stay at the office late and went back to the hotel, pleased to find a small package waiting at the reception desk. He'd not dared carry it on the plane but had paid extra to have it delivered to him there in Perth. He went to bed early.

When he woke up at five o'clock the next morning, he knew he'd not get back to sleep, so began to do some more research online about this Cousin Sarah and Thomas Norcott.

It was disappointing in one sense. As far as he could tell they were both squeaky clean in their business dealings. It was usually easier to deal with folk who weren't behaving perfectly. He liked to have a handle on people's weaknesses.

He waited till Marie was likely to be awake to phone her. He wanted to ask her how things were going. Unfortunately, she didn't answer her phone. What was she doing? He hoped her mother wasn't getting at her.

He'd have to go down to see them as soon as he could get away to check on the general situation.

Since the office was running smoothly, he'd arrange to take tomorrow afternoon off.

He texted Fleur to say he'd be coming down then to chat about their daughter's future, but she didn't respond. What was she doing? Avoiding him or had she gone out already?

He didn't like being kept in the dark. He'd have a quiet word with Marie next time and tell her to keep in touch with him more often.

Chapter Thirty-Two

Marie's mother woke her early and took her to the shops at eight o'clock, saying, 'I have things to do today so we'll have to fit this in now or not till tomorrow.'

Since they only wanted a few casual clothes, it didn't take long. But her mother seemed to have an eye for colours that would look good together and they didn't disagree about anything.

'Thank you,' Marie said as they queued at the checkout.

'You're welcome. And anyway, I can't let you wear business clothes to mess around in. It'd look silly and I'd not do that to you.'

Marie studied her. 'No, you wouldn't, would you?'

'Besides, if I'm brutally honest, it'll annoy Terry and that'll amuse me.'

'You've changed.'

'Have I? How?'

The truth came out before Marie could stop herself. 'You're standing up to him.'

'It was about time I did, don't you think? The money I inherited has given me confidence, I must admit.'

'Unfortunately, I'm still dependent on him so I have to do as he says.'

'Only till you find yourself a job.'

She looked at her mother and grimaced. 'I had a part-time job and even if I'd worked full time as a shop assistant, I couldn't have afforded a flat of my own.'

'Maybe you'll find a way – if you want your freedom badly enough.'

'Freedom. Ha! I should be so lucky.'

'Is it my imagination or has your father grown more autocratic since we split up?'

Marie frowned, thinking hard. 'Maybe, no, definitely.'

It didn't make much difference to her situation, though. She was still trapped.

Portia had gone out by the time they got home. With strict instructions from her father to behave, Marie didn't dare refuse to do anything and anyway, her mother didn't ask her to do anything unreasonable.

When she'd put away her new clothes and changed into more casual gear, her mother waved at a bookcase. 'You're welcome to borrow anything you like or watch TV. Up to you. Unless you'd like to help me with these.'

She took Marie into a room full of papers and mess. 'These are the old family papers and photos. Cousin Sarah left a letter asking us to sort them out. They've just been piling up for decades.'

'I wouldn't know where to begin. I've got some hand-washing to do, if you don't mind.'

'Of course I don't. The lines are at the side of the house.'

After she'd finished her washing, Marie couldn't settle and went to ask, 'Would it be all right if I went out for a walk round the nearby streets, Mum? I'm supposed to be on an exercise programme and you know what Dad is like about that sort of thing. He told me I was too flabby.' She sighed at the thought of that, then remembered she wasn't supposed to sigh.

It was doing her head in being careful every time she opened her mouth.

'Of course it'd be OK but thank you for letting me know. You'd better go straight away because it'll be too hot later on and you don't want to get sunburnt. Borrow one of my broad-brimmed sun hats from the stand in the hall and put some sunblock on and you should be OK. There's a tube of it in the downstairs cloakroom.'

Marie nearly refused to wear a stupid sun hat, but she supposed that was what everyone did in a hot country and she certainly didn't want to get burnt.

She set off briskly, arms pumping, head high, in case her mother was watching. As soon as she was away from the house she slowed right down and when she found a small park with a shaded seating area, she went into it and sat down, this time letting herself sigh.

What was her father planning for her? Whatever it was, she was sure she wouldn't like it.

After a while she began to wonder what the two people to one side were doing there. The guy was fiddling with some fancy photographic equipment and the woman was waiting near a sort of shelter that looked like a big umbrella with skirts hanging from it down to the ground.

A panel was lifted and a young woman came out of it, wearing casual clothes that were obviously too small for her. The older woman looked surprised, then angry.

The two of them began arguing and it was like an old silent movie, with people gesticulating and the model going back into the changing tent.

A few moments later, Marie saw the younger one creep out of the tent by lifting the back flap up.

She started running as soon as she was out, hurling what looked like a bundle of clothes into some bushes as she ran past them.

What on earth was going on?

The other two were still speaking in low voices, then the woman called out and when there was no answer, went into the tent. She came out again, yelling loudly, 'Oh, hell! She's done a runner and taken the clothes with her, Rusty.'

Marie went across and retrieved the bundle that had been hurled into the nearby bushes, taking them to the woman, who was searching in the wrong place. 'Are these what you're looking for? Your, um, friend threw them in the bushes as she passed me.'

They broke off and the man said, 'Oh, thanks! We're going to—' He broke off abruptly to stare at Marie, nudging his companion. 'I think fate has just given us a helping hand, Jan.'

The woman also studied Marie. 'Wow, yes.'

'Do you have a minute to chat?' the photographer asked.

Marie was completely puzzled but anything was better than sitting around on your own. 'Sure.'

'You aren't a model, by any chance?'

'I wish.'

'You look like one.'

'Me?'

'What size of clothes do you take?' the woman asked and when Marie told her, she beamed at the guy. 'Perfect.'

They both studied her again, then Jan asked, 'Would you like to have a try at it?'

Marie was puzzled. 'What, modelling? I wouldn't have the faintest idea how to do it.'

'We could show you. Most of today's work only involves standing still in different sets of clothes. We'll tell you how to stand; your job will be to look natural and happy.'

'Why are you so desperate for a fill-in model? Don't you have others to turn to, ones who know what to do?'

The guy continued to study Marie, his eyes running up and down her body, though not in an offensive way.

Jan said, 'The woman who left so suddenly was our fill-in for a sick model, but it turns out she's pregnant and is now bigger than she used to be, so she didn't look right in the clothes. How about you put some of them on and if they fit you, which I think they will, we could try a few shots?'

'We'll pay you the going rates,' the man said.

When he said how much that was, Marie was surprised and couldn't resist the thought of earning some money. 'Well, all right. I'll give it a go.' It had never occurred to her to look at modelling as a career option because her father spoke so disparagingly about fashion and 'scrawny catwalk zombies'.

'Actually, it might be better for our purposes if we train you ourselves. We do a lot of work for one particular company and we know exactly how they like their clothes displayed. What's your name?'

'Marie Davies.'

He frowned. 'You've got a Pommy accent. Are you on holiday here? If so, the government won't allow you to work.'

'I have dual nationality, Aussie and British, so I should be all right to work here. I've lived in the UK since I was a baby so this is like my first visit.'

'That should be OK, then.'

Jan held out the clothes. 'We need to take advantage of the light. Could you try these on quickly? You can change in the tent. Be careful not to knock against the walls, though. It falls over easily.'

The clothes were a good fit, so a bemused Marie found herself letting Jan make her up and do her hair.

She enjoyed doing the job greatly. It was easy and they were fun. All she had to do was move this way and that on their instructions, and smile or look dreamy or whatever they told her. They explained what they wanted so clearly that wasn't hard. And they praised how quickly she caught on, which made her relax a bit. It sure beat studying dull old books.

After the first few shots, Rusty said, 'Are you sure you've never done any modelling?'

'Of course I'm sure. Why?'

'Well, the camera absolutely loves you and you're a natural for moving slowly and gracefully. We'll pay you what we agreed for this shoot and maybe you'd like to try doing some other work for us? We've lost a couple of our favourite models to marriage and maternity recently, you see.'

For a moment she could only gape at him, then she smiled suddenly. 'I'd love to do some more work. It's fun and I've enjoyed wearing these lovely clothes.'

'Good girl. We'll get your details down and if things continue to go well, we'll draw up a contract.'

That's when she wondered whether her father would let her do this. He put a big effort into his so-called image and used the word 'classy' a lot. Surely he wouldn't mind her earning some money so easily, especially if she asked his advice? 'It's fine by me, but I think my father would prefer to see any permanent contracts before I sign them.'

'We're not at the permanent stage yet. You need to prove you can cope with a full range of the work we undertake before we'll do that.'

'That should be all right, then.' It certainly beat working in a supermarket for peanuts.

Since it was getting really hot now, Rusty offered to drop her off at her mother's house on the way so she went back into the tent to change into her own clothes, hating how old-fashioned they looked.

Jan came into the tent as she was finishing. 'Just wanted to tell you that Rusty is happily married and he's a great guy. You won't get any inappropriate behaviour from him, unlike some people in the industry.'

'That's good to know. Thanks.'

As she was about to get out of the car, Rusty gave her a couple of his business cards and smiled at her. 'I think you're going to be good at this, Marie, possibly very good.

And if you are, you'll want someone experienced to act as your agent. I could do that for you.'

'I'll bear that in mind.'

She hoped she would be good enough at it to get a few more jobs, although she wasn't sure about making a career of it, even if her father approved. She'd never been very good at anything in her life that she could remember, though she was quite good at sewing and mending, thanks to her mother's training and her own love of clothes. But that was easy. Anyone could do it.

Still, a few modelling jobs would be really good. It was terrible not having any money.

Fleur was just about to go looking for her daughter, afraid of her getting sunburnt, when Marie came in. She was beaming, which was a surprise because she'd been scowling as she walked out of the house. In fact, it had been a few years since Fleur had seen her daughter this happy.

'Well, you look as if you enjoyed your walk.'

'I did, Mum. I had an absolutely marvellous time. You'll never guess what happened.'

'Sit down and tell me.' She patted the seat next to her on the sofa and Marie flung herself down on it, waving to Portia, who was doing something in the kitchen.

'By sheer accident I ran into some people doing a photoshoot for a clothes advert in that little park you told me about. I saw the model who was supposed to wear the clothes run away crying. It turns out she was pregnant and had got too fat for the outfit to look good on her. I saw where she threw the clothes and when the people started looking for them, I took them back.'

'Good for you.'

'When they saw me, they stared and then the man said I had the right looks and asked me to try out because they'd had to postpone this shoot once already and urgently needed to get it done today.'

'I didn't know you were interested in modelling.'

'I wasn't, but they offered to pay me so I had a go, and guess what? The photographer said the camera loves me and would I like to try working with them again? They pay far more than that grotty supermarket did and they were fun to work with, so I said yes.'

She ran out of steam, bounced to her feet and twirled round, still fizzing with excitement.

'That's a bit of luck. Well done you.'

'I'd better phone Dad and tell him about it.'

Fleur stilled. 'Um, are you sure? I doubt he'll approve of a job like that.'

'Why wouldn't he?' Marie fumbled in her backpack and pulled out the phone he'd given her, then thought about it and said slowly, 'I think I'll wait. I want to see his face when I tell him. I want him to be proud of me for once.'

She shoved the phone back in her bag and stood up. 'I'd better go and wash my face. Jan put this make-up on me and it feels all sweaty and greasy now.' She ran up the stairs.

Fleur stared at her cousin, who must have overheard all this.

'Aren't you pleased for her?' Portia asked.

'I think it's a great chance for her to have fun and earn money at the same time, but Terry has a way of taking over and sucking the life out of something if he doesn't approve of it. You saw how vibrant and bubbly Marie looked today. I bet those people's praise is part of what made her look good on camera.'

'On the other hand, she might do even better financially with someone like him who knows about business and money standing behind her.'

'Not if that someone is Terry. He likes to take the starring role. You'll see when you meet him. He'll try to charm you. Don't fall for it. It's only social window-dressing. He's about as charming as a rat with jaundice.'

'You know, you've never said anything good about him, not one thing.'

'No. He could be fun when I first met him, but the older he got, the more self-focused he became and only wanted me as a housekeeper. And he changed, became more arrogant and a bit strange at times. I don't think he likes people, just uses them. My son doesn't get on with him at all.'

'From the photos you've shown me, James looks to be a rather gentle person.'

'He is. Kind and brilliant with his hands. I miss him but at least he gets in touch regularly by email, even if his messages are only short.'

Marie re-joined them and sat staring into space, smiling slightly.

She fell asleep soon after tea, not stirring till Fleur shook her gently and suggested she go to bed. 'You're still jetlagged.'

Chapter Thirty-Three

The following morning, Marie looked at her mother as they were finishing breakfast. 'Do you think you could buy me some pretty underwear? Just a couple of sets. If I'm changing clothes, what I'm wearing will be on show, you see.'

'Sensible reason. My pleasure.' Fleur took her daughter to a local chain store famous for its underwear and bought her several sets, and a packet of pretty knickers.

Marie looked at the nightwear longingly, then shook her head. 'I'd better not buy anything too fancy. Dad won't like them.'

'He won't be wearing them. And why would he even see them?'

'He went through all my clothes as we packed.'

'Had he nothing better to do?'

'He's grown very controlling about every detail, far worse than he used to be. Besides, I can't pay you back, Mum. I won't have any money to spare till I've done a few more jobs.'

'No need to pay me back with money. You can do that by making a success of this job opportunity and not wasting the money you earn.'

Marie brightened up. 'Do you think I can make a success of it? Really?'

'Yes, I do.'

'Then why did you insist I went to university?'

'Me? I didn't. It was your father who insisted.'

'But he said you—'

'I don't lie to you. You know that. It was your father's decision. Helping you with your expenses was a way of bribing you into going.'

Fleur watched Marie gape in shock then grow quieter and frown into space. She wondered if her daughter was having second thoughts about telling her father the news, and she hoped so, but in the end that was up to her.

'We'd better go home now because Terry's due soon.'

He turned up a little later than the time he'd given them, which was typical of him. She went to open the door, not surprised to see the handle turning before she got there as he tried to come straight in. While he was in Australia, she'd make very sure that the front door was kept locked.

If he tried to boss her around, he was in for a surprise, but she was more worried about what he might do when Marie told him about her new job. He was such a snob these days.

She smiled as she deliberately waited till he knocked again to open the door. Childish but satisfying.

Portia had gone round to Thomas's but was worried about Marie and Fleur. She looked at the clock, wondering how they were getting on with Terry, who sounded to be a horrible man.

'Is something wrong?' Thomas asked.

She hesitated, not sure how much her cousin wanted to share about what was going on with her ex. But she really valued Thomas's opinion so she told him what was happening. 'Is there anything you think I should do to help her?'

He was quiet for a moment, then grinned at her. 'How about we go round there now and butt in, for a start?'

Ethan looked from one to the other. 'Do you think that's wise?'

'I think it's what Sarah would tell us to do. What do you think, are you in for that, Portia?'

From somewhere she found the courage to say, 'Yes. I do think Fleur might need our visible support, from what she's said about him.'

'We'll all go,' Ethan said at once.

Thomas shook his head. 'Not this time. You're in no state to face a bully and you've been told to take things easy. Besides, we don't want to leave the girls on their own.'

'You'll look after Portia? I don't want anyone upsetting her.'

'Yes, of course I'll look after her. I think I can still summon up the chill barrister expression I used to intimidate folk who were trying to twist the law in their favour.'

As they walked briskly along the street, he said, 'There need only be trouble if he causes it, you know.'

She was comfortable enough with him to say, 'I suppose so. I'm not used to standing up to people, but I'm starting to feel more confident. And Fleur has been so nice to me. I have a feeling she might need some visible support, at the very least.'

A few streets away, Col was pacing to and fro, also worrying about Fleur, going over what she'd said about the current situation. She'd insisted she didn't need his help, saying it'd only confuse things to have an outsider there when she was dealing with her ex.

'Are you sure?' he'd asked.

'Terry and I have done this before, quarrelled, I mean. Only, well, I used to chicken out and give in to him. I shan't do that this time, which may throw him off balance. At the very least it'll make me feel better.'

She'd sighed. 'The trouble is, Marie has always adored him, even though he hasn't deserved it. He used to undermine my authority very cleverly, but from what I've heard from her and James, he's not being as careful about how he deals with people these days. His more powerful work roles have gone to his head, I think. Well, something seems to have done.'

'I still wish you'd let me help you.'

'No, I'll be all right, Col. Really. I think university has changed Marie more than he realises. That said, he's clever at getting what he wants or he wouldn't have obtained such a high-powered job.'

After a short pause, she added, 'I do hope she won't let him stop her taking these modelling jobs, because I think they'll do her good. But in the end it's her choice.'

'You seem sure he'll try to stop her.'

'Fairly sure. It'll not be classy enough for him, having a daughter who's a lower-level photographic model.' She grimaced. 'That used to be one of his favourite words, only his idea of classy wasn't mine. "Handsome is as handsome does" is still a good rule.'

Thinking about that conversation afterwards, Col couldn't settle, didn't like to think of her facing up to a bully.

When he could stand the anxiety no longer, he got into his car and drove round to her house. There was a large luxury car just pulling up outside it. He went past and stopped, watching a tall man with thinning blond hair and a sour expression get out of it and go across to try the door, then scowl and ring the doorbell. When no one answered, he hammered on the door with a clenched fist.

Col wondered what, if anything, to do. He didn't want to poke his nose in if there was no need for an intervention but he did want to see what was happening and be available.

Then he suddenly remembered that the Buchanans were away and he had a key to both their house and their side gate because his company did the cleaning for them.

He turned round and parked in front of their house, getting the keys out of the locked box in his boot.

I'll keep an eye on things, just in case, he told himself. No need to intervene . . . unless it seems necessary to protect Fleur.

It was then that he admitted to himself how important she had become to him. He already felt to have gone past the 'getting to know one another' stage.

Chapter Thirty-Four

Terry walked into the house, moving past her so quickly he'd gone on ahead into the huge living area before she'd realised what he was doing. She had to push past him to get into the room.

He stood looking round, assessing it all. 'Very nice interior as well as location. You fell on your feet here, Fleur.'

'Did I? How nice to know that you approve.' She mimicked one of his favourite actions and held up one hand to stop him speaking. 'As far as I'm concerned you're here to discuss Marie's future. I've no desire for idle chit-chat. She's out on the patio. I asked her to wait for you there.'

He studied her, eyes narrowed, as if her sharp response had surprised him, then shook his head slightly, obviously dismissing it as irrelevant. 'She was in a really bad state when she came to me. She's not fit to be let out alone, so I expect you to back me up on sorting her life out. She's proved she can't be trusted at university.'

'She's fit enough to do something she's interested in, something non-academic, but forcing her to go to university was stupid. I'm sorry I let you push her into it.'

'Well, that's in the past now. For the present she'll have to stay with you for a while. I'll only be in Perth for part of the time and I'm in a hotel, so it's not at all suitable for her to stay with me. If you and I act together we can help her sort things out.'

'I'd rather you discussed my future with me before you decide anything, thank you very much.' Marie's voice wobbled as she spoke.

Fleur moved forward. 'We'll come out and join you on the patio then, shall we?' Unless she was very much mistaken, the quick glance Marie gave her was grateful.

She walked across and put her arm round her daughter's shoulders, feeling her trembling. It was hard for anyone to stand up to Terry when he got into his troubleshooter mode. No wonder his company valued him for solving crises round the world.

'Yes, let's all sit down. And it wouldn't hurt to offer us a drink, Fleur.' Terry moved past her again.

'I'm not offering you any hospitality. You're here on family business or I'd not even have let you in. Let's just sit down and sort things out with Marie, then you can leave.'

'Your manners haven't improved.'

'Neither has your arrogant way of treating your family.'

He made a scornful sound and took a seat. 'A family is an expensive thing, in both time and money. I don't like to waste either so I cut straight to the point.'

She sat down and he continued talking at them.

'I've been making enquiries about finishing schools. The best ones aren't in Switzerland these days but there's one in Paris that people in the know speak well of. There are various jobs that can be accessed if you have highly developed social skills.'

Fleur gaped at him. One thing their daughter did not have was social tact. She looked at Marie, who was staring at him in horror.

'What? I hated French at school, Dad, I can hardly remember a word of it.'

'You'll soon pick it up when you're living there.'

'I'm useless in formal social situations, too, so I'm not even going to try that suggestion. Anyway, I've found a job, so I don't need it.'

'So quickly?' He shot a quick, suspicious glance at Fleur.

'Mum didn't find it for me, I did.'

'Doing what?'

'Modelling. I've got an offer from a local agent to represent me because I've done one job for them already, a paying job, and it turned out well.'

'Modelling! I'm not having my daughter parading around in skimpy garments for everyone to gawp at. You might be quite good-looking but you haven't the wits to get to the higher levels in a career like that.'

'She's over eighteen,' Fleur said quietly. 'She can make her own choices.'

He turned on her, his voice glacial. 'You keep out of this.'

Her tone was just as sharp. 'No. You try listening to others for a change.'

'I don't need to listen to her views. She has no idea what's best in today's world, and nor do you.'

'And you do? You're a dinosaur, Terry. Finishing schools, indeed! You'll suggest wearing crinolines next.'

'Making good connections and knowing how to behave socially can still put people ahead in life.'

'Well, I'm not going to any sort of school,' Marie said. 'Never, ever again.'

'You'll do as you're told, young lady, if you want one penny more from me.'

'You can stay here for the time being, Marie, and earn your own money,' Fleur said.

As he opened his mouth, she could tell from his expression that he was about to lay down the law again, so she stood up. 'I think I'd like you to leave now. If you're going to be rude to me and ignore what Marie says, you're wasting our time, Terry.'

He surprised her by going across to his daughter, grasping her arm and jerking her to her feet. 'I made a mistake bringing you to your mother's, Marie. The inheritance has clearly gone to her head. I'm taking you back to the hotel with me now and if necessary I'll hire someone to keep you safe.' He deliberately twisted her arm behind her to start her moving.

'Ow! You're hurting me!'

Fleur moved quickly across to them. 'Let go of her this minute.'

He pretended to be amused but his tone was vicious. 'Oh, my! Are you going to make me?'

When she tried to pull him away from Marie, he gave her a hard shove with his free hand that sent her staggering backwards.

As she fell across a chair then bounced to the ground, the patio door was slammed open and Col rushed in. He helped her up, putting an arm round her shoulders.

'Are you all right, Fleur, love?'

She realised what he was doing and nestled against him. 'I am now you're here, darling.' She wished she could have taken a photo of Terry's shock at this exchange of endearments.

Col gestured towards Terry with his free hand. 'This the ex?'

'I'm afraid so.'

'Does he always manhandle women?'

'If he has no need to charm them, it has been known. He doesn't beat them, but he's good at pushing them around. Literally.'

Marie had seized her opportunity to jerk away from her father and was now standing close to her mother.

'Are you all right, Marie?'

She rubbed her shoulder. 'It really hurt when he twisted my arm but I'm not going with him, whatever he says or does.'

Terry was carefully straightening his clothes and studying Col, as if trying to work out who he was, while at the same time scowling at Fleur.

The doorbell rang and she hesitated. 'I'd better answer it. Don't let him grab Marie again, Col.'

She hurried across to the hall and opened the door, sighing in relief when she saw Thomas and Portia standing there. 'I'm so glad to see you, Thomas.'

'Trouble?'

'Yes. My ex is trying to take our daughter away with him forcibly. She doesn't want to go. She's twenty, not a child any longer, so surely he has no right to do this.' She glared across at her ex as she added, 'And he just knocked me to the floor.'

For once, Terry seemed at a loss for words, except to mutter, 'It was an accident.'

'Any witnesses?'

'Two. My daughter and Col.'

She glared at her ex and gestured towards Thomas. 'This is my lawyer, by the way.'

'You're turning into a clever bitch. But I'm not going to let you ruin our daughter's life.'

'You no longer have a say in what either of us does. Please leave immediately.'

He moved slowly forward and she tried not to flinch as he stopped near her and jabbed one finger towards her, just avoiding touching her face.

'I'll be in touch again when you've had time to calm down. We still have to decide what to do with Marie.'

'No, she has to decide what she wants to do.'

Col moved closer. 'Fleur asked you to leave. Do you need help finding the door, Mr Davies?'

Terry ignored him. 'I'll be in touch, Fleur, once you and our daughter have had time to calm down. I do not intend her to do any more low-level modelling jobs, whatever you say or do. She can do better for herself and the family than that.'

'Please stop threatening my client, Mr Davies,' Thomas said quietly but with authority.

Terry didn't respond, just walked out and left the front door open.

'Petty-minded, isn't he? Let me.' Col went out into the hall, waited until the car had driven away, then closed and locked the front door.

Fleur let her breath out in a long, slow exhalation. 'Thank you for intervening, Col.'

'My pleasure.'

She smiled at Portia. 'And thank you for bringing Thomas round.'

'I was worried about you.'

Thomas waited till everyone had sat down, then said quietly, 'You'd better tell me exactly what happened here today. Don't leave any detail out.'

So she went through it again, feeling somewhat embarrassed. 'It was like a bad B-rated movie.'

'Your ex looked furiously angry when he left,' Thomas said. 'You'd better be careful. Bullies don't like being denied what they're after.'

'I know. Good thing my daughter is here in Australia with me now, isn't it, or who knows what he'd have got away with doing?'

Marie suddenly clapped one hand to her mouth. 'Oh, no! Dad's still got my passports, both of them, the English one and the Australian.' She looked at her mother. 'He took them from me after we arrived in Australia. I didn't dare refuse to hand them over.'

'As your lawyer, I can send him a letter, asking formally for them to be returned,' Thomas said.

'He'll refuse.'

'If you're twenty, you're legally an adult and have every right to manage your own passports.'

Fleur said, 'Thank you for your offer, Thomas, but I have to agree with my daughter. Terry will simply refuse.'

'Once he's done that we can apply for new ones. People do lose passports from time to time, or they get stolen.'

'I bet we have to resort to that. Now, the least I can do is offer you a cup of coffee or some other drink.'

Portia patted her arm. 'I'll deal with the refreshments, Fleur. You're bound to be feeling a bit churned up after that confrontation. Your ex is a big man, isn't he? He gave me the shivers and he wasn't even looking in my direction. If looks could kill, you'd be dead now.'

Col moved towards the patio door. 'I need to go back and lock the side gate at the Buchanans' house. I'll come back the front way, so it'll be me ringing the doorbell in a couple of minutes.'

When he'd gone, Thomas looked at Portia. 'It's just about wine o'clock, don't you think? You look like you need a stiff drink after that.'

'Good idea. Red or white?'

'White.'

'I'll get them.'

Marie looked across the patio at her mother. 'I didn't realise that you and Col were together.'

'It's, um, quite new.'

'I like him. He seems gentle but he's not frightened of Dad.'

'I'm not so much frightened these days as wary of your father. It was unlike him to use violence so openly, which just shows how furious he was and how he's changed.'

'Why do you think he's so against me doing any modelling jobs? I'd have thought he'd be pleased.'

'One of the women he got together with towards the end of the time he and I were still married was a model, quite a well-known one.' Fleur gave a wry smile. 'She ran rings round him, then cheated on him and married his boss. He's never forgiven her but he didn't dare try to get his own back on her. He found a job elsewhere as soon as he could.'

Marie's mouth was a big O. 'Didn't you mind him being unfaithful?'

'Of course I did. It was the final straw to discover how often he had hooked up with other women. I was one of the last to know. Luckily he decided he could do better than me at this stage in his life so was happy for us to split up – less happy when my lawyer found the money he'd secreted away. Or possibly some of the money. I'm sure he got away with some. He was always switching money round.'

Marie let out a long, low whistle.

'If you want to try modelling, don't let him stop you.'

'I did enjoy it, but it's too soon to know if I want to have a big push at it, don't you think?'

'Yes. Give it a preliminary try.'

She looked at her mother. 'I'm sorry for how I've treated you. If I'd seen him more often, I might have realised what he was like. Was he always so bossy?'

'He was more subtle about it when we first married. I didn't realise till later how he was using me. The more successful he became, the less subtle he grew in dealing with those he regarded as inferiors. And I was useful in those days for looking after his clothes and children.'

'I feel so stupid.'

Fleur shrugged. 'He's fooled cleverer people than you or me. Learn from it and move on. We'll have to be on our guard from now on, though. He'll try something else, I'm sure. I hope he doesn't stay in Australia for long.'

The front doorbell rang. 'That'll be Col.'

'Give him a great big thank you kiss for me, Mum.'

Fleur smiled at that instruction, then decided to follow it.

Col didn't protest and it was a few minutes before they joined the others.

By that time Ethan and the twins had been summoned to join them and it all turned into a very pleasant evening.

Chapter Thirty-Five

When Thomas tried to contact Terry the following day, the woman acting as his secretary in Australia said he'd had to fly up to Singapore suddenly.

'How long will he be away?'

'Just a day or two. He wasn't quite sure.'

'Oh dear. I wonder if you could help me, then. He was looking after his daughter's passports. She has dual English and Australian nationality so there are two of them. She needs them now for her job. Would you know where to find them?'

'I can't possibly give you anything belonging to Mr Davies without his permission, Mr Norcott.'

'They don't belong to him. She's an adult and they belong to her. He's just been looking after them for her. I'm her lawyer, by the way.'

'I still can't do it.'

'Then perhaps you could just check that they're safe? She's going to need them, you see. She's a model and must be able to fly to jobs elsewhere in this region. And like her father, she doesn't always get much notice.'

There was silence, then she said, 'I suppose I could check that they're there. There's only one place they could be, after all.'

There was silence, then she came back online. 'They're not in the safe or in the locked drawer of the desk he's using while he's here, I'm afraid. I can ask him about them if he calls.'

'Please do that and get back to me straight away.' He put the phone down, not liking the sound of this.

Four hours later, Thomas received a call from the secretary. 'I spoke to Mr Davies and he says he's already given her passports back to her and he's worried that she seems confused about that and a few other things.'

'Well, he hasn't given them back to her, and I've seen no sign of her being confused about anything. I'll make a note of his response though, in case it's needed in court.'

She sounded panicked. 'Why would it be needed in court?'

'Because he insisted on looking after the passports and seems to have lost them. Is he usually so forgetful?'

'I have to go. There's another call.'

She ended the call.

He shook his head sadly. How petty could you get? What a control freak this Terry Davies was! Indeed, it was strange behaviour for a man in his position.

Well, Thomas wasn't letting him get away with controlling a young woman just finding her way in the world after a rocky start. Definitely not.

He would put on his lawyer's hat and send a letter to the company office asking for the passports back.

An early phone call the next day from Rusty brought an offer of another job, another one to replace the pregnant model, and Marie accepted instantly, listening to his instructions and taking notes.

When the call ended, she beamed at her mother and raised one thumb triumphantly. 'I've got another modelling job this afternoon. It's just outside somewhere called Fremantle.'

'That's about forty minutes' drive from here. How are you going to get there?'

'I'll have to call a taxi.'

'That'd be expensive, not to mention you'd be needing a taxi to come home afterwards, so you wouldn't earn much. And I can't drive you as I've made other arrangements.' Anyway, she didn't want to set a precedent. She had a quick think. 'Let's see if we can find a cheapie car hire place instead. I'll pay for one.'

'Really?' Marie gulped, looking emotional. 'That's very kind of you, Mum.'

'Grab some breakfast quickly. I'll go online and find a car hire place, then phone and see what's available.'

Marie hesitated, gave her mother a quick, rather embarrassed hug without looking her in the eye, then went into the kitchen to grab a bowl of cereal and an apple, which she ate standing up.

She paused suddenly, spoon in the air. 'You don't think Dad will come after me if I do this job, do you?'

'How will he know what you're doing or where you are?'

'He's cunning at finding things out. And he's boasted to me more than once in the past year or two about getting his own back on people who've crossed him. I never thought he'd turn on me but now I'm a bit worried about that, to tell you the truth.'

'We'll keep you safe.'

Marie didn't look convinced.

By midday they had a small car hired for a month and Marie was over the moon to have her own transport.

'I don't know why you're being so kind to me, Mum. I don't deserve it.'

'I know. But you're still my daughter. You won't get me funding you for another chance if you don't make the best of this one, though.'

She got another of those almost furtive hugs for that. 'I won't need another chance. I'm not stupid, I'm just no good with book stuff.'

That made Fleur wonder. Now she knew that Portia was dyslexic, she had to wonder if the tendency ran in the family. This wasn't the time to look into that, though.

Ethan phoned Portia late that afternoon. 'I know this is short notice, but do you fancy having dinner with me?'

'And your family?'

'No. Just you and me.'

'Why?' She clapped one hand to her mouth. Would she never learn not to rush in so bluntly?

'Several reasons. The main one is that I don't get the chance to chat to you on your own and I'd like to. Dad will be around tonight to keep an eye on the girls and I'm longing to go out in the evening without a wheelchair. I'm not supposed to walk far, but I am supposed to walk increasing distances each day.'

'Oh, well, I'd love to have dinner with you.' Strange how she'd been instantly attracted to him, whereas Ben, though a nice guy, hadn't stirred her emotions at all.

'Good. Is there anything you can't eat?'

'No. That's Fleur. I love all sorts of food.'

'I'm going to have to ask you to drive me.'

'That's fine.'

'And I still get rather tired by mid-evening so could we go quite early?'

She chuckled. 'Suits me. I get hungry quite early anyway.'

When she put the phone down, she went rushing to find Fleur. 'Ethan's just asked me out to dinner. Can you get your own meal?'

'Yes, of course. That'll be nice for you.'

She nodded, smiling blissfully. 'What should I wear?'

'Let's go and look through your clothes. What type of restaurant are you going to?'

'Oh. I don't know.'

'Then you'll need an outfit that can go anywhere. You look so happy about it.'

'I am.'

'He seems a nice guy.'

Her cousin beamed and nodded. She looked like a different person from the tense, awkward woman Fleur had met in the airport.

* * *

By the time she sent Portia off to pick up Ethan, Fleur was feeling like a mother hen with a particularly fussy chick. Marie hadn't come back yet but had phoned to let her know she was going out for a coffee with Rusty and Jan.

Fleur sat down, relishing the peace and quiet. If Terry was out of the country, there was little or no chance of being disturbed.

Only a few minutes after she'd thought that, there was the sound of breaking glass followed by a car accelerating away down the street. She rushed into the side of the house they rarely used, where the only window looking out onto the street was situated, and found that a brick had been thrown into the room there, smashing the window and scattering shards of glass everywhere.

She felt utterly certain that Terry had arranged this. She'd overheard him organising similarly annoying tricks once or twice before they split up and been disgusted that he'd stoop to such petty nastiness. Damn him! She hated having him and his annoying ways back in her life again.

She found a twenty-four-hour emergency glazier and arranged for the window to be boarded up temporarily and the glass replaced the following day. It was going to cost a lot but hopefully their house insurance would cover it. Good thing it was still light.

Then she gave in to temptation and phoned Col, telling him what had happened.

'I'll be round in a few minutes.'

'There's no need.'

'I want to see you – and also to find out exactly what happened.'

'Someone chucked an old brick through the window. End of story.'

'Have you touched anything?'

'Actually, no. I was too upset to clear up, then I found a glazier who'll be here shortly. He says to leave the mess to him.'

'Let me come and look at it before anyone touches it. I'm on my way.'

She wondered why he wanted to see it. One brick was just like another as far as she was concerned and she couldn't see anyone getting fingerprints from such a rough surface. But she was happy at the thought of Col coming round. His caring about her was such a bright, shiny new gift.

Thomas stayed with his granddaughters till Ethan came home with Portia. They both looked happy and the girls instantly exchanged meaningful glances with him.

They took the opportunity to remind her that she'd asked if she could draw them and made arrangements to go round to her new studio the next day and let her do some preliminary sketches.

Thomas hated to upset the happy mood but he felt it'd be better to warn Portia about the brick that had been thrown through one of the windows of her house. It was sad to see her joy fade so quickly.

'Fleur's ex must have arranged the brick to be thrown,' she said. 'Who would do something nasty if they weren't getting a benefit from it?'

'Some people enjoy creating mayhem for no reason,' Thomas said. 'But you may be right about Terry arranging it. He's a strange one. But he's out of the country at the moment so there's not much chance of blame sticking to him.'

'Can we go and see the damage?' Nicole wanted to know.

'Yes, let's,' Liane said. 'We can suss out your studio while we're there, Portia.'

Portia looked at the two men. 'Will it be safe for them to go there, do you think?'

'Of course it will,' Ethan said and Thomas nodded agreement. 'You can give me a ride and you can take the girls, Dad?'

Before they set off, Portia managed to snatch a moment's privacy with him. 'Thank you for my outing. I had a lovely time. That was some of the best Japanese food I've ever eaten.'

'And the best company I've had, which was much more important.'

'I enjoyed your company too.' She'd never met a man so easy to talk to.

'So we'll do it again?'

'Love to.'

It was only a short drive round the street. There was a glazier's van outside the house and two men seemed to be just finishing work as they drove into the garage. The shards of glass had all been cleared up and a panel fastened over the gap, so there wasn't even much to see.

'They've done it quickly!' he said in amazement.

Fleur was standing by the front door, speaking to the glazier. As he nodded and got back into his van, she turned to Portia. 'They can put in new glass tomorrow. He told me about some glass that can be smashed into crazing but won't break into pieces. It's more expensive but I told him to go ahead and get that sort.'

'Definitely.'

'Let's go inside and join Thomas and the girls.'

She was frowning as she sat down next to Col. 'Has this sort of thing ever happened before round here, Thomas? It's always seemed so peaceful.'

'The Buchanans had a bit of bother from a guy who wanted to buy their house, but it quickly turned into a farce. Otherwise, no. And I've lived on the other side of this canal for a few years.'

'We should install CCTV outside, then if it happens again, we'll get a shot of who's doing it,' Ethan said.

'I can buy the camera and fittings first thing tomorrow,' Col said. 'I know where to get one and how to fit it.'

'Thank you.'

'It feels as if we've become a family,' Liane said quietly. 'We might not all be related but we feel connected somehow.'

'I agree,' Thomas said. 'And I think we'd better leave you two in peace now we know you're going to be safe.'

'Do you want to stay for a nightcap?' Fleur asked.

Nicole looked at her father and shook her head. 'Dad's tired. This is quite late for him.'

Ethan sighed. 'Sadly, they're right.' He turned to Portia and kissed her cheek before leaving.

The girls winked at her as they followed him, and Fleur went to see them out.

Portia realised she was still standing there, hand on the warm spot – well, it still felt warm to her – where Ethan's lips had touched her skin.

Fleur came back and gave her a warm smile, but they didn't say anything, thank goodness.

Portia knew she was blushing. She could feel the heat in her cheeks. 'I think I'll go up to bed now.' She ran up the stairs, leaving Fleur to farewell Col.

There was dead silence from downstairs and she smiled. She'd bet anything they were having another kiss.

She hoped she and Ethan could have the privacy for a proper kiss next time. She felt quite sure there would be a next time. There was none of the doubting she'd had with other men about whether he'd meant it about another date. He was very special.

And so were those two girls. How mature they were for their age!

The next day passed quietly. In the morning, Fleur had a sudden idea and showed Marie what was left of Sarah's clothes.

She pounced on them. 'What beautiful materials. The styles are a bit, well, older-woman-ish. Would it be all right if I altered a couple of them to fit me? And used up the scraps of leftover material?'

'Go for it. Take the lot. We were only going to give them to a charity shop.'

'You mean it? I can really have them all?'

'Yes.'

'That's fantastic. Is there a sewing machine in the house? These jobs are too big to do by hand.'

'Yes. But we haven't used it so I don't know if it's in good working order.'

'Can I try it out?'

'Of course. Do you still enjoy sewing?'

'Yes. But I had to do it by hand at uni, so I was a bit limited in what I could make. It's the cheapest way to get what you want and anyway, I love making clothes. I know Dad thought I made stupid things, but other people at uni admired them.'

'Well, the sewing machine is in the hall cupboard under the stairs. There may be some sewing stuff there. Be my guest with that too.'

From the yell of triumph that floated up the stairs, she guessed the sewing machine had won Marie's approval. Sewing was one of the few interests they'd shared, but Terry had hated her wearing home-made clothes.

Oh, she grew so angry sometimes at how she'd put up with the way he'd treated her. But he'd been away a lot, so it hadn't impinged as badly as if he'd been at home all the time.

It had still impinged, though. And she'd let it.

Portia was waiting for her downstairs and they managed to sort through some more folders of papers.

'Is Marie as good at sewing as you are?'

'She used to be. It was one of the few things we never disagreed about. I gave her the rest of Cousin Sarah's clothes. I'm sorry. I should have asked you about that before I did it.'

'I'm not into sewing and I've already taken the things I liked. Good luck to her. She's stunningly pretty when she's happy, isn't she? Why didn't you let her take a fashion and design course, or whatever they call it these days?'

'Terry.'

'Ah.'

Col rang to say he had to sort out a small crisis at work but could come round in the early afternoon to fit a CCTV system.

Fleur stayed outside, chatting to him and passing him things, enjoying the safe feeling it gave her to have him there.

Terry was throwing a long shadow, she felt, and she couldn't help wondering what he'd do next.

By teatime the surveillance system was installed.

When Fleur went inside again, she found Marie waiting to show her the patchwork skirt she'd run up from some of the bits and pieces of material left from Fleur's alterations to Sarah's clothes.

Portia joined them. 'Wow! You're good! That's a lovely skirt.'

'I'm going to wear this tomorrow to go to the shoot. Did I tell you I have another job booked to replace that pregnant woman?'

'Only about three times,' Fleur teased. 'You must be doing something right.'

'It's about time I did.'

'We've all been – let's call it hampered during the past few years. I was not only short of money when your father and I split up, I was short of time to spend with you and James. This inheritance has been a gift in other ways than financially. I'm just sorry your father came to this part of Australia.'

'I'd not be here if he hadn't.'

'That's the only good thing about it.'

She didn't share with Marie how worried she was about what Terry would do when he came back from Singapore. She was quite sure he wouldn't leave them alone. Would he even accede to the lawyer's letter about the passports?

Who knew? He'd become very unpredictable. When she looked back, she could see the way he'd changed over time.

Why? Were her former suspicions true? Surely he wasn't that stupid?

Chapter Thirty-Six

In the middle of that night, a vehicle drew up outside the house. Marie, who'd been sleeping fitfully, wondered why a car would be stopping there and peered out of her bedroom window. The car had no headlights on and it didn't move away.

What now?

Feeling worried, she ran along to her mother's bedroom and shook her. 'Wake up! There's a car stopped outside the house.'

Portia jerked awake as she heard them run along the landing. She got quickly out of bed and ran to join them at the window of Marie's bedroom.

'Keep back!' Fleur whispered. 'We don't want them to see us.'

'Why has it stopped there?' Marie muttered.

'Probably to disturb us. Can either of you see the number plate?'

'No. It's got something covering it up.'

'I bet they're just doing it to upset us,' Fleur said angrily.

'It's my fault you're getting bothered, Mum.'

'No, it isn't.' Portia gave Marie a fierce look. 'You didn't cause the trouble, so how can it be your fault?'

'It has to be Dad doing it because of me, don't you think? Who else could it be?'

'It's likely to be him behind it, but he'll be paying someone else to do it,' Fleur said. 'He'd not actually risk doing it himself, even if he has come back to Australia.'

'Don't switch any lights on,' Portia said. 'We shouldn't give them the satisfaction of knowing that they've disturbed us.'

Someone got out of the car and rang the doorbell, then jumped back quickly. The car began moving off before he'd even shut the passenger door.

'I wonder if the CCTV picked up anything useful?' Portia said thoughtfully.

'Who knows? Come back to bed. It's no good us staying up. We can't stop people driving round.'

No other vehicles stopped outside the house but none of the three women slept well that night.

They all gathered in the kitchen as soon as it was light.

'Should we report this to the police?' Fleur wondered aloud.

Portia shook her head. 'I don't think we should do anything without asking Thomas.'

'I feel as if we're besieged. And it would have only cost Terry a hundred dollars to do it. Where does he find people to do this sort of thing? I'd not know where to start looking.'

'Who knows?'

'I wonder if he has come back from Singapore.' Marie shivered. 'What about my job this afternoon?' she worried.

'You'll go and do it, of course. And smile all the way there and back.'

'Well, I'll have to go shopping. We're running out of fresh fruit and veggies,' Portia said.

'And I need some thread.'

'Go to the shops with Portia, not alone,' Fleur told her daughter. 'Safer that way.'

'What about you?'

'I'll be sure to keep all the doors locked.'

Shortly after the two women had left for the shops, Thomas phoned to ask if he and Ethan could leave the girls with Fleur while he took his son to a physio appointment that had suddenly been changed.

'Of course you can. I enjoy their company.'

'Thanks. They keep saying they'll be all right on their own, but I'm not happy to leave them, given all that's going on round here. We'll be there in about ten minutes.'

When the car drew up outside, Nicole got out of it and went straight into the house.

Liane dropped her backpack and several items fell out, including a bag of coins destined for an animal charity she supported, so she crouched down to pick them up, calling, 'Sorry to delay you.'

A van had driven slowly past but its driver seemed to have no interest in them and was listening to the radio from the way he was bobbing his head to and fro. There seemed to be no one else around.

'Oh dear, a few coins have rolled behind the wheel. Sorry to be so long,' Liane apologised.

'Doesn't matter,' her grandfather said. 'Take your time. We've not got far to go.'

Liane stood up, checking the ground. 'There. I think I've got all my coins all now. See you later.' She retrieved her backpack from the rear seat of the car and followed her sister into the house.

A couple of minutes after Thomas drove off, the van returned and parked further along the street.

One of the men inside it spoke into a mobile phone to someone stationed across the canal opposite Fleur and Portia's house. 'We're ready. Tell us when it's all clear.'

'It's clear now. One has just come outside and is sitting by the canal, watching some birds. There's an older woman upstairs fiddling with a flower arrangement and someone I can't see clearly in the room at the end of the canal side of the house. But the one outside has long dark hair as per the description and is on her own.'

'Good. With a bit of luck we'll get in and out quickly.'

The van edged along the street and stopped on the drive close to the front door. His companion pulled a mask over his face and got out of the back of the van. He fiddled with the door lock and got it open in only a minute or so, laughing softly at how easy it was.

He paused just inside to listen carefully then ran lightly through the house and out onto the patio. The lass outside was still sitting staring at the water. She had the long dark hair he'd been told to look for. When he went outside, she must have assumed it was someone from the family because she didn't turn round.

'Shh. Move quietly. There's the most gorgeous baby bird calling for its mother to feed it and—'

He clapped the impregnated pad across her mouth quickly and held it there in spite of her struggles till she sighed into unconsciousness. Then he picked her up and ran back through the house, pausing briefly to check that there was no one passing by in the street before going out and shoving her into the back of the van.

She was already beginning to stir.

'Go, go, go!' He slammed the back doors of the van shut and as it drove off, he held the pad over her face again.

'Just over four minutes,' the driver said with a chuckle. 'You win the bet.'

'It all went our way. People are rarely as watchful in daytime. Wonder what old bossy-boots wants with her?'

'Who cares as long as he pays up? Truss her up. It'll take us nearly an hour to get up to Perth.'

When Fleur came downstairs after re-arranging the silk flowers she'd bought a couple of days ago, she saw that the front door was slightly open and went to peer outside, puzzled. There was no sign of anyone, so she closed it and went to look for the girls.

She found Nicole still in the documents room but no sign of Liane.

'Where's your sister?'

'Out on the patio last time I looked.'

'Well, she's not there now and the front door was open.'

'What? We shut and locked it when we came in, truly we did.'

Fleur began to feel uneasy. 'Will you go and check upstairs? I'll look in all the downstairs rooms.'

It took them only a couple of minutes to do that and they met in the kitchen.

'She isn't in the house,' Nicole said. 'What can have happened to her in such a short time?'

They went outside onto the patio and found a can half-hidden under one of the chairs and a puddle of what looked like cola round it.

'She'd have cleared that up,' Nicole said slowly. 'She's Mrs Tidy and anyway we don't leave things around that attract ants. Why would she have dropped it?'

'Something's very wrong. I'm going to phone Thomas.'

He answered at the third ring and she explained that Liane was missing.

'We're at the physio. I'll get Ethan out of his session and we'll come straight to your place.'

'It'll probably be nothing but— Oh, that sounds like the garage door rolling up. Let me go and see who it is before you ring off.'

Fleur ran across to see Portia and Marie coming into the house but they hadn't seen or heard from Liane, so she told Thomas.

'We won't be long.'

Nicole looked at the others. 'Liane wouldn't have left the house without telling us.'

'It has to be down to Terry, then,' Fleur said.

'That doesn't make sense!' Portia said. 'Why would your ex want anything to do with Liane? He doesn't even know her.'

'To use as a bargaining chip, perhaps? To get Marie to do as he wants.'

'Kidnapping is a serious offence. Would he have risked that just to stop her doing modelling jobs?'

'I'd not have thought so, only he's been acting strangely ever since he arrived.'

Thomas and Ethan turned up then, but were just as baffled as the others about why Liane would be the person missing.

Ethan frowned. 'If the door was open, then someone must have come in from outside.'

Nicole shook her head. 'I don't know how they got in. We didn't leave the door open, Dad. Honest, we didn't.'

'Let's look at it.'

'There's a magnifying glass in the office.' Portia rushed off to bring it.

Ethan examined the keyhole. 'Those could be faint scratches. Hell, what do I know about breaking into houses?'

'We'd better call the police,' Thomas said.

'They'll say it's too soon to worry.'

'Leave that to me. I know one of the senior officers. He'll know I don't call them in for no reason.' He took his phone out of his pocket and walked away from the others.

Chapter Thirty-Seven

The two men drove into a garage and once the door had rolled down, the man in the back dragged Liane to the edge of the van floor, then hauled her over his shoulder and carried her into the house.

As he put her down, she promptly vomited over him. Cursing, he shoved her away.

She was sick again as the other approached her. 'Allergic to . . . anaesthetics,' she gasped. 'You could kill me.'

They exchanged startled glances.

'Need . . . water.'

Giving her a disgusted look, the second man got her a glass of water and held it out to her, keeping a careful distance away.

The other one was trying to wipe himself clean, using the dishcloth. 'Never mind her. Phone bossy-boots and tell him we've got her.'

'You keep an eye on her, then.' He wagged one finger at Liane. 'Shut up and stay where you are or you'll get thumped. And I'll be first in the queue to do it.' He went into the next room.

She was shaking, so took a gulp of water and put the glass on the table. She tried to listen to what he was saying in the next room but all she could hear was a murmur.

He came back and wrinkled his nose at the mess on the floor. 'Let's go into the front room.'

'He said to stay in the back, where no one can see us.'

'You can stay here but I'll be the one throwing up if I have to hang around in this stink.' When he picked her up and carried her into the living area, she didn't struggle and looked bone white, which had him exchanging worried glances with his companion.

'We should tie her up. And gag her.'

'What if I . . . choke? Could kill me.'

'We'll just tie you up but if you try to shout for help, we will gag you.' He produced some rope and tied her hands behind her back. 'Keep an eye on her, Jack, while I clean myself up.'

He went back into the kitchen and there was the sound of running water, then he came back with damp but cleaner clothes.

'Is bossy-boots on his way?'

'Yeah. Said he'd be here in about half an hour and to have his package ready.' He grinned. 'Nice little earner altogether, this job.'

The time seemed to drag to Liane. The men refused to talk to her, her mouth felt sour and her hands were getting numb. She still didn't understand what was going on, not at all. Why would anyone want to kidnap her? And who was this bossy-boots person they kept mentioning?

Eventually there was the sound of a car pulling up outside and the front door opened.

Liane turned her head to see who it was and gasped in shock when she saw him.

The newcomer gasped even more loudly and strode across to stare down at her. 'What the hell are you two playing at? This isn't the one I asked you to bring me.'

Both men gaped at him, then stared at one another in puzzlement.

'She was where you said, and she looks like the photo – long dark hair tied back.'

Liane decided this was no time to be brave and began to cry, an art she and her sister had perfected as young children. She'd recognised Marie's father from a photo her new friend had shown them, but she pretended not to know his identity. 'Who are you? Why am I here?'

Terry thumped one hand against the door. 'You damned fools. You've brought the wrong girl.'

Then he moved across and began to untie Liane's hands. 'There's been a mistake. I'm sorry for that. I'll take you back home, but if you value your safety, you'll not recognise any of us again.' He grasped her shoulder tightly, digging his fingers in, hurting her. 'Is that clear?'

She let out a sob or two and nodded vigorously.

He went into the kitchen and came back with a tea towel, fastening it across her eyes. 'I need a gag.'

'You can't gag her. She says she's allergic to anaesthetics and she keeps being sick. She might choke.'

She listened intently but all she heard was a curse. She could have shaken the blindfold off but made no attempt to do that. To her relief, he didn't gag her. She really was allergic.

He guided her outside and sat her in a car, cramming some sort of sun hat over her head to hide the blindfold.

'Do not try to remove this or uncover your eyes, or I'll knock you unconscious. Nod if you understand me.'

She nodded.

'Understand this. I am saving you from those two. I did not ask them to capture you.'

He was playing this like an actor in a poor movie, she thought, and sounding rather strange, speaking far too quickly. Well, the minute she was free of him she'd tell everyone who had ordered the kidnapping.

She shuddered. If he let her go. She hoped he really was going to release her.

Fear shivered through her as the car moved off.

There were traffic noises and they felt to be going quite fast. She didn't try to remove the blindfold, could have rubbed it off against the seat but much as she was longing to do so, it'd be better to save that till she was desperate to see what was happening.

Two police officers came to Sarah's house and listened to an account of Liane's disappearance, asking questions.

'How can you be absolutely sure there's not someone playing a trick on you?' one asked.

'She's my twin. I know her.'

'I'm sure too,' Thomas said. 'I'm a retired lawyer and I'm not in the habit of playing tricks on anyone, let alone calling in the police for no reason.'

'First thing we'll do is to put out a warning to look out for a missing girl.' One of them went outside and came back shortly afterwards. 'They're sending it out to all cars.'

Thomas had been thinking hard. 'You might try looking out for a car leased to a certain Terry Davies.' He gave them the name of the company Davies worked for.

They phoned but it was clear they were finding this hard to believe and if it hadn't been a well-respected lawyer who was a friend of someone in a high place, they'd not have been giving it much attention.

When they'd noted down the relevant details, they left.

'I doubt they're going to try very hard,' Thomas said.

Nicole burst into tears and her father put his arms round her.

'I feel so helpless,' Fleur said.

Liane heard the sound of a siren in the distance. Was it the police or an ambulance? It came closer and closer, and she desperately wished her hands were free and she could flag them down. A sob escaped her.

'Shut up, you.'

She edged the tea towel down a little and glimpsed a blue light flashing at the edge of it.

Terry cursed as a police car loomed up in the rear-view mirror, siren blaring, lights flashing. He glanced down at the speedometer and realised that he was speeding and started to slow down.

Furious at his own stupidity, he slowed to a halt and reached out for the tea towel, yanking it quickly down to Liane's neck. 'Do not say anything to them. You understand? I've not hurt you and I won't. I just want to take you back to your family.'

She nodded. He seemed to have forgotten that he'd tied her hands behind her.

One of the police officers opened the driver's door and bent down. 'Could you please get out, sir?'

The minute Terry was out of the car, Liane yelled, 'He's kidnapped me. Arrest him. Look. My hands are tied.' She rocked as far forward as she could to show them.

Before Terry could do anything, the officer slammed him against the car and warned him to stay still. The other officer ran round to the passenger's side and opened the door.

'Her hands really are tied!' he called.

Before Terry could do anything, handcuffs were snapped on his wrists.

'I wasn't the one who kidnapped her. I was taking her back to her family!' Terry yelled.

'We'll discuss that at the station.'

The officers called in what was happening and were told to take Liane and Terry to the nearest police station, which was in Mandurah. She was glad when they left her in the car with one officer driving, and the other drove with Terry, now handcuffed to the side of the rear seat of the police car.

As they escorted her inside the station, Liane suddenly found herself crying for real, out of sheer relief, and couldn't stop.

'Is there someone we can contact?' a female officer asked gently.

She managed to stop sobbing for long enough to give her father's phone number, but the tears continued to roll down her cheeks.

A doctor came to examine her and verified that she hadn't been assaulted. After that, the kind female officer sat beside her, assuring her that her reactions were normal and her family was on the way to pick her up.

Gradually, Liane began to regain control of herself.

By the time her father and grandfather arrived, she was sipping a hot drink with a blanket wrapped round her.

She dumped the cup on the table and flung herself at her father, once more reduced to tears.

In another part of the police station, Terry refused to say anything till he'd phoned his company and asked them to send him a lawyer.

After he'd done that, he gave a brief outline of what had really happened, insisting that he had not intended to kidnap Liane but to get hold of his daughter.

'You're still saying you plotted to kidnap someone?' the woman asked incredulously.

'It was my daughter and it wasn't kidnapping. I wanted to look after her. She had a breakdown in the UK, so I brought her here for a holiday. But my wife is not the person to deal with Marie and was making things worse. You can ask the girl who was in my car if I didn't try to take her home again the minute I realised they had the wrong person.'

'Then why did you tie her hands?'

He felt weary and dizzy and the lawyer's voice seemed to be coming and going, now loud, now soft. He struggled for words, struggled to think straight. Suddenly the room began to whirl round him and he cried out as he felt himself falling down, down into blackness.

* * *

The ambulance sped on its way to hospital, siren blaring, with the man in the back hallucinating and having to be restrained.

When they got to A&E he was taken straight through, but the two police officers stayed with him, just in case.

As they took his outer clothes off the doctor said, 'The only other time I've seen symptoms like these, it was a drug overdose.'

'Presumably you can test for that?'

'Yes. We'll test for several things, but I don't think it's a heart attack or anything like that.'

It was two hours before the results came back and during that time, Terry began shouting that the brightness was hurting his eyes, and jerking backwards as if he thought someone was about to hit him.

At no time did they dare leave him unattended.

The doctor looked at the results and nodded in satisfaction. 'I was right. He must have taken a hefty dose recently.'

'What of?'

'Cocaine in some form or other, I should think.'

'What can you do to treat him?'

'It's not always easy when they've got to this stage. He must have been snorting it for years. Look at his nose. I think we'd better admit him to the psychiatric wing. The risks some people will take for a high make me sick.'

Thomas's phone rang and he looked at who was calling, then slipped out of the room.

He listened intently to what the police officer told him. 'Hellfire! Cocaine addiction! I'd never have thought of him being stupid enough to get into that.'

'You'd be surprised at how varied the backgrounds of addicts are.'

'Well, what's going to happen to him now? I don't want him coming after his daughter again. She's just getting her act together, has even found a part-time job. Indeed, her mother has taken her off to a photoshoot at the moment.'

'Davies has been committed to a psychiatric unit. She'll be safe for a few days because we daren't let him out after he's hallucinating so badly. He'd be a danger to himself as well as to others. Can you tell anyone who needs to know?'

'Yes, of course. It'll be his ex and his daughter who're most affected, the young woman he claims he was trying to look after. Thank you for sorting this out, Gerald. Much appreciated. I owe you one.'

'We're happy to have helped. I knew you'd not call me unless it was genuinely important. See you next week at the meeting.'

Thomas took a minute to compose himself, then went back to join the others and tell them what had happened.

'Shall I tell Fleur for you when she brings Marie back from the job?' Col asked.

'Yes, please.'

'It speaks well for Marie that she's still doing that job.'

'She didn't want to let them down. But Fleur wasn't allowing her to go off on her own this time, wanted to be sure she really could cope after such a shock.'

Thomas smiled at his friend. 'Looks like you're getting on quite well with Fleur.'

'Extremely well. I didn't think I'd fall in love again, but it looks like I've got a keeper there. In fact, you're surrounded by lovers, my friend. Ethan and Portia seem to be getting on rather well too.'

'Yes, I'd noticed. And she might seem a bit shy sometimes with adults, but she's brilliant with the girls, which is a huge bonus. They're at an age where they need an older woman to talk to.'

'And Fleur told me that guy whose child she looked after is still in touch. Apparently, Mandy is now treating her like a favourite auntie.'

When Fleur brought Marie back from the photoshoot, she found a message from Col asking her to contact him.

She phoned him while Marie was changing into her new skirt and a T-shirt.

'They've got Terry. It'd be better if I told you the details in person.'

'Come round.' She turned to see Marie looking at her anxiously.

'What's happened about Dad?'

'Col's coming to tell us in person.'

'Can't be good news, then.'

'No, not likely.'

He was with them five minutes later, and surprised Marie by putting an arm round her as well as her mother and guiding them both over to the sofa.

Gently he explained about Terry's drug problem and the resulting current health difficulties.

Fleur closed her eyes, shaking her head. 'Should I have known? I did wonder once or twice, but dismissed it, thinking he'd not be so stupid.'

'You'd probably not have known unless you've got experience of drug addicts.'

'Good heavens, no! You sound as if you have.'

'A little and not directly. A friend's son got involved. It didn't end well, I'm sad to say.'

They both looked at Marie, who was staring down at her hands. She looked up and gave them a sad smile. 'You don't have to worry about me. I had one go at a minor drug at university and hated the way it made me feel – as if a heavy cloud was sitting on my head.'

'I'm glad to hear that,' her mother said. 'And I've just realised that we'll have no difficulty getting your passports back now. I'm sure they'll be in the safe at his office.'

'Good.' The smile became genuinely amused as Marie added, 'And when we were living with you, don't think we didn't notice how you kept an eagle eye out for us getting involved in drugs. I know now that you can't see through walls, but I did wonder sometimes, you were so quick to get on to us if you thought we'd done anything wrong.'

'I did my best.'

Marie nodded. 'That's a good motto for life, don't you think? Do your best.'

'It's all you can do. No one can ever achieve perfection.'

'I know it's early but I think I'll go to bed now. I'm exhausted and you two lovebirds need a bit of privacy.'

Col stretched his hand out to stop her going. 'Thanks. You don't mind me and your mother being together?'

'Would it make any difference if I did?'

'Not to me, but it might make things more difficult.'

'Well, I don't mind at all, actually. Mum deserves some happiness and you're not anything like Dad.'

A week later, Thomas informed Fleur that Ethan was not pressing charges on condition that Terry went into voluntary rehabilitation in the UK. He'd therefore been released by a magistrate and would be escorted to the airport and accompanied on the plane journey.

'He's not likely to be allowed back into the country.'

'Thank goodness for that!' Fleur said. 'I won't have to be always glancing over my shoulder.'

Marie came in later and made a similar remark, adding, 'And I have my passports back now, thank goodness.'

Thomas left them with formal printed invitations for a weekend in a luxury hotel in Perth at which a very special gathering was to be held.

It ended with: *Formal dress required*.

When they asked what it was in aid of, he merely smiled. 'It's another of Sarah's gifts, the final one. And that's all I'm going to tell you till we get together.'

Epilogue

Fleur answered her phone. 'Liane! How are you?'

'I'm fine now, well, most of the time. But we both need your help.'

'What can I do?'

'You're the best person we know about clothes. We need something that can be called "formal dress" and Dad hasn't the faintest idea about clothes. He's just going to hire a penguin suit. Pops already owns a penguin suit.'

Fleur laughed. 'You want me to go shopping with you?'

'Yes, please.'

'Portia and Marie have asked the same thing. How about we all go out tomorrow morning and see what we can find?'

'Great idea!'

'We can all fit into Portia's car, which is bigger than mine.'

The five ladies hit the big shopping centre as soon as it opened. It took a total tour of the fancier dress shops, then a revisit to a couple of them, and lots of trying on before they could all be satisfied.

After that, Fleur insisted on taking them all out for lunch and could see even Liane relax completely.

'We're going to knock the men for six,' Nicole said gleefully. 'And this is the most grown-up dress I've ever had.'

Which made Fleur worry that it was too grown-up. Too late now. It had been bought and you'd not get it out of Nicole's hands again. She'd even noticed the girl patting the bag it had been packed in before she put it in the car boot.

On the afternoon of the party, the group of five women went to the hairdresser's at the hotel then got ready together in Fleur's suite.

'Pops still won't say what this party is in aid of exactly,' Nicole grumbled, watching herself in the full-length mirror as she moved to and fro and swished her full skirt about.

In another suite, the three men were ready rather more quickly, so they sat sipping glasses of champagne.

'Don't you think you should tell us exactly what this is in aid of now?' Col asked.

Thomas grinned. 'Nope. The big reveal will only take place in the so-called Sky Suite, with all of us present. It's got a room for dinner parties with an adjustable table, which will be set to just the right size for our group. And I'm not telling you anything till we've got rid of the waiting staff.'

There was a knock on the door of the ladies' suite and when Fleur answered it, a woman handed over a box, saying,

'With Mr Norcott's compliments. If you can be ready in ten minutes, I'll come back and escort you to the Sky Suite, madam.'

Fleur opened the box to find corsages of delicate orchids, which somehow managed to match the colours of their gowns.

'You don't look surprised. Did you tell Pops what we'd be wearing?' Liane looked at Fleur. 'I thought we were going to surprise him.'

'He just wanted to know the colours and I saw no harm in that. He has no idea of the styles of our outfits. We're still going to wow them with our splendour. Now, hurry up. I can pin the corsages on for you lot, but someone will have to do mine.'

They were ready just in time for the second knock.

This time it was a man who looked like a maître d'. 'If you ladies are ready?'

He escorted them up in a special lift, which needed a key to access it.

The twins' eyes were big with wonder and, looking at Liane's smiling face, Fleur thought this was some of the best medicine that could be found to cure the nervousness she'd displayed occasionally since the kidnapping. Clever Thomas.

The gentlemen were waiting for them and they were escorted into a room with an elegant dining table.

'There's a phone over there that you can take photos with,' Thomas said.

Portia pounced on it and said, 'How about starting with a group photo?'

'I have a professional photographer coming to take a group photo in a minute or two,' Thomas said. 'This camera is to snap cute moments.'

Nicole giggled. 'It sounds funny when someone your age says "cute", Pops.'

'Get used to it.'

The photographer came just then, arranging and re-arranging the group, and taking several photos. Then she left.

Thomas waited till they were sitting down to ask, 'Do you want the speech first or the food?'

'The speech,' Fleur said. 'I'm presuming you'll be telling us the purpose of this gathering?'

'Yes. Very well then. I think I can sit down to tell you.'

When they were all seated and gazing at him expectantly, he began. 'Sarah's final provision in her will was in case her fondest hopes were fulfilled, which I was to judge, and I truly think they have been.'

He looked round. 'She thought some members of the family and some of her friends were rather isolated socially and wanted to pull us together and make us into a new family but attached to the Blakemeres. She told me she trusted my judgement absolutely and she hoped I'd become the senior member of that new family.'

He smiled. 'I think we have gradually drawn together closely and I'm quite sure she would be delighted about that.'

After a brief pause he started speaking again, his voice husky with emotion. 'Our surnames being different doesn't matter; it's our love for one another that is the important thing. Her various gifts were carefully thought out during her final months and the task gave her great pleasure. She gave what she thought was necessary to help us draw together and I think we have done that, don't you? She didn't expect the glitch your ex provided, Fleur, but I'm sure that has been safely dealt with now.'

Fleur swallowed hard, because she felt near to tears at Cousin Sarah's kindness. She caught Portia's eye and exchanged smiles with her cousin, thinking how different Portia looked these days. And so happy.

'Would anyone object to being considered part of this family?' Thomas looked round.

'Even me?' Marie asked. 'I wasn't in Sarah's plan. I've never met her.'

'She left the exact composition of our new family to me, and I'm very happy to include you, Marie. I'd have included your brother if he'd needed help, but he seems settled in his ongoing work and studies. Are you happy to join us?'

'Yes. Very.' She fumbled for her handkerchief, couldn't find it and mopped her eyes on her napkin instead. 'Sorry!'

'Nothing to be sorry for. Now, let's drink to our new family.'

He rang a bell and footsteps approached the room. The maître d' came in with a bottle of champagne accompanied by a woman holding a tray of glasses.

'Australian champagne,' Thomas said. 'She specified that. And also, only an inch or so of bubbly for the twins. She never really thought in centimetres.'

They nudged one another and exchanged grins.

When the champagne had been poured, the maître d' bowed and took his assistant out of the room.

Thomas stood up. 'I think this is a toast we should drink standing.'

He waited till they'd all stood up, then raised his glass. 'To Sarah's gifts and to the new family that has resulted for us.'

'With all our gratitude,' Fleur dared to add.

Thomas nodded approval, then they raised their glasses and sipped.

Portia tapped a spoon against her glass and took what was for her a very brave step, announcing, 'I think we need another toast. Here's to Thomas, who has helped and guided us to this new stage in our lives and I for one am totally grateful.'

'To Thomas.'

The room seemed full of light and joy, and for a moment no one moved, then they sat down and began eating the sumptuous meal Sarah had also specified.

As he got ready for bed later, Thomas looked upwards, his eyes unfocused, and said quietly, 'This has been one of the happiest days of my life. Thank you, Sarah. Your gifts have had the result you hoped for. We have all benefitted.'

He'd have sworn the lights in his room flickered in response.

ANNA JACOBS was born in Lancashire at the beginning of the Second World War. She has lived in different parts of England as well as Australia and has enjoyed setting her modern and historical novels in both countries. She is addicted to telling stories and hopes to celebrate the publication of her one hundredth novel in 2022, as well as sixty years of marriage.

annajacobs.com